Alidor

Written by Matthew Hillsdon

Self Published

First Edition

First published in Great Britain in 2024

A record of this book is available from the British Library.

Cover illustration: Bobooks
Edited by: Emma Hillsdon
Back Cover Illustration: Robert Wright
Map Illustration: Kesara B

Few quests worth undertaking can be completed alone. Worthy endeavours will struggle to find a satisfying conclusion without a helpful guide. Crumbling mountains will need an extra set of hands to climb and even the most fearsome of villains is soon bested with a trusting gang alongside. So this is for those who follow along in the hope of greater stories to come.

Author's Note
The Forgotten Hero is a prologue to *The Unlikely Allies* and is best read after reading;
The Balmoth Brothers
The Starborn
The Rotting Thief
Available in Stolen Tales for Cunning Thieves Part I.

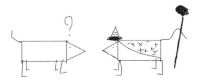

The Forgotten Hero

Chapter One
Wars Eventually End

Death was all those of Alidor knew. For so long the human's purge lasted, going on like a raging storm that cast woe over the lands. Leaving few unaffected by the horrors that followed in the wake of warring armies battling for power. Peace though had finally returned. Sadly the alliance of elves, dwarves and dragons that brought it about quickly crumpled away once no enemy remained to unite them. The Seer's hold on power had been ensured with the Crown City cast to the sea and encaged. The Human's King Harold Hargo along with his rebellion had been vanquished, only one hold of the banished King remained and nine years after the Crown City's fall still stood against the Seers.

A fortress the Afeun was, one with many towers and great stone battlements scored with iron spikes. In the north it sits, deep within the Seer's own land. A great number of miles lies between there and the Seer's city of Duniesa. Although on a clear day one with particularly keen eyes would be able to look out over the ocean and just about make out boats sailing to and from Duniesa's harbour to the east. Knowing what force the Seers had would now be marching for the fortress to lay siege, the Commander, one Christian Barker had hoarded enough food for the occupants to last as long as they'd need. For a number of years he and his small force had waited for their enemies to advance on the fortress, but little about the Afeun was of interest to the Seers within the Golden Tower. With wars raging in every direction it was easily overlooked. Even after the Crown City fell so many other issues drew the Seer's eyes. When they did finally see fit to raise a force and march on the fortress in the spring of the year Six Hundred and Eighteen they were met by a constant stream of catapult and ballista fire. Prepared well Commander Barker had, so after six months of laying siege and multiple failed attempts to storm the gates Seer Elidom Godborn was compelled to pull the force that had been sent from Duniesa back. Forcing him to summon a pair of wood elf rangers, who along with their companions had won their names during the human's purge and in time would form a group that would become known as The Watchers.

'An impending fort it is,' Banbury Bale said. A dwarf with a terrible stutter he was and as he pulled himself up he brushed off the mustard yellow tunic and trousers he wore. 'What are you doing? Get down, they'll see you,' Richard Balmoth ordered, pulling Banbury back down by the end of his long, dirty brown beard. The pair were lying on a bank, the night was heavy and the only light came from the torches pacing up and down on the Afeun's menacing battlements. 'They can't see sh…Sh…Nothing,' Banbury stuttered.

'We don't know that, just stay down and keep quiet.' Rolling over Richard looked down to the bottom of the bank to another wood elf who stood beside two pure white zatifas horses. Caspian and Fiona, Richard had named these steeds. The wood elf wore the same green ranger's uniform and cape as he. Brothers the pair are, but their uniforms and the short swords on their belts are the only similarity they share. While Richard's brown hair was short and scruffy with stubble over his chin, his brother Jhona's hung down to his shoulders and swayed like his hair had never known a nasty knot. 'Still waiting on your thief Jhona.'

'He's not late yet,' Jhona Balmoth snapped back to his brother. 'There look,' Banbury said tugging on Richard's cape. On top of the wall a different light now shone. All the others glowed orange, but this one was a bright white that quickly faded. 'That's the signal, let's move,' Richard ordered and the three of them left the steeds and hurried to the wall.

Towards where the light had flickered they went and as they approached the Afeun two ropes fell down from on top of the towering wall before them. Jhona quickly put the bow he carried over his shoulder and took hold of one. Instantly his rope was pulled up the wall, leaving the others to climb the one that remained. 'Will the rotter pull us up also?' Banbury asked securing his father's scythe in the holster he wore on his back. To most Banbury's scythe appeared to just be a metal pole which sits nicely within the harness he wore over his back. Flick the switch concealed on its side however and it doubles in length springing out a razor sharp blade as it extends. 'I wouldn't count on it. Get going and don't slip. Last thing I need is your rear crushing me,' Richard replied. At the top of the battlements the last member of this odd little band made himself known. A rough green hand greeted Jhona, helping him over the wall and onto a wooden walkway. 'He said I was late didn't he?' The owner of the hand remarked. He was a goblin wearing a mucky, old black tunic and baggy trousers beneath a hooded black cape. All of which helped conceal him in the dark and hide the many harnesses that covered his torso. His long wart covered nose twitched as he spoke and the one protruding tooth that jetted up from the right of his lower jaw made him look rather sinister. Fear however was the last thing Jhona felt upon seeing him. 'Don't fret about my brother Wasiz,' he remarked as he squeezed his old friend's cheek. 'Did you find the Commander's room?'

'Sneaking into a young man's room, dear Jhona what sort of thief do you take me for?' Wasiz blustered.

'Don't joke, where is he?' Jhona asked again as the others heaved themselves over the battlements. 'Took your time,' Wasiz said with a bent grin as they did. 'Let's just finish cleaning up this mess. Have you at least found him?' Richard complained.

'Go with Bale and get the gates open for the others. Myself and Richard shall handle the Afeun's master,' Wasiz said and after learning the way to the gate they spilt up. 'Is he well guarded?' Richard asked. 'No. Nothing we can't handle,' Wasiz replied. 'There's less fighters here than your Seer's letter said and not a wolf in sight. Might've been best to leave this one be, while we still can. You don't have to go running every time the Seers call you know.'

'You're fully aware why we can't. This war has to end and the La Sores will never see it as over while Barker still rules here. Enough of your worrying, let us hurry and end it before more have to die,' Richard said as they stepped over a pair of guards who Wasiz had previously knocked unconscious. 'Let's just get our hands on him and this war will finally be over and we can all go home.'

To the gate Jhona and Banbury went. The handle of Banbury's scythe caught the guard's chin before he could react, throwing him back and letting the pair pull on the winch to open the gate. Releasing the winch Jhona took his bow and an arrow from the quiver on his back and fired it at a guard who was approaching on the wooden walkway above the pair. The arrow slipped past the floorboards and stabbed through the guard's boot impaling itself in his foot. A yelp from the guard followed and then a thud as he fell, knocking himself out as he went. With the guard unable to raise the alarm Banbury soon had Afeun's gates open, and beyond hidden by the night and camouflaged in the tall grass by their green uniforms the Balmoth's rangers waited. As the portcullis raised and the gates opened they picked themselves up from the dirt and ran to the open gate. Bells rang out as they were seen and soldiers grabbed their arms and ran from the Afeun's barracks. The calm courtyard Jhona and Banbury stood in was quickly crowded and the pair were surrounded by spears. The ranger's bows soon pointed at their enemies as they stormed through the gates and silence once again returned as the two forces both waited for the other to make the first move. Before any blood was spilled or even a harsh word uttered a cry from Commander Barker's balcony drew them all. There he stood, grey was his hair and untamed beard for little of the young man who first took command of the Afeun remained. His old, wrinkled hand shook as he raised it and spoke. 'Lay down your arms. Lay them down I say. Elf and wood folk, human and wolf, our war is done. The Afeun is breached and we cannot hold its keep any longer. The Balmoths have offered a truce and I shall take it. Lay down your arms and we will be left here under the golden tower's rule,' Commander Barker declared making his weary soldiers slowly drop their swords. None wanted to continue fighting and few who could put up a fight remained. Most had grown old like their Commander. Forlorn men with grey beards his host were while their young knew nothing of war. Bows and swords were dropped breaking the silence in the courtyard and but one human still held his spear. 'Put it down, let this be done,' Jhona said as he approached. Unlike his brother whose face showed their many years of fighting Jhona's was unblemished with rosey red cheeks and a smile so fair it would make most knees weak. 'Is it woody, is it?' The man replied. 'I am not as young as others, I still remember. I will not be a slave for your Seers again. I shall not kill for them, nor shall my sons or daughters,' the man said as loud as he was able. A fierce fighter rested within him but his body had grown weak with age. As his strength failed him his spear began to pull him down but he was caught before he fell. 'It is done. I swear it,' Jhona said. 'Free men you and your kindred are. Let it end with us, for this war is over.'

The morning came quickly and the names of all the soldiers were taken, leading Richard to discover the fort contained few. Most there were former slaves or their young, few battle harden warriors of the Crown City remained. 'Why so many women and children?' Richard asked the commander. 'Most fled here when the war began, few men of fighting age are left. Mostly widows and babes. The few soldiers we had have grown older than myself,' Christian joked then took a harsher tone. 'They will be treated fairly, I have your word. You shall see to it yourself?'

'I will, you have my word and that of my rangers,' Richard replied.

'Good, for there are few things in this world to rely on, but a promise from a Balmoth I'd say is one,' Christian said taking Richard's hand and shaking it with what little strength he had. 'You know of me?' Richard asked. 'Your name goes before you ranger and that of your brother. If any other had snuck into my room a very different ending we would have ourselves, but for the best this is. If the Crown City is truly gone as the rumours say. A sad thing it is, but for the best maybe, let the blood spilling between us all end and leave us mortals to live what lives we're left with,' Christian said. With the siege of Afeun over the job

The Forgotten Hero

Richard and his companions had been sent on was done. So finally after months of weeding out militias, trapping spies and ending blockades they were all more than ready to return to their homes.

For the Balmoth brother's home was a farm that had been passed down to them when Richard's parents suddenly died. Although it had been many years since either had been able to return there. Only children both were when Richard's parents passed and neither had the green thumb needed to run a farm. Thankfully a kindly Seer was to hand, one who took them under his wing, schooling and training the pair until they left him as rangers. Banbury Bale originally hailed from Kogginston, but after a rather unexpected event regarding a greedy earl found himself married not to one but four sisters. They had made him take out a hefty mortgage on a fairly impressive cottage that lay a few miles from the dwarven city of Orashon's gates. 'We'd be protected there in the shadow of the great gates, especially when you're off galavanting,' one said to convince him. 'Good growing land also, you'd always have a fine roast waiting when you get home if we lived there,' another would go on until finally he gave in. Wasiz however had no humble home to return to, thieves such as he rarely do. He did however have a pair of apprentices, who unlike he had wisely invested the coin they'd procured into a run down tavern on the outskirts of the sleepy little village of Chiptun. Hardly a day and a half's ride from the Afeun, this is where they all now rode to for one last drink together before parting ways.

The Flipped Swan usually has a line of patrons waiting at the door to see what performance the owners would put on that night. The high ceiling allowed for incredible acrobatic displays that amazed diners. Often causing astonished gasps as women fell from the chandeliers and were slowly unravelled by the yellow ribbons they were wrapped in. While some patrons waited to creep to the back rooms where a great deal of men and women would happily fritter away their earnings over a green cloth clad table. Tonight though was not a normal night, no patrons waited at the door and the few who dared draw close found themselves chased away by chattering bats. For tonight the skies above the Flipped Swan were darker than usual. Upon the roof bats scurried while others swarmed around the chimneys and dangled from the tavern's gutters. Within only one patron waited along with Wasiz's apprentices for the Balmoth's party to return. A pale face she had, one that held no life and as she waited the owners timidly tended to the bar. 'How much longer? She's making even my blood chill and she hasn't ordered one drink,' Efrain Umbiter said.

'Not too long I hope,' her partner Fandisco Carriguan replied. The sound of hooves and scattering bats then drew their eyes to the door opening and both breathed a sigh of relief when Banbury stormed in past the flapping pests. 'There's a real chill a-about here,' he stuttered and then saw the pale woman. 'Ah that explains it.'

'Master Bale, how did it all go?' Fandisco asked rushing to greet him. 'As well as it could have I suppose,' Banbury replied going to the fireplace to warm himself. 'Don't suppose you have a spot of rum and some pork chops for a weary fellow who's been pickity peckish for three days now do you?' Pouring him a glass Efrain took it to him. 'Rum yes, but food will take awhile.'

'Guess you have no need to heat the stove with only h-h-her here,' Banbury stuttered.

'Fandisco fetch my pipe,' Wasiz ordered as he and the others entered. 'About time you got here,' the pale woman said, speaking for the first time since she'd arrived at the tavern. Standing and marching before Richard she took his arm. 'Are you really so eager to see me my lady?' Richard replied as he was pulled by her to the staircase and up it. The sound of a door slamming closed followed as Jhona and Wasiz sat down. 'If the blood sucker's here there must be some trouble right. You said you were done after all this. You promised you were in fact, the both of you did,' Fandisco said handing Wasiz his pipe. 'Shh,' Wasiz said pulling him down and clipping him round the ear. 'She will hear you calling her that. Let her have her way and let us hope that's all she's here for.'

'As long as she's gone before the other rangers return,' Jhona said.

'Don't worry yourselves, it is your bellies we should fret for. A young lady such as you Efrain should have at least a pot of stew ready for us chaps when we return,' Banbury laughed to himself.

'And it's thanks to that comment you'll be cooking your own dinner,' Efrain replied pinching Wasiz's pipe from his mouth and putting her feet up at their table. 'Would you get your own?' Wasiz complained snatching it back. 'Go on then Bale get the stove on, takes a while to heat up, be waiting until morning for some food at this rate,' Jhona chuckled.

'No point even putting it on for you woodys. I'll just get some bush leaves for you to graze on,' the jolly dwarf said whilst marching into the kitchen. 'What happened then? Let's hear it. What adventure have the pair of you been on?' Efrain asked and waited with Fandisco for Wasiz to tell them tales from their journey. The young pair were both massive fans of Wasiz and his stories. 'Are you two not tired of this fool's nonsense yet? He heavily embellishes most of our travels you know,' Jhona said.

'I'm afraid there's no exciting tale to tell anyhow. All went as we hoped it would and we didn't even come across any decent loot,' Wasiz complained.

'Speaking of loot,' Fandisco said getting up and going to the bar. Reaching over he grabbed an envelope from the shelf behind. 'This finally returned.'

'About time as well,' Wazis said opening it to reveal it contained a small silver whistle. 'Is that a zatifas whistle. Where did you find it? Only twelve were ever made' Jhona asked.

'A what?' Efrain wondered.

The Forgotten Hero

'You ask for tales but don't bother to pay attention when I do tell one. I have told you before of this whistle's song,' Wasiz complained. 'The high elves and their steeds the zatifas each wanted a way to find one another whenever they would need, no matter how far they were parted. So a master silversmith created these. Twelve he made and gifted one to each of the five Seers. Two he gave to the royalty within the Evertree and another three went to the first elfin lords who returned to Duniesa after the first's war ended. The final two they say he kept for himself, one for him and another for his partner.'

'But why do you have one?' Jhona said as the whistle was rolled over the table to him. 'As you say I have no need, but I hoped you'd find a use for it,' Wasiz said as Jhona picked it up to see Wasiz had sent it away to have the words *dear Jhona* engraved along the side. 'Oh Wasiz,' Jhona said smiling to him as Fandisco went back to the bar gesturing for Efrain to follow as he went. Reluctantly she did leaving the pair at the table grinning to each other until Jhona said. 'You can't keep doing this you know. Magic whistles, a bow from the finest craftsmen in Meceller. Not to mention all that trouble you caused when you stole that Duke's saddle for Fiona.'

'Didn't hear you complaining about the boots,' Wasiz chuckled, eyeing the heeled black leather boots Jhona wore. 'You can't keep stealing things for me,' Jhona complained once his blushing cheeks had faded. 'It's not like I go out of my way to. I found that when we were dealing with those ruffians who'd taken

control of La Sore Castle in the last days of the war,'
Wasiz said. 'You got it from the La Sore's that's even
worse. Seer Marlos is hardly the forgiving type,' Jhona
complained. While Wasiz laughed off Jhona's worries
the door to the tavern flung open and the rangers left at
the Afeun began piling in. 'At least wipe off your
boots,' Fandisco yelled at them as his clean floors
became covered in mud and he did his best to contain
the rowdy bunch that were filling the Flipped Swan.
The heavens had opened during their ride and each
ranger that entered was wetter than the last. 'You there,
Malcolm. What has you back so soon?' Jhona asked.

'Did you not hear Captain those new fellas
showed up to relieve us. They carried orders with the
Seer's mark,' Malcolm said.

'Elites that's what they call themselves,'
another ranger added. 'That's right looked like right
berks they did. Norcea knows why the Seers sent them,
we'd already done their job,' Malcolm laughed with
others and none but Wasiz noticed the look of horror
that covered Jhona's face. 'Don't, it will be the Seer's
doing, best not get involved further,' Wasiz said. Not
hearing him Jhona was soon on his feet and blowing
the whistle as he went to the door. 'Jhona wait, it can't
be helped.' Silent the zatifas whistle was to all but
Caspian and Fiona. Outside rain poured down as
Caspian came running reaching Jhona with a roaring
neigh. 'It's just a whistle, is it really that loud?' Jhona
asked as he climbed up while Caspian continued to
complain. 'Wait Jhona,' Wasiz yelled running after him,

but Caspian was already turning to leave forcing Wasiz to leap onto the steed's back so he wasn't left behind.

While his companions rode away or fought with coals to heat the stove Richard Balmoth lay on a warm bed with a cold body beside his. 'This is how it always starts,' Richard said as Calenir Pearce rose from the bed. 'What do you mean?' She replied as her black hair was brushed from her cold cheeks. 'A smile and a kiss, then you tell me about something awful. After draining me of a pint of blood that is. I'm right am I not?' Richard said. If the bats scuttling over the roof and Fandisco's reference to blood suckers hadn't already given it away Calenir was in fact one of the undead. A vampire, one of the Grey Count's own. The truce created by the pair had lead them to skulk away for numerous secretive meetings over the years. Today however the pale lady would ask more of him and his small fellowship than she ever had before. 'He's found something, my father's generals are sure it's what they need to create an eternal darkness,' Calenir said.

'No offence, but even the Grey Count can't do such things. No matter how powerful you believe your father is,' Richard said.

'I thought so too, but he has help now. A man not even I have seen. Someone's pulling his strings. Whoever he is, he's made my father a puppet. He has almost all of my father's generals under his control and together they plot. If I had anyone else who I could go to then I would. Failing turning myself in to the Seers to be turned to dust you and your friends are all I have,'

Calenir said. Sitting up Richard asked, 'What exactly are you asking us to do?'

'We have waited as long as we can and may have just delayed the inevitable with our alliance. You must remove him so I can take his place and stop whatever this man is doing before it's too late,' Calenir said. 'You're asking for more than we have ever done. It is no simple feat, even with the Count's own daughter aiding us,' Richard said.

'I swear it Richard this is the only way. I don't want his power or his position but it's the only way now. The Seer's war with their former slaves has weakened the elves. My father's generals see it and will force him to act before you can rebuild. You know as I do, your people can't stomach another war. When the clouds spread those of Meceller, nor Duniesa, not Kogginston or even the Balmoth's valiant rangers will have the strength to halt their advance. But if we work together. If we go against him before they have time to assemble the armies of the Vale we could save both our people from this,' Calenir said.

'We were lucky to survive the war and now Amunden's dragons have broken their alliance with the Seers. We will have them to deal with before too long. I hate to say it, but you're right,' Richard said rubbing his forehead. 'It will take time to prepare and I feel we would need more hands than my small band has. I cannot ask my rangers to ride so far from their homes.'

'I have a few loyal to me, if you can remove my father we shall handle his generals. Then together we can finish this puppet master's games. Only you do I need Richard,' Calenir told him.

'What makes you so sure there's another? This could just be the Count's doing,' Richard inquired. 'Because of the way he speaks. It doesn't sound like him anymore, hasn't for months. It's like another has taken his face and is just wearing him,' Calenir whispered as if the man she spoke of may have been listening. 'I shall speak with my brother, if he and the others are willing we will help,' Richard said. Calenir fixed the final button on Richard's uniform to hide the wounds her fangs had left and told him, 'I will return to Paratis and delay him however I can while I can still move freely around the fortress. When you're ready go to a town outside of the Vale called Vurcun. Once there find the stable master, he will be expecting you. We shall decide our next move when we are reunited,' Calenir said. 'So be it, be safe until then my lady,' Richard said and with a smile to him Calenir bit her finger and as the deep red blood oozed out she spoke words Richard didn't know and a blood red light filled the room. A second later Richard heard the window open and the sound of a bat's wings fluttering away.

Faster than any other horse were the zatifas, a fact Caspian proved. With haste he returned Jhona and Wasiz to the Afeun and as they had arrived previously it was the dead of night when they approached. Dismounting the pair sent Caspian away while they entered the fort to find elves in golden armour marching about it and tall fires burning all around.

Elites these were, a new force created by Seer Marlos and Eloise La Sore to replace their former slaves. Going before the largest fire Jhona smelt flesh burning and then saw the bodies of the Afeun's people piled within. Past the flames corpse's burnt leaving Jhona weeping before the fire when he saw the melting face of the old man he'd helped stay standing. 'The bastards, those sodding Seers,' Jhona raged as the wind began to whizz about him. 'Oi woody get away from there,' an unsavoury Elite bellowed to him, but before he drew close to the grieving ranger Wasiz blocked his path. 'Think who you speak to, for a Captain of the rangers is he.'

'No bloody rangers should be here,' the Elite spat as he gripped Wasiz and tossed him aside. What he didn't know however was that in fact Wasiz was aiming to protect him. For as soon as he was thrown down the winds that were whizzing about Jhona sung past Wasiz to the Elite. Such an incredible speed did the winds reach that they sliced through his armour, leaving deep gashes in his flesh and blood spurting from his many wounds. As his agony filled cries rang out more Elites drew their swords and began rushing to the pair. Wielding his bow Jhona fired arrows all around. Using the wind he controlled he could manipulate them so he didn't even have to aim. As soon as the arrows left the end of his bow the element took control, guiding them to their targets. Taking a dagger in each hand from the harness beneath his cape Wasiz ran to intercept a pair heading to Jhona's back. Tossing a dagger to the face of one Wasiz tripped the other as the Elite's sword swung letting him stab the Elite in the back of the neck as he fell. While the fires continued to burn and the sun rose the Elites who had slain the people of the Afeun were felled.

Blood covered the pair and as the morning's light bathed them Wasiz took Jhona's hand and let the heartbroken ranger sob on his shoulder whilst the fires slowly faded. 'It was done, they were no threat to any. Elidom's won his war, why would he?' Jhona wept.

'Even Elidom's rage wouldn't lead him to this, it's as you say, he'd won his war. In another's hands this evil lies,' Wasiz told him. The wind had still been singing about them until a shadow cast over the pair. On top of the Afeun's wall the master of the skies, the great griffin Charlemagne had landed silently. He glared down to the pair as his wings folded over his back. 'How dare you interfere with the Seer's order,' Charlemagne bellowed down to them. Wiping his eyes Jhona went before him as his sorrow left him and he yelled. 'How dare we. You watch the skies and see us, but happily ignore their cruelty. Send your Seers, tell them Jhona Balmoth waits for them and we shall see which of those high cowards would dare face me,' Jhona yelled up to the beast. 'They will not let this lie son of steeds. The young in the golden tower don't see you as the old do. The days of Seers draws to a close and little sway will my master have over the ones who come next,' Charlemagne replied.

'Let them see me however they wish,' Jhona muttered turning from the beast. With that the great griffin's wings flapped and he was away to the sky.

To the gate the pair went and there they sat as Wasiz puffed on his pipe. No Seers did come, only their friends returned. Richard and Banbury had soon heard the same from Malcolm as the others and with Fiona had hurried back to the Afeun. 'I'm sorry, I just couldn't stop myself,' Jhona said as Richard looked over the bloody courtyard. 'No more blood was meant to be spilled here,' Richard said.

'In our defence the golden sods started it,' Wasiz added. 'The Seers won't see it that way and with what we now have to do I was hoping to have their aid,' Richard said. 'Aid for what?' Wasiz asked.

'We must go to the Forgotten Vale,' Richard announced. 'Straight from your bro-bro-brother's mess to one made by your mistress,' Banbury stated.

'It's not like that. If what she's saying is true we may have the chance to stop another war that will cover the lands before it starts,' Richard said.

'Going through the Vale is no easy feat and getting into the Count's fortress will be another challenge altogether. The Paratis has never been breached, even the dreaded Amunden stayed clear when he rained fire down on the Vale,' Wasiz said rubbing his chin. 'A task made considerably harder now the Seer's ain't going to aid us,' Banbury blustered glaring at Jhona. 'They wouldn't help even if we went to them. Neither Elidom nor the La Sores care for the south. They will let it burn as they always have before. They will sit in that accursed golden tower of theirs and do nothing once again. I'm not asking any here to join me, but if we had this chance years ago. The chance to stop the human's purge before it began would you say you wouldn't take it,' Richard said.

'We'd be dead after taking just two steps into the Vale, even worse they could change us. There's no cure to their bite you know. This could just be some elaborate trap for your pale lady to turn you,' Banbury said. 'I doubt even she could stand him for an eternity,' Jhona joked. 'I did hear a story a little while ago, about three healers. Rumour is they can cure any ailment, fix broken bones all with just their hands some say. Nothing do these tales tell of the blood sucker's curse, but I feel we will need some good healers if we are to take on this quest for your pale lady,' Wasiz said.

'Stronger weapons we will need also, my scythe can cleave through a wolf but silver will be required for this foe,' Banbury told them.

'Quite, but silver is easily sourced. Healers however are not. Where are they Wasiz? We shall try and get their aid,' Richard said.

'Well there lies the problem. They're being held in Accultian,' Wasiz said.

'So to embark on one perilous quest we must go on another first. Blooming blood suckers, now that god awful Countess,' Banbury complained.

'I think I may be able to think up a worthy plan to free them. If they will help us though, well we shall just have to leave that to Balmoth charm.'

Chapter Two
Stealing the Sisters

Accultian lay in the north past black mountains and over bubbling seas. Upon the Dragon's Rest did Countess Elander's fortress stand. Built upon the side of the dormant volcano that was said to have birthed the dragons themselves. A harsh journey laid before any who would dare try to pass the sea to reach it. One that the feeble rarely survived and even tested Richard and Jhona Balmoth as they rowed over the rough seas. 'Your thief has outdone himself this time. We will both end up on the end of a rope following his stupid schemes,' Richard said.

'He's not my thief,' Jhona blushed. 'Moan all you like Richard, but I didn't hear you coming up with anything.'

'Nor have I heard you offer to row,' Richard complained. 'Look there's the dock, hurry and put on a smile,' Jhona interrupted, quickly changing the subject as he did. Approaching the dock an old elf woman waited to greet them. As pale as the Lady of the Forgotten Vale was she, like most they saw as they climbed wet stone steps to be lead into a dimly lit hall where many women in grey robes shuffled about. All those of Accultian dressed the same aside from one, the Countess. In a throne she sat like a queen watching every step they took as they were lead across the room.

The Forgotten Hero

Her heavily painted face twitched and she bit her rosey red lips as they approached, leaving lipstick smeared over her yellow teeth. 'The Seers say you wish to make use of my mages,' the Countess said proving she had believed the forged letter Wasiz had sent to her. 'Yes my Lady. Healers we need, for there are still many of the Crown City's wolves plaguing the Seer's lands and skilled hands we need to mend the damage they do,' Richard said. 'Healers are rare young ranger and extremely expensive. So rare and so dear they are I wonder why the Seers don't come to make this request themselves,' the Countess said.

'For safety's sake my Lady. They believed it best we receive them. That way we can quietly return them to Duniesa and avoid any unwanted eyes noticing us,' Richard said.

'Unusual, but to be expected. Elidom has grown so weak he's forced to beg me for help once again. To think of that high and mighty clown quivering in that tower of his while his former slaves run amuck is rather amusing. Why would I bother to help anymore? I made him his wall, I caged his problem away and he dares still ask more of me,' the Countess spat as she lifted herself up and sauntered over to Richard. 'I would not call him weak my Lady, but wars change much. Things in the Seer's city are not as they were and the people of the south, my people. Well they fair even worse. Forget the Seers for a moment if you will. Turn your mind to them, the wood folk and others who suffered through a war they wanted no part of. Think of how they'd praise you and your mages. Think of the love they'd show in return for your help in their time of need,' Richard said.

'Praise matters little to those of the Rest ranger. Most here don't even have names for the masses to hail,' the Countess remarked. Forcing his way past the stink of the vile woman's perfume Richard lent in and spoke lightly. 'They may not, but you my Lady have a grand name. One the people of Meceller will cheer harder for than their own queen.' With a cruel grin the Countess continued to chew her lip until she suddenly clicked her fingers and announced. 'So be it, an example of their skill I believed you would want. I have prepared a test for them.' Gesturing for them to follow she lead the pair away and down a dim passage.

Into the very bowels of the volcano they were taken until before them a pit lay and there waiting in chains was a woman covered in tattered cloth, with bright red hair. 'This is the one you can purchase. I had them prepare her earlier. She's feisty, be sure to keep her underfed and in chains or else she heals nothing and just tries to escape,' the Countess said.

'I was told there were three,' Richard replied. 'There are three, but only two have the skill. The third is best used as a tool to motivate the others,' the Countess said waving her hand and a door in the side of the pit opened. Another wood elf woman with light brown hair and the same basic attire was pushed out followed by one of the Countess's guards. Drawing her sword the guard pushed the woman down and ran the blade along her back leaving a deep cut as it went.

29

'Stop this,' Jhona yelled, but Richard's hand to his quelled him. 'Do not worry, see,' the Countess said as the wounded girl was dropped before the one in chains and she began to heal the wound that ran up her sister's back. 'Incredible,' Richard said trying to keep up the pretence that he was enjoying this ghastly show. 'But what of the other, we would rather have them all if we could.'

'Even the useless one, whatever would you want with her,' the Countess spat.

'An extra set of hands is always useful,' Richard said. 'However, I do find business such as this is best done over a bottle,' he went on with a grin to the Countess. 'You must have many rare bottles stored here I'd say.'

'So be it, let us get away to my office. I have a rather nice blend there,' the Countess said almost forgetting about Jhona as they went to leave. 'Oh you can stay here if you wish or wait at your boat,' she said in a hurried tone too eager for the attention of the handsome young ranger was she.

While the Countess's eyes were firmly fixed on the Balmoths Wasiz and Banbury had found another way to infiltrate the island. As the waves crashed to the shore a pellawhale was pushed to the beach. The second largest creature of the sea these monsters of the ocean are. Wielding huge grey bodies, and a mouth large enough to fit many a boat within. Opening its enormous mouth Wasiz and Banbury stepped out. 'What a way to travel, mighty good of you Ponky. Stay close you hear, we shall need a lift back to the mainland so don't swim off too far,' Banbury said.

'I find it hard to believe you were ever a sailor Bale,' Wasiz said shaking his arms to remove the pellawhale saliva that covered them both. 'Well I wasn't for long thanks to a certain rotter,' Banbury joked slapping Wasiz on the shoulder with his saliva covered hand. 'Just long enough to meet lovely Ponky here.'

'Let's be quick before any in Accultian see this big fish,' Wasiz ordered and the pair made their way to a drainpipe with a locked grill over it. 'Your turn tea leaf,' Banbury said. Going into his pocket Wasiz pulled out a black key. Patches of rust covered it while the top had been bent into a crude skull shape and the teeth along the bottom were jagged and sharp. To look at you'd struggle to imagine what sort of door a key such as this would unlock. A relic created by an ancient being this key is, one Wasiz stole away long before he ever felt the warmth of the sun upon his green skin. Holding it before the lock the teeth of the key began to bend and it reshaped itself to fit the lock it had been held before. Just the sight of this made Banbury's stomach turn. 'Hurry it up, can't stand that thing,' Banbury complained as the lock fell away, allowing the pair to open the grate and enter the drain.

'Smells awful in here thought an island of ladies would have cleaner drains.' Banbury's complaining continued until Wasiz stopped him and said. 'Here this should be it.' Pushing a manhole aside the pair climbed up and into a room filled with the tools used to torture the Countess's mages. 'Been many a year since I've seen a limb splitter,' Banbury said looking to a blood covered device used to lower a large stone chisel to the legs of the one sitting in it. Once in place the weight above is released cleaving the occupants legs perfectly in two. Even more heinous devices than this filled the room and as they made their way past them Wasiz found some still had bodies within them. A burnt corpse in a metal tube then drew Wasiz's eye. 'What do you suppose that one is?' Banbury asked.

'It's one of her experiments, someone must have told her that this poor sod could wield the flames,' Wasiz said. 'So she burnt them alive?' Banbury queried. 'It's how she tests them, tortures them until whatever hidden abilities they have are revealed so she can steal them away. If none appear I imagine this is the fate many share,' Wasiz told him. Going to a locked cabinet with glass doors the pair could see it contained many vials of black liquid. 'Magic isn't just fancy spells that make sparks you know and only a handful of elementals like Jhona will you find these days. The Countess and her mages are something else entirely. Something the Countess created herself by stealing the gifts of others and passing them to her own. She's become terribly powerful thanks to all her work and the Seers turning a blind eye to her antics.'

'Then why come rob her,' Banbury blustered.

'Don't fret or fear Master Bale, there is no villain so powerful to stop me from pinching from them,' Wasiz chuckled to himself. Going on they found a corridor leading to a stairway that descended down many slim steps to a dungeon. 'Not hers are you?' A foul voice spluttered as they passed the first cell. 'W-what in Alidor is that?' Banbury said as the man stumbled to the bars of his cell. 'A high master I am, but what are you?' A high elf this man was but barely resembled one. His ears had been cut leaving only puss covered holes to remain. His glassy eyes made him appear blind and every movement he made caused what grey hair was left upon his head to fall away. 'Here to aid a friend are we. Would you aid us also and tell us if the three wood elf sisters are here?' Wasiz asked. Slamming himself to the bars they both saw he only had stumps for hands. 'Ahh yesss,' the man said as drool ran over his bleeding black lips. 'Come for the Starborn have you?' Vile laughter followed from him. 'So it's begun the shadows have awoken once more.'

'What shadows do you speak of?' Banbury asked. 'You shall see soon enough Banbury Bale of Kogginston,' the man chittered.

'What do you know of me fiend?' Banbury said clanging the bars. 'Leave him, he's just a trickster,' Wasiz said. 'No Rotting Thief, no tricks do I play and I'll prove it. Down there is the Starborn you seek,' the man said using his stump to point down the row of cages to the end where a solid metal door lay. 'There is the healer you're looking for, but freeing them will only delay your end. The shadows that come can't be stopped for their master would never allow it,' the man went on. 'They best be there fool, if not we shall be back for you,' Banbury said and they left the man as he laughed through his broken teeth.

Opening the door with his skeleton key the pair went in to find a wood elf woman with her hands bound by chains tied above her head that held her dangling above the ground. 'That her?' Banbury asked.

'Leaflin is what I heard your family name is, was that right?' Wasiz asked walking towards the woman. 'Easy thief, as tricky as that other scoundrel I feel she is,' Banbury insisted as Wasiz drew close.

'Leaflin that's you yes?' Wasiz asked again but she remained still with her face covered by brown matted hair. 'Release her,' Wasiz ordered Banbury and pointed to the hook that held her chain aloft. 'On your head be it then,' Banbury replied knocking the chain from the hook and letting her drop down to be caught by Wasiz. 'Come now, you can speak can you not?' Wasiz asked. She didn't speak just rose her hand as ice covered it and gripped his throat. You see for around two weeks this young woman had been hanging from the chain, but this was by her own design. Knowing what punishment would follow from acting out as the Countess would say, she'd formed a plan of escape. For days she'd been rubbing her palm over the chain creating enough friction to make her palm sweat. Finally after she felt the sweat drip to her forehead she was ready, unfortunately she hadn't expected a strange couple to barge into her cell. 'See I told you,' Banbury said raising his scythe. 'Stop, please we mean you no ill. Your aid is what we seek,' Wasiz said.

'What use would you have for me? Only a weapon I am to men like you,' she said as the sweat she'd formed into ice began to cover Wasiz's neck. 'I swear it, only your skill as a healer we need and only one of you we will beg to aid us, but all three will be freed. I swear it,' Wasiz promised.

'She would never free us all. You must know the Countess to be here and know she'll never give away her only hope at everlasting life,' she said.

'Which is why we came a calling.' Wasiz said as his breath left his mouth in clouds of freezing air. 'Release him or lose your head lady,' Banbury demanded as doors beyond her cell slammed.
'Quickly, others are coming and we will be discovered soon. You must decide Leaflin. Try and free yourself if you wish, but only my scheme will see both you and your kin free of this hellish place,' Wasiz insisted.

As the guards approached the door to the Leaflin's cell they saw nothing amiss. Opening the door she looked to be tied aloft as she always was, so in they went without a second thought. 'Wakey, wakey ya brat it's dinner time,' the guard said as she and her partner wandered into the room and went to their prisoner. While one lifted up her head the other filled a spoon with the most unsavoury looking slop from the bowl she held. 'Come on eat up. Chef spat in it special, just for you,' the woman mocked as the spoon rose to meet her lips. Just as it did the ice hidden in their captive's palms that had until now been holding her palms to the chains melted away and she dropped down. In a flash each hand was covering a guard. Ice spread over their faces then moved around the back of their heads until they were frozen solid. Releasing them the pair fell back and as they hit the ground the heads of the guards shattered into chunks of frozen bone and melting brains. 'You said they were healers,' Banbury blasted out as he and Wasiz emerged from hiding behind the open door. 'I am a healer master dwarf, the best there is. Free my sisters and you will have my aid,' the woman announced. 'A fine deal and one I shall see to honour,' Wasiz said.

'And you are?' She asked.

'Wasiz my lady. They call me many names in even more lands, but the Rotting Thief is the one I'm best known by around these parts.'

'Do not tell her much, witches like her can curse you with just a name,' Banbury said. Ignoring him the woman held out her hand to Wasiz saying as she did. 'The Rotting Thief you shall have to tell me the story that gave you that name. Sadly mine is far more simple, Bethany Leaflin.' As they shook hands the woman seemed slightly warmer to Banbury, but the headless bodies soon made him forget this as they left the cell. 'Careful now Leaflin. Follow them and your fate is for sure. Death and dismal lives is all that awaits you and your kin. For she knows you fell. She has not forgotten her Starborn,' the vile man yelled as they passed. A comment all ignored and quickly forgot as they left the dungeon behind.

'It's over there by the dresser,' the Countess said waving to a trolley of bottles in the corner of her office. 'I shall be mother then,' Richard said going to the trolley and as the Countess cleared furs from an ample heavily cushioned long chair Richard snuck a pill Wasiz had given him into her glass. A fine farmer was Wasiz and the pipe weed he grew and constantly smoked had many a use. Once he would have to fill a room with such smoke to pacify his enemies. After meeting Efrain however, who was rather skilled at alchemy they developed a new strain and were able to distill the effects of the plant into a pill. This pill Richard hoped would keep the Countess asleep long enough for them to flee with the three sisters in tow. 'Here we go, a fine scent to it,' Richard said sitting beside the Countess. 'Now what of the mages,' Richard asked handing the Countess her glass. 'You have fine taste for wine ranger, but your taste in mages is poor. Why come all this way for them? I have others who would fight these wolves you speak of. Fire mages who can burn them to ash in mere seconds,' the Countess said. 'Fire mages, few of them remain, the last true were of the first were they not?' Richard asked. Putting her unused glass on the table before them the Countess said. 'Not true. I have elves who can now wield them. Before long we will be able to pass it to even your folk,' the Countess said.

'Flames and wood folk are not a good match my Lady, but it is healers we need. The Seer's order it so it must be done I'm afraid,' Richard said wracking his brain for a way to make her drink. 'Have it your way, but one is all I will give you and more gold than you and your brother carry will it take for the redhead,' the Countess replied. 'The Seers will see you paid whatever you ask. Send your price to the golden tower. Whatever coin you wish for you will get, but I must insist on her sister's aid also. Keep the other healer by all means, but I feel the redhead will be of more use if a noose is around her sister's neck,' Richard said with a wicked grin making the Countess giggle and edge closer to him. 'A fine idea that is. I shall send a bird to the Seers and in the meantime we shall just have to entertain one another,' the Countess said.

'Quite, but before let us drink to a deal soon to be completed,' Richard insisted raising his glass.

'So be it, to the Leaflins,' she smirked as she retrieved her glass and the pair emptied them. Barely a second after Richard removed the glass from his lips the Countess's were upon his. Thankfully only a minute or two did he have to endure the Countess's slobbering tongue invading his mouth before she fell fast asleep on top of him. Forcing her and her bloated dress aside he got up and stormed over to the drink's trolley, taking the bottle as he went for the door. 'I shall need more than this to forget the taste of her,' Richard muttered to himself as he necked the bottle and hurried back to the pit.

Soon after Richard lead the Countess away most of her guard followed leaving just the one waiting in the pit with the sisters. It was silent and only moisture dripping from the stones made a sound. Until the wind began to sing about them and the yell of the guard drew both their eyes to her. A stone had been whizzed through the air knocking out the guard and allowing Jhona to drop down into the pit. 'Hurry, release your sister and let us be free of this place,' Jhona said taking the keys from the guard's belt and tossing them to her. 'But, wait. What's happening?' The girl asked.

'He's freeing us you idiot just get me down,' the redhead spat to her sister whose hands uncontrollably shook as she took the keys and tried to unlock her sister's chains, whilst at the same time trying to stop her torn dress from falling away. Taking the string from his bow Jhona went to her back. 'Get yourself free I shall tie this,' he said.

'Watch your hands boy,' the redhead snapped.

'Do not fret, for neither of you are any interest to me,' Jhona said as he threaded the bow string through the tears at the back of her dress and tied it so it wouldn't fall away. With her hands free she soon released herself and then her sister, who once unchained reacted in much the same way Bethany did. Pushing her sister behind her she stood tall before Jhona and then ducked past him to retrieve the sword the guard had wielded. 'Whatever game this is we won't be playing it, begone. We shall get ourselves free of this place.'

'Wendolin don't, he seems like he's here to help,' the other said.

'Then he won't mind leading us out with a sword to his back will he,' Wendolin replied.

'Stop it sister,' another voice said from past the open door. 'We have a deal and we are all now leaving,' Bethany ordered as she lead Wasiz and Banbury into the pit. 'Agreed,' Richard yelled, shouting to them as he ran along the top of the pit. He slid down the ladder to them seemingly more eager to leave than the sisters were. 'You missed some,' Jhona joked as he rubbed bright red lipstick from Richard's cheek. 'She was a beast, next time you do the charming part,' Richard said. All of a sudden the eyes of the sister whose name none had yet to ask caught his. Hazel green they were and to him they twinkled as if stars danced within them. 'What brings a woman such as you to a place as grim as this?' He asked.

'Excuse me if that's how you ask someone's name, it's a fairly strange way,' she replied.

'Later for your ego Balmoth let us be off. Ponky won't wait forever,' Banbury said ushering them on to the manhole both he and Wasiz had entered through. As they waded through filth Richard moved to walk beside her and said. 'I suppose this is an even worse time to ask your name.' Distracting her with his question she slipped, but before she fell into the running sewer Richard caught her making her splutter her reply in a mild panic. 'Stephanie.' As her hair was pushed from her eyes his smile charmed her until she was pulled away. 'Don't be so clumsy,' Wendolin snapped going between the pair as they walked on to the open grate.

'Come on now girl. It's not like her to be late,' Banbury said. Just as the others joined him the pellawhale emerged. 'There you are, had me worried for a second you did.' As its gigantic mouth opened the sisters stopped dead in their tracks. 'This is a joke right,' Wendolin said. 'Well we could hardy leave on a barge,' Jhona replied. 'It doesn't look so bad, just sticky,' Stephanie said. 'Don't whine Wendy anything's better than staying here,' Bethany insisted pushing her on with Stephanie. Climbing into the pellawhale's mouth they heard bells and whistles ringing out from within Accultian. 'No more dilly dallying, they're on to us,' Banbury said. With that the Leaflin sisters were finally free of Accultian, not one of the three knowing what to expect when the beast they now travelled in opened its mouth.

Chapter Three
The Fangs of the Forest

Disembarking from the pellawhale's mouth Wendolin's mood grew increasingly worse as she fell from it to a pebble beach. 'This is ridiculous, what sort of rescue was that?' She said as she wiped the pellawhale's saliva from her face. 'The sort that sees you free, thanks would normally be called for,' Jhona said. With her eyes clear and greenery now plentiful Wendolin's wrists flicked and vines sprang from the ground and rushed to them. Water suddenly flew from the sea freezing the vines as they went. 'Stop it Wendy,' Bethany ordered. 'Don't call me that,' Wendolin whined. 'Do you think we would fight like that if we were blood?' Jhona joked to Richard.

'Let's all just sit back, have a smoke and it will all be made clear soon enough,' Wasiz said but he soon found his pack had been soaked in the pellawhale's mouth. 'Where are we? Felt as if we were at sea for days,' Stephanie asked going to Richard's side.

'We had to pass to the south. I'm afraid the Seers are none too fond of us at the moment and returning to their lands would have been fairly risky. It has been just over a day. I hope the journey wasn't too taxing,' Richard said as he began to look to the trees that bordered the pebble beach. 'It was fine, their fighting was worse than the slime,' Stephanie told him.

'Good work there girly, you go off and get yourself home safe you hear,' Banbury said waving to Ponky as the giant submersed beneath the waves. 'Banbury, you were meant to take us close to Rafsing's dock,' Richard shouted over as he realised where the pellawhale had taken them. 'Is this not the Rafsings?' Banbury asked. A howl then drew every eye to the trees and dread filled them all. 'The Fang. Of all the places you dumped us before the Fang. You idiot excuse for a sailor,' Jhona yelled running to Wasiz he reached into his bag and pulled out a spare bow string. 'It's too late for that,' Wasiz said as Jhona tied it to his bow. From the foliage that surrounded the trees snarling wolves began to emerge. 'Stay close,' Richard ordered pushing Stephanie behind him and drawing his sword. Without warning they pounced, charging from the woods and encircling them all. Roots and vines rose before Wendolin, as water from the sea flowed about Bethany, but before one wolf could pounce another howl stopped them in their tracks. Back to the woods Richard looked and there stood a wolf with dark black fur, tall and broad he was and to his side a white wolf with a bead of black over her left eye stood. 'Rangers are not welcome here,' the black wolf howled down to them. 'And we do not mean to be,' Richard said stepping forward. 'Only by mistake have we come by you Fang Lord. A simple misdirection by a fairly useless guide.'

'I won't have that, Ponky's a smarter beast than any of these m...M...Dogs,' Banbury stuttered.

'It is you I speak of you fool, be quiet,' Richard snapped through gritted teeth. 'Not had woody flesh in years, and these smell so good. Especially the women, let us eat them and drown the dwarf,' a wolf with black fur that had patches of grey said. He was still marching in circles around them. 'Enough Fengal, let them by,' the black wolf ordered making Fengal snarl to them as they passed. 'Lucky you are and thankful to the Fang Lord you should be. Spared by the word of Balvor the Mammoth Slayer, best you hope his White Light keeps it so.'

'Why come here ranger, was a pact not made?' Balvor the Mammoth Slayer asked. 'It was and made by him so why would we come to break it,' Banbury said getting increasingly frustrated with the wolves whose pups had now joined them and had begun trying to nip at Banbury's long beard. 'Away with you devils.'

'Let the dwarf be,' Salene, the White Light of the Fang ordered as she nudged the pups away. 'Including me, three have lead the pack since Barramore's day. The face of the ranger is forgotten but the name remains, you are the Balmoth?' Balvor asked.

'I am. We are sorry to intrude but now here we must wait for our friends to find us before we go on,' Richard said. 'More rangers?' Salene asked.

'No just two horses, of the zatifas they are,' Jhona said. 'Only two for so many,' Balvor inquired looking over their large group. 'Yes there is only two, other steeds we will hopefully find in Noress,' Richard told him. 'You will find no steeds there, it is a town of ghosts. None dwell there or would dare to,' Balvor said. 'No one ever returned after the war,' Salene added.

Stepping aside Balvor went on. 'Make camp to the far east of the forest and don't stray from your fire when night falls.'

'Thank you Fang Lord we will be away as quickly as we are able,' Richard promised. The wolves then left them and after a trek through the Fang they came to a ridge that overlooked the deserted town of Noress. Little did any know that the wolves had still watched their every step and now a brown wolf with a missing left ear spied on them as they began to make camp.

'The sun will set soon, let us make a fire to dry ourselves. I can still feel that whale's saliva under my shirt. Once dry we shall speak of our trials ahead,' Wasiz said. 'After some food also,' Banbury insisted.

'Fine, but only until you have made up for the sorry way you saved us will I stay,' Wendolin said. Taking the hatchet from his belt Banbury went to chop wood for a fire, before he swung however his hatchet was stolen by a vine that swiped it from his hand. 'Don't cut the trees,' Wendolin said in a menacing tone.

'Then how am I to build a fire,' Banbury replied. With a click of her fingers broken and dead branches fell from the trees all about them. 'Use them, not the live ones,' Wendolin said leaving Banbury to pick up sticks. While the others found fallen logs to push around the fire Banbury was making, Wendolin clicked her fingers once again and a throne of vines covered in blooming flowers rose from the ground for her. After blowing the zatifas whistle there was little for them to do as they waited for Caspian and Fiona to find them. The little food they carried with them was passed to Banbury and he set about preparing a meagre meal for the hungry party that crowded around the fire as he cooked. 'That can't be all the food you have,' Wendolin complained watching Banbury pour the sorry looking beans into a pot. 'Quiet Wendy, it's better than nothing,' Bethany said. While they picked at their food the sun set, a sight none cared to see until the glimmer of white on the horizon drew their eyes to it. Both Fiona and Caspian had passed over the east bridge days ago and had been happily amusing themselves until the sound of the whistle called them back. Whilst the steeds were greeted by the others only one of the Leaflins showed any interest. Leaving her sisters to continue bickering Stephanie walked over and found herself staring to the tall white steeds. Never had she seen horses such as them and the white coats all zatifas horses share are bright enough to mesmerise any. 'She is Fiona,' Richard said standing beside her as Caspian reared up. 'Yes I was getting to you. The moody chap is Caspian.' Timidly she went on going before Fiona. She held her hand out as she drew close and let the horse move her nose into it. 'She almost glows,' Stephanie said.

'She seems to have taken quite a liking to you my lady,' Richard said.

'I do hope it's not just her who's taken a liking to me.' As these words left Stephanie's lips she felt her cheek's burn with embarrassment. Thankfully, Wasiz quickly distracted them both from the steeds and Stephanie's burning cheeks. He had vanished shortly after they found a place to camp and now ran to the fire carrying a tied joint of pork. Hopping about like an excited fool he was and when Banbury saw he'd returned with meat he soon joined him. After travelling so long with wood folk both were slapping their lips as they put it over the fire and watched it sizzle. 'As savage as they get these are,' Wendolin sneered as Bethany sat on the arm of her throne. 'They are good people Wendy, they seem to be anyhow. Stop complaining and think where we are. We are finally free of her, we can go home,' Bethany said.

'We can't go home, not until we help them. They will keep us until we stop being useful same as she would have. Besides that we don't even know if we have a home left. Mother and father are long gone,' Wendolin said. 'Stolen you are red, but do not fear, for no group of callous Countesses are we,' Wasiz announced tossing the bag he returned with to Wendolin's lap. 'Where did you find all this?' Wendolin asked, looking inside to see a variety of clothes. 'That town's not totally deserted, seems a few traders were passing through and dropped a couple of bits. I do hope something fits, never had to dress a lady before so I just grabbed a handful of garments,' Wasiz told them.

'See, they are not so bad,' Bethany said. With a huff Wendolin called Stephanie over and waved her hands once again. This time creating a wall of vines covered in sharp thorns to conceal the three of them. 'Do you remember when we pinched the Duke of Bushcroft's prize hen? Oh the meal we had that night,' Banbury said. 'I seem to remember eating pork that night also, after you said I couldn't eat that plump hen,' Wasiz smirked. 'W-w-, but it had such big sad eyes poor thing,' Banbury laughed.

'Would you look away for a second?' Jhona said grabbing Richard's arm and pulling him to the fire to join the others. 'Look away from what?' Richard spluttered. 'You know very well, you've been staring at that poor girl ever since we found her,' Jhona said 'True, not like you to be so taken Richard,' Banbury added. 'Perhaps he has found his eternal love,' Wasiz joked, but all their joking stopped when the wall of thorns fell and Stephanie walked forward. Her brown hair was now plaited down her back revealing its true length. Tied with a green vine it was and a soft green dress covered her with a golden rope around her waist, that held the small purse that rested on it. Looking to her the others saw a smartly dressed woman walk over, but Richard saw her quite differently. Each step she took that drew her closer to him would make his heart jump like it was ready to pound itself from his chest. To him her hair sparkled and just the sight of her smile made him weak. Never had Richard been struck in such a way and the feelings that now rushed about his heart and mind couldn't be controlled. 'Thank you Wasiz. The clothes are perfect I cannot even remember the last time we had something clean to wear,' Stephanie said. 'Save your thanks for the poor lady whose washings gone missing,' Wasiz said as he and Banbury began slicing up the pork. 'You, well you look. It's really nice,' Richard said stumbling his words like a lad would if trying to charm someone he's particularly taken with. 'What my brother is trying to say is the dress suits you my lady,' Jhona said in a sarcastic tone. 'Well tell your brother thank you,' Stephanie joked as her sisters rejoined them. In black leather trousers and a red shirt with frilly shoulders Wendolin was now. While Bethany was left with bright blue overalls, the sort you'd commonly find a farm hand wearing. 'We shouldn't have let her pick first,' Wendolin complained as she tore the ruffled sleeves from her top. 'Could you not steal from someone with better taste?' She went on.

'They're still better than the rags we were in,' Bethany reminded her. 'So are we to just watch the savages eat or will you finally tell us why you all risked your necks to save us from the Countess,' Wendolin said. 'Quite right and now is as good as time as any,' Richard stated. 'Further south is the Forgotten Vale where the vampires dwell. Ruled over by one called the Grey Count. We aim to travel there and remove him from power so whatever endeavour he's currently waging can be stopped before another war begins.'

'So why do you need us? If you can infiltrate Accultian this Grey Count's hold should be easy enough,' Bethany said.

'I'm afraid it won't be, even if I can get us in quietly we will not get out without a fight,' Wasiz explained. 'We only need the aid of one of you. The others can wait at my apprentice's pub until our return.'

'If you return,' Stephanie muttered.

'I should not worry, the Balmoths have never failed me in the past.' A voice said that shocked them all and made even the horses spin their heads to see a tall man in a white gown with long golden hair. Seeing him Richard's companions leapt up to join him while the girls simply wondered who he was. 'You have clearly been busy,' the man said.

'How far away did you get your pet to drop you Godborn?' Jhona said looking at the mud over the bottom of the man's gown. 'Had to be a fair distance to stop me noticing him.' He went on as the wind whistled around him. 'Please Jhona, I only snuck up on you to stop you fleeing before we could speak,' Seer Elidom Godborn insisted. 'I imagine we're in trouble,' Richard said. 'You weren't. I was able to quell the La Sores, but now you're kidnapping girls,' Elidom exclaimed.

'Do we looked kidnapped?' Wendolin remarked from her throne. 'I don't suppose you do, where is it they found you three anyhow?' Elidom asked but then he noticed her throne. 'Are they mages?' He said spinning to face Richard. 'Not exactly,' Richard mumbled. 'I'm not,' Stephanie said raising her hand. Grabbing Richard's shoulder and leading him away from the others Elidom snapped. 'This is a joke right, you didn't take them from her did you?'

'We had no choice the Grey Count is planning something,' Richard said.

'Someone is always planning something Richard. You Balmoths can't keep trying to solve the world's problems without thinking about your actions,' Elidom said. 'Where is Avlor? What does he have to say about these Elites and I doubt he'd care we'd upset the Countess,' Richard said.

50

'Seer Tranem and I have less power than we did Balmoth. The La Sore's have the people's trust now. Did you hear they wish me to be a King?' Elidom said. 'I heard but believed they were only rumours,' Richard said. 'I'm afraid not.' Another's voice interjected and a high elf with a wrinkle covered face and balding head shuffled over using a cane to keep himself stable. His hands were heavily scarred and his fingers twisted, making it difficult for him to keep hold of the cane he wielded. 'They wish to see Elidom King, but keep the army they're creating for themselves. Even Seer Dune has been swayed by them.' Seeing the man join them Caspian and Fiona soon rushed over to greet him with Jhona close behind. As Fiona nuzzled the man's cheek Jhona said in an extremely respectful tone standing to attention as he did. 'Seer Tranem.'

'Very funny boy now come here before my stick finds you,' Avlor said embracing Jhona as the pair laughed. 'Whatever happened at the Afeun? I didn't teach you to use your gifts in such a way.'

'It wasn't all my doing, those Elites brought it on themselves,' Jhona said.

'I'm inclined to believe you my boy, but you best stay clear of any more,' Avlor told him.

'Who are these two?' Bethany asked. Increasingly curious about the pair she was and after getting close and seeing Avlor's mangled hands she was full of questions. 'Seers,' Richard scoffed.

'Thinks he's our boss that one does,' Banbury yelled from the fire. Neither he nor Wasiz cared to leave their meal to argue with Seers. 'A pointless use of precious time it is to try and convince one who claims to know all that you're right,' Wasiz would say of them.

'No man would wish to be boss of you Master Bale, of that I can assure you,' Elidom said not noticing Bethany reach for Avlor's hands. Taking them in hers she asked. 'How did this happen?'

'Gnomes I'm afraid, bunch of right nasty buggers they were too my lady,' Avlor told her. 'A tale your new companions will tell you I'm sure. For I would not be here if not for the Balmoths there.'

'Your wounds are fairly old I'm not sure I can cure the scars completely, but we can try,' Bethany said. 'Try what my dear?' Avlor asked as the water that dripped from the leaves and rested on blades of grass around them was drawn to their hands. With his hands in Bethany's and the water spinning about them Avlor began to giggle as whatever Bethany was doing tickled his hands wildly. 'Please my dear, I shall laugh my old tongue out of my mouth at this rate,' Avlor said through giggles as Elidom watched on amazed. 'That's impossible,' he mumbled to himself as they watched the water fall away. Avlor clenched his fist like he had never felt his hands before and if you didn't know they were once mangled you would never have known. 'So many aches and pains I still had from them, but now they're like anew. This can't truly be,' Avlor said looking over his hands. Elidom though just stared to Bethany as her smile charmed him without her even seeing. 'Oh my dear how am I to thank you, for such a gift you have given me.'

'Gold and a lot of it,' Wendolin yelled to them making Wasiz lean in to Banbury and in a whisper say. 'She's my favourite sister.' As they shared a laugh Bethany said. 'Do not fret me nor my sisters need any thanks.'

'Let me see,' Avlor said rubbing his hands together. 'It may be pushing it a little, but let us try an old trick of mine.' Holding up his cape and hiding himself behind it, Bethany saw his hand shuffle a little. Then dropping the cape back down he revealed a red and white checkered blanket. 'Now how did it go next. Ah yes, that was it.' With that he cast out the blanket and it began to separate and change colour, breaking up into three bright blue hooded capes. 'Here we go, one for each,' he said handing two to Bethany and then placing the last over her shoulders. She span in her new cape and shook Avlor's hand to thank him before handing the others to her sisters while Elidom rubbed his eyes with his hands. 'You've really done it this time Balmoth. Least we found you before this went any further,' Elidom said.

'It must go further. If the Forgotten Vale's curse is allowed to spread we shall face an enemy worse than the wolves or humans,' Richard insisted.

'We are done fighting wars Balmoth,' Elidom said. 'The Grey Count won't be able to challenge the force the La Sores will create. They just need time to do it. Do not stir the Grey Count now when the world has so many other problems. Go home, your farm waits for you.'

'And what of them if we do,' Jhona said looking past them to the others around the fire. 'You know what, the Countess will try to take them back before long and will eventually succeed. There isn't anything we can do to control that woman as you well know. She won't let a prize like them slip away. Many a mage have I seen, but not since the days of the first have I seen an elemental mage who can heal with just their hands alone. Your thief would last as long as he can hide himself from the many enemies he's managed to make and the dwarf not much longer than that I'd imagine,' Avlor said.

'So we give in,' Richard said.

'It is for the best Richard,' Elidom told him, words that sparked a memory in Richard's mind.

'You said the same that night,' Richard said in a whisper so only the four of them could hear. 'The night you left for the Crown City and nearly didn't return. I don't forget as easily as you do Elidom, difference is I don't ride to start wars as you do. We ride to stop them and will go with or without your blessing.'

'Enough, I don't wish to speak of it any further and dredging up the past will change nothing. Our course is set Seer, it is as I said to your pet. Stand against us if you dare, but if not don't block our path with pointless lectures,' Jhona said. Pulling Richard away and leaving the pair of Seers the brothers went to return to their friends around the fire.

'So will I just have to sit here and listen to them eat or will you tell us what's next on this quest of yours?' Wendolin asked shaking her hands sarcastically. 'Ar… Ar…Weapons,' Banbury stuttered. 'That's what's next, finding some silver blades to deal with those blood sucking devils.'

'After the pair of you decide who will be joining us that is. I have prepared a contract of sorts,' Wasiz said going into his pack and pulling out a scrunched up piece of parchment. In short it said they'd be paid a trunk of gold in return for healing any of the party should the need arise. 'You can make that two trunks,' Wendolin told him, after reading a portion of the contract. 'We shan't need a contract or anything like it. I will travel with you in thanks for freeing us. All I ask in return is you find a place for us after. One far away from Accultian,' Bethany said making Wendolin kick Wasiz and say. 'Give me a quill, I'll be the one going. I won't have you lording it over me or the guilt if you don't return.'

'I won't be left behind, if you're both going so am I,' Stephanie insisted.

'You can't go Steph,' Bethany said brushing her off. 'Why not? I'm smarter than the both of you,' Stephanie protested. 'Yes, but can you do this,' Wendolin said as roots sprang from the ground around Stephanie lifting her up and creating a seat of roots that held her aloft. 'Very funny, put me down,' Stephanie demanded. 'Stop your witchcraft. Come, d-d-d-don't come. It matters little if we haven't got silver,' Banbury insisted. 'There are few swords that will be useful against the Grey Count's own. Even a silver blade won't be enough to kill him,' Elidom said shocking them all, for all there believed he had left. 'So you do want to help then?' Jhona said.

'You're a friend Jhona and always will be. If your hearts are set on this I will do what I'm able. Little though that will be. For if a war rises from this the Seers must be seen to have had no part in it. Weapons I may be able to help with however. You know of King Lex Darum yes?' Elidom asked.

'Died in the Weeping Woods did he not?' Banbury said. 'Yes Master Bale, but never found was he or the weapon he forged,' Elidom said.

'A fable it is, the Kalarumba was never truly forged, just a story to scare you Seers,' Banbury told them. 'I wish it were so. I do not know what killed King Darum or the army that followed him but we believe we have found where they went,' Elidom said and moved to sit at the fire beside Bethany. Clicking his fingers the fire jumped up and began to form shapes. 'The west bridge?' Richard asked as the structure appeared in the flames. 'It's in Aceonse.'

'Close, from the south side of the Lavender Lake and a few more miles east there is a cave in the canyon's wall. Within the locals say they have seen ghostly spectres. Sure they're dwarves they are but any who dare try to enter haven't returned,' Elidom warned.

'What do these Elites know of it?' Jhona asked.

'Nothing. I have had Charlemagne looking into it. If that weapon is out there no other will you need against the Grey Count,' Elidom said.

'It will be days out of our way, but the chance to nab a dwarven king's horde is one I'm certainly up for,' Wasiz said.

'Maybe thief, but my scythe is as useless against sp... Sp... Ghosts as blood suckers,' Banbury said. 'You all sound fairly useless, but lucky for you we are here now,' Wendolin said rolling up the signed contract and dropping it on Wasiz's head. 'We can head off after some sleep.' Turning away she twirled her hands and where the wall of thorns grew now a mound of them spawned. As a doorway opened in it Wendolin called for her sisters to follow. With a huff Bethany did while Stephanie quickly turned to the group to say before following them. 'I really am sorry about them Wendolin doesn't mean to be, well so mean.' Sharing a quick smile with Richard she soon hurried after her sisters. 'Bed it is then,' Jhona said.

'Yes and you best get on before you're missed,' Richard said to Elidom. He remained though but only to lean in close to Jhona and ask. 'The name, that one who healed Avlor what was it?'

'You mean Bethany the woman who healed Avlor,' Jhona corrected him.

'Yes her, she makes me feel terribly odd. How do you suppose you speak to one?' Elidom asked.

'If by one you mean a girl I'm hardly the one to ask, as you well know. I did think we shared that,' Jhona said. 'Never mind it, probably just an iffy stomach. A spot of bad celery perhaps,' Elidom replied. He then left to catch back up with Avlor who had already began shuffling his way back to where the master of the skies waited. Jhona noticed though as Elidom went his body seemed to sway like he was in an odd daze of sorts.

Going to bed so early meant the Leaflins woke as the sun rose. Stephanie was awoken first by a bead of sunlight piercing through the tangled roots. After throwing her new cape over her she left her sisters to wake. Outside the sun was slim on the horizon and cast a warmth over the forest. Only one other sat awake before the dying fire. 'Did you not sleep?' Stephanie asked Wasiz who was looking over a map. 'Oh yes I did a little, but whenever my eyes close his night song starts,' Wasiz said. He then closed his eyes and a roaring snore came from Banbury. 'See what I mean,' he joked. 'What is it you're looking for?' Stephanie asked. 'A faster road to the west bridge, but all are too well watched. We shall have to keep to the smuggler's paths to stop too many eyes seeing us,' Wasiz said then Stephanie noticed the map begin to fade until the parchment went blank. All apart from the name Jhona Balmoth written at the bottom. 'What happened to it?' Stephanie asked. 'A very special map is this, was searching for it when myself and Jhona there first met. That's why I popped his name down on it to ensure I'd not forget it. This map here knows every path this world has, even secret ones,' Wasiz said.

'Will it show me places?' Stephanie wondered.

'What would you like to see?' Wasiz asked.

'The Humtees, it's where we're from. It's probably not even there anymore. The Countess said it wasn't anyhow,' Stephanie sighed.

'See for yourself,' Wasiz said handing her the map. 'Just ask it to show you.'

'Could you please show me the Humtees,' Stephanie asked and black squiggles began to cover the page until a map of the village formed. 'It's all there. Look there's Peacock Lane and that's where our parents cottage is.'

'It is easy for people like the Countess to claim something when you haven't the means to find out for yourself,' Wasiz said. The pair looked over the map until the others began to wake. With Wendolin giving orders they were all on their feet and would soon be off on their journey to find the Kalarumba. The eyes of wolves though had been watching them through the night and not only Elidom Godborn had friends in the sky. While preparing Caspian's saddle Balvor made sure Richard saw him as he passed by, leading the ranger to leave his group. 'There was a Seer here,' Balvor growled once the pair were alone. 'I did not summon them and nothing do they know of you wolves or our pact,' Richard said.

'You're pushing your luck ranger,' Balvor snarled. 'Not only do you bring Seers to my forest you neglect to tell us of the Afeun.' As crows chattered to one another in the treetops above them. 'If the crows tell you of the Afeun then you know it wasn't our doing. We took that fort without spilling a drop of blood,' Richard said.

'Enough, the crows saw it all and your brother's actions are the only reason the pack is yet to hear of it. Your Seers may condemn him but death is the only cure for men such as these Elites. When the others do hear you must be far from here for I can only quell them if no rangers are around to make easy prey of. It is your quest that concerns me most Balmoth. If the blood suckers are riled up it will not be the Seer's lands that suffer, but ours,' Balvor said.

'That's precisely why we must act now. I have the ear of the Count's own daughter. He's already planning his war and readying his generals for it. If we don't move against him now we may never get another chance,' Richard said. This lead Balvor to grumble and after a few seconds of silence Richard asked. 'Why not join us Fang Lord? Not only your nose but your strength will be of great help.'

'No, I can't leave the pack and little help would I be. Off with you now before the crow's chattering reaches the others.' With a nod to the Fang Lord Richard returned to his companions while Salene joined her mate. 'We should join them, show the rangers we can be trusted,' Salene said.

'We have shown them and left be we have been, best not show ourselves to the Seers,' Balvor said and left her to watch as Richard's party began to walk away from the Fang.

Chapter Four
The Seer's Elites

'How much more walking? Do you even know where the nearest stable is?' Wendolin complained.

'Yes I'm sure there's one nearby. Only a mile or so once we pass the plains we should find it,' Richard said. 'That's not nearby,' Bethany added. Almost half way across the barren grounds that was the Plains of Nore the party had gotten. To their backs the trees of the Fang grew smaller with each step. North west they went over the cracked ground and while the Leaflins had been rather jovial when they began their trek, Bethany and Wendolin grew increasingly grumpy as they realised just how far they truly had to walk. 'Well we will need a rest soon, poor Steph's feet can't take it,' Bethany insisted as she and Wendolin fell behind the others. 'I'm fine, they're just being babies,' Stephanie said taking Richard's arm to walk with him. Hurrying forward Wendolin pushed them apart and said. 'No she's just trying to look tough. We can stop there for a rest,' Wendolin said pulling her sister away. 'Hardly been marching for a couple of hours and already they whine. Exactly why you don't take the fairer sex on quests such as ours. Only a dwarven lass could handle it,' Banbury blustered.

'Then why is it we have never seen any dwarf ladies adventuring on our travels,' Jhona asked.

61

'They are far too clever for that, know how their bread's buttered they do. Content to leave the heavy lifting to silly sods like me,' Banbury said.

'I fear you know little about even dwarf women Banbury,' Stephanie chuckled with Richard after shrugging off her sister with a dirty stare. 'Bite your tongue young lady. I am the only man here to know the embrace of a loving wife,' Banbury replied. 'Really, who was mad enough to marry him?' Stephanie whispered to Richard. 'Not one but four suffer from that madness,' Richard said.

'Four, he has four wives,' Stephanie said. 'Was one not enough,' but her whisper had grown louder than she expected from the shock. 'You react as if it's so sordid. It's terribly common for my kind to take multiple wives. Take my uncle, Cherrytoe Buggerings for example. He had a wife for everyday of the week,' Banbury said. 'It's hard to know who to feel most sorry for is it not lady Leaflin. Do you feel for the many women having to share their hearts only to be passed by the next day for another. Or the man who has to cope with eight wives,' Wasiz giggled.

'Don't you mock. It's your doing I ended up with so many as it is,' Banbury said.

'My doing, the sailor blusters. You didn't have to accept their hands. You were fairly eager from what I can remember,' Wasiz snapped back.

'You have some peculiar friends Richard,' Stephanie quipped. Storming ahead Wendolin went until she suddenly stopped and sat down. 'That's it, we must rest for a minute at least,' she insisted.

'Not here we have to go on until we pass this cursed place,' Jhona said as a landmark caught his eye. Since the day it was left sand had began to cover it, to most who passed by it would look to be just a rock. 'He's right,' Richard said. 'We can rest soon, but we best not dally here.'

'Why not, this is a good a place as any. Could use a few trees though,' Wendolin said.

'Just get up we don't have time for this childish nonsense,' Jhona snapped.

'What happened here that has you so riled up?' Bethany asked. 'Ask Wasiz, he likes telling pointless tales,' Jhona scoffed and continued walking as the Leaflins looked to Wasiz. 'He's right, it's not a tale worth telling and hardly paints us in a fair light,' he said. 'I think we have all had enough of you watching us and picking what's best to say,' Bethany said.

'Exactly, tell us something we actually want to know for a change. What happened here?' Wendolin added. 'Fine, walk and I shall tell you,' Wasiz ordered and in a flash Wendolin was on her feet and all three sets of eyes glared to Wasiz.

'It took months of planning. The whole time we never expected it to work, but through schemes, manipulation and the biggest bucket of lies I could find we did it and we won,' Wasiz said as they followed Jhona who now walked ahead beside the horses. 'What did you win?' Stephanie asked. 'The war, the human's purge. What do you know of it?' Wasiz asked.

The Forgotten Hero

'Not a lot, events in the real world seemed to not really matter much while she had us,' Wendolin said. 'In short we were losing, well the Seer's were losing I should say, but a tide was turning thanks to the Balmoths and their mighty steeds. Courageous Balmoths and pesky thieves were never going to be enough however. So Seer Godborn hatched a plan that he hoped would end the war and leave the Crown City under the Seer's control. We had no idea what it would turn into when he summoned us. No part did we play in the battle but the sight will never fade. They were never meant to burn. When the dragons arrived we were as shocked as most in the Crown City. Flames fell upon them before any within the City could even scream. Elidom had even managed to manipulate the dreaded dragon Amunden. He and his kin showed no mercy. With the city ablaze Seer Godborn advanced hoping to secure his victory, but another had beaten him to it. None know why, for he is trickier than even I but the Wizard June appeared before the City's gates. I could only see faint shapes on the horizon, built for the dark underground eyes such as mine and Bales are. The Balmoths saw it clearly though as your woody eyes would have also. Just there they once stood,' Wasiz said gesturing to the east. 'There where the land cuts into an oval, that is where it broke away and was cast to the sea. With just the slamming of his staff to the ground he sent the very mass of land the Crown City rested upon sailing to the east as if it was but a fly he'd swotted away. We never expected he could possess such strength. This sent Seer Godborn into a rage we had never seen within him. So fierce was his hunger for revenge we expected him to strike down the Wizard right there. Before he was able the Wizard June vanished, leaving his staff behind and us by the shore watching the City burn as the sea pulled it away, past even a wood elf's sight. Not content with his victory Elidom went to Accultian, there he had your Countess create the King's wall that will imprison them within their City forever more.'

'Elidom that man from last night, he worked with the Countess?' Wendolin said.

'I'm afraid so. Her mages were vital during the war. She was able to put the Seers in her pocket long ago and still keeps them there today,' Wasiz told her. 'So that's why you didn't end her when you could have, to keep him happy,' Wendolin snapped. Looking to Richard Stephanie noticed his face had become pale, his bottom lip shook and he stared to the ground hoping none would see his bloodshot eyes. 'What is it?' She asked brushing the back of her hand on his. 'It would have been done without the dragon's aid,' Richard said in a whisper. 'It would have ended without blood or ruin. They'd sent them away, their wolves. Those in the Fang are descended from the wolves who were sent away that day. After the battle was done we discovered King Hargo had known dragons flew to his city. How he forced Barramore and his kin to flee we still don't know, both the humans and wolves were so loyal to one another. Rarely would you find one without the other. So when we arrived and saw only humans stood before the City I became sure this war would end with a truce.

Then the dragons arrived and these plains burnt,' Richard stopped and looked to where the Crown City once stood. 'You could hear the wails of those in the City, their cries still ring in my ears like a bell getting slammed with a hammer time and time again.' Taking his hand Stephanie pulled him close as tears dropped down his cheeks. 'He promised us it wasn't meant to be this way. Promised us this was their doing, but before the war even began Elidom had become a man none of us could recognise.'

'What was it that changed him so?' Stephanie asked. 'Later for that, I've told enough sad stories for today,' Wasiz said reminding the pair they weren't alone. Ahead Jhona walked quietly beside Caspian until he heard footsteps running to his back. 'I didn't mean to upset you, how was I to know what happened here?' Wendolin said. 'Is that your way of saying sorry?' Jhona wondered causing Wendolin to shove him and say. 'I'm trying here ranger, it's not like the last few years have been easy on us either.'

'You're right and maybe I am being a bit self centred. How long were you in Accultian anyhow?' Jhona asked. 'Too long, must have been thirty years at least. We were only children when she took us and that story paints me in a worse light than yours does you,' Wendolin told him. 'Well next time we pass a grim spot you will have to tell me and we can be miserable together,' Jhona laughed with Wendolin as they carried on over the Plains.

Finally dust turned to mud and grass as the party left the Plains of Nore. Finding a path they went on north west and soon found oaks and willows all about them. 'Not much further, once in Lonas we should be able to find some horses to make the rest of our journey less taxing,' Richard said.

'Is that this Lonas up ahead?' Wendolin asked as she pointed to a cottage. Ahead where the road broke into two, a charming thatched cottage had been built between the two paths. A clean white picket fence enclosed the front garden where four beds of white and blue flowers grew. The owner had been tending to the flower beds but after seeing the large party approaching she rushed to her gate and began waving to them. 'Dearie me. Dearie me,' the portly woman said as they approached. 'Whatever has you all out and looking such a sorry state,' she went on as she stormed past her gate to the girls. 'Poor thing, poor dear things you are.' Licking her finger she wiped Bethany's mucky cheek. 'We are just travelling to Meceller,' Richard fibbed hoping to quickly brush her off, but this lady clearly had ideas of her own. She had already begun to usher the Leaflins through the gate to her front door. 'In with you all, no sort of mother would I be letting you carry on as mucky as you are. Go on now, my Gerald will take care of your lads but a hot bath is what you girls need,' the woman said persuading them on. While Stephanie took Bethany's hand and gingerly walked to the door, Wendolin almost ran when she heard the offer of a hot bath. 'This is strange Richard, we passed here less than a year ago and there was never any cottages here,' Jhona said.

Once within the cottage the Leaflins found it almost empty. Only a round table, a stack of a barrels and few candles sat around it and as soon as the door closed the woman's demeanour dramatically changed. 'Where's the bath?' Wendolin complained.

'Shut it,' the woman said drawing a long jagged knife from beneath her apron. 'Gerald, Graham get out here,' she ordered and two men appeared from the only other room the cottage had. Gerald was an old elf whose hands wobbled as he unraveled a length of rope, while Graham appeared to be their son. Both had withdrawn faces that contorted as they readied themselves to carry out the grim deeds they had in mind. 'What is this you old witch?' Bethany shouted pushing Stephanie behind her. 'Quiet, the Elites will be here soon for your rangers, but they said nothing of you,' the woman said as she waved her knife about. 'Hurry and bind them Gerald be useful for once,' the woman spat. 'Right you are Enid, get here you,' Gerald said. Reaching for Wendolin, the old elf tried to grab her hands but she pulled them away and said. 'No one will ever cage us again and I swear you will die if you touch me.'

'Shut her up and tie her,' Enid snapped.

'You won't just die, you'll suffer a pain few others will ever know. I will tear your body into as many pieces as I...' Suddenly Wendolin was cut off by the back of Graham's hand striking her across the face, dropping her to her knees. Grabbing her hair Graham pulled Wendolin's head up so she faced him and put the rusted blade of the dagger he held to her throat. 'Let me gut this one mother, please. She would squeal so nicely,' Graham licked his foul lips as he spoke but Wendolin ignored him and asked her sister once he had finished making his gruesome request. 'Will you complain if I kill them?'

'Just do it, leave the old man,' Bethany ordered and the cottage started to shake. 'What's that?' Enid yelled putting her knife to Bethany's throat. 'She did try to warn you,' Bethany replied as roots burst through the floorboards. Gerald's body was scored by the many roots with such force his guts were pulled out as they shot through him. Graham had been spared this fate instead the roots cocooned themselves around him and as he wailed he was pulled beneath the broken floorboards and buried under the cottage. 'I told you to spare the old man,' Bethany complained as Enid fell back. Dropping her knife she ran to the front door, but when she reached it she found vines that sprouted bright red flowers over them had begun to cover the doorway. 'Sorry I got a bit carried away,' Wendolin remarked as some of Gerald's innards fell from the ceiling. 'I'm still remembering my own strength. It's been so long since we've been able to use our abilities without being beaten or starved after.'

'Never mind, she can tell us,' Bethany said.

'Tell you what?' Enid replied as fear gripped her and roots began to spin about her legs. 'Who you really are?' Bethany said.

'Crows,' Enid yelped as she tried to bat the roots away. 'You don't look like a crow,' Wendolin said. 'Crows of the Wilds, we're mercenaries. Hired by the Elites,' Enid replied as roots spun around her, gripping her legs and pulling her up to hang upside down from the rafters. 'Hired to do what?' Bethany asked. 'They had word the Balmoths travelled this way, they wanted us to delay them, that's all. We meant no harm,' Enid lied.

'Why are those Elites even after them?' Stephanie asked. 'Do you not know? They're murderers. The lot of them, killed a fort full of Elites he and his brother did,' Enid said.

'That's not true, it can't be,' Stephanie mumbled. 'We'll find out for ourselves,' Wendolin said. With a flick of her wrist the vines crawled away from the door letting the Leaflins leave Enid to be pulled into the rafters where the roots cocooned her away.

Storming out of the cottage the Leaflins rushed back to the others with Wendolin leading the way. 'So you are just a bunch of rogues,' she yelled and as she went the flowers in the beds rose to follow her. 'Rogues, what b-b-bluster. Him maybe, but the rest of us are certainly no rogues,' Banbury said gesturing to Wasiz.

'What happened? We tried to get in, but the door was barred,' Richard asked.

'She said she was a Crow of the Wilds some sort of mercenary. They had this plan to stall you for these Elites and they tried to kidnap us,' Stephanie told them. 'Never mind that. Is it true? You're just a band of killers?' Wendolin said snapping her fingers before Richard's face to win his attention. 'Whatever has she told you, we are no such thing,' Richard said.

'So you didn't kill a fort full of Elites, see I told you,' Stephanie said, but as she turned to scold her sisters she caught Jhona's eye. 'It's not true, is it?' Before Jhona could answer her Wasiz quickly sprang up to his defence. 'They left Jhona and myself with little choice. We took the Afeun from its Commander without even a life being taken, and we left after making peace by giving them nothing but a few sore heads and a stubbed toe. Save your accusations of murder for the ones who truly deserve it. These Elites brought their end on themselves. Barely a second had we returned before they set on me. Giving Jhona and myself no choice but to defend ourselves.'

'You weave so many fables it's hard to know if you ever speak the truth,' Wendolin replied as she grew increasingly irritated with her companions. 'It's the truth, but we don't have time to convince you now. We must be off before the Elites arrive,' Richard insisted. 'From what they said it sounded like they were fairly close by,' Bethany told them.

'If they're in the saddle it won't take them long to catch us,' Banbury added.

'I have an idea, but it's risky,' Wasiz said going past the girls to the door and looking in. 'Call us murderers, have you seen the state of this?' Wasiz announced as he saw the blood covered walls. 'Quickly, find a brush we must get this house clean.'

The Forgotten Hero

As Captain William Slade lead his unit of twenty men before the cottage it seemed to him the Balmoths had yet to show. Climbing down from the grey stallion he rode he removed his golden helm to reveal his messy blonde hair and beard, along with a war torn face and deep piercing green eyes. Leaving his men to prepare the cage that sat on the tumbrel they had pulled with them. Captain Slade hoped to soon have the Balmoth brothers within it and be on his way to Duniesa to collect the hefty bounty the La Sores had placed on the pair. Rushing through the gate he barrelled to the door only to have it open just as he reached for the knob. He had expected a sour faced Crow of the Wilds to greet him, but he was taken back when a rosey cheeked wood elf opened the door. 'Good day sir, can I help you?' Stephanie asked. 'Quite,' William said as he composed himself. 'Where are the owners of this cottage? I have urgent business with them.'

'That would be my mother and father sir, but only myself and my husband are here. You're welcome to wait until they return sir,' Stephanie said welcoming him in. Thankfully they had managed to clean the blood and guts of the previous owners from the walls. Banbury had done his best to repair most of the broken floorboards, while they had covered the rest of the damage to the floor with a dirty brown rug. Before William was able to inspect the room further Richard emerged from the other room wearing Bethany's blue overalls and a tatty straw hat. 'This is my husband, Tony,' Stephanie said using the first man's name that came to mind. 'I'm sorry but I didn't get your name.'

'Captain William Slade of the Elites,' he said holding out his hand to shake Richard's and asked as he did. 'Did your in-laws tell you of our mission?'

'Oh yer they did at that,' Richard said in a strange voice that made Stephanie wince. 'Very well, my men will conceal themselves around the cottage, fetch me a drink while we wait would you?' William said. 'I can do that for ya sir,' Richard said going to the barrel beside the door. When Richard uncorked it he found it contained tarter slop, an awful smelling drink that stunk out the cottage as soon as the cork was removed. Taking a goblet from the floor Richard filled it and handed the frothing drink to William. Extremely disappointed by his beverage he turned his nose up at it and then looked up and down the man he had been told was called Tony. 'What do you know of the Balmoths?' He asked glaring to Richard. 'Only as much as the next,' Richard replied. 'Do hear they're awfully close with those Seers of yours, makes me wonder why you're bothering with them.'

'What makes you say that?' William asked.

'Well by the time you get them there may not even be a bounty to claim,' Richard said.

'Maybe so, but even if their Seers save them the La Sores will praise me for capturing the pair. Those brothers and their rangers have been left to go about unchecked for far too long. My Elites will knock that playboy Richard and his queer brother into the dirt at the very least,' William declared.

'You certainly are rather miffed, their actions in Afeun must have really riled you and them men of yours up,' Richard said noticing William's eyes were now fixed to his. 'Not at all,' he replied with a huff. 'Those men weren't my Elites, the La Sores have had to reach far to fill our ranks. Sadly a few undesirables had to be recruited, but in time only the finest of the elves will carry these blades,' William boasted resting his hand to the long sword on his belt. A fine steel blade it was, with a golden handle that held the emblem of the Seer's Elites upon the pummel. A golden helm was their mark, one that resembled the helmets Slade and his Elites wore. 'Funny how you wood folk think his rangers are some sort of saviours. A band of scrawny rogues is all they are,' William went on as Richard lent against the barrel. 'Only those with particularly tiny minds would see the rangers as rogues. Some even say your golden city would be ash without them. Once the bridges were built the people of the north did little to nothing to hold back the purge. Where were you then Captain? While rangers fought and died to save whoever they were able. When wolves tore down doors and devoured the innocent,' Richard said as a grin uncontrollably spread over his face. He was all too aware William had cottoned onto their ruse and was rather enjoying watching him becoming increasingly uncomfortable as he spoke. Flinging his shoulders back and standing as tall as he was able William tossed the goblet down laughing as he stepped towards Richard. 'I was safe. I was in the north and only stories did I hear of the war. That's all you are Balmoth, nothing but a story. You're no hero over the lake. Maybe you were one day, but those days have passed,' William spat.

'Walk away from this Captain. You're getting yourself into something far beyond your capabilities,' Richard insisted. 'I shall decide that ranger,' William replied and tilted his head gesturing for Richard to leave the cottage. In the other room Jhona had been listening to their conversation through the thin wall. Realising their ruse had been discovered he silently opened the door and began to draw an arrow back in his bow. 'Get moving Balmoth, bluster all you wish from the cage,' William ordered.

'Walk away from this Captain,' Richard said again spying Jhona creeping across the room. 'There's no need for this fight.' Unfortunately William hadn't taken his eyes from Richard's and saw his gaze quickly darting to Jhona and then back to him. Guessing it was Jhona Balmoth sneaking up on him he quickly lunged forward, grabbing Richard by the collar with one hand while pushing over the barrel with his other. Spinning on his heel he released Richard letting him slide over the tarter slop covered floor and crash into the round table. Reaching for his sword William was quickly knocked back and pinned to the wall. An arrow had pierced his sleeve, slipping past his armour it had cut through the cloth beneath to hold him in place. Jhona's foot then pushed his half drawn sword back into its scabbard. Before Jhona could retract his foot William's free hand grabbed it and with all the force he could muster he threw Jhona back. Lifting the light wood elf into the air, leaving him to land in the pool of tarter slop. Snapping the arrow to free himself William tossed the end at Richard just as he'd regained his composure.

Making him slip back down pulling Stephanie with him, who was desperately attempting to pull him to his feet whilst also keeping herself standing. Running to the door William hurried to summon his Elites as Jhona leapt up to follow. Opening the door he charged out, yelling to his companions as he went. 'Draw your swords the Balmoths are...' His yells stopped however, once he saw his Elites crammed into the back of the cage and two women stood before it. 'It shouldn't be the Balmoths that worry you Captain,' Wendolin chuckled. Before William could react the flowers in the beds about him rose and weaved themselves around him. Dragging him over the floor Wendolin made the flowers wrap through the bars of the cage suspending William from the ground and tying him to the side. 'Who, who are you?' William yelled as he was restrained. 'Never mind that,' Wendolin said as the others left the cottage while Wasiz and Banbury lead three of the horses the Elites had arrived on from hiding. 'The rest of your steeds are wandering somewhere. I'm sure they will free you soon enough, but continue to follow us and we won't be so kind next time,' Bethany threatened feeling rather powerful in Richard's uniform. 'Don't get yourself mixed up with the Balmoths, the La Sores will be after your heads next,' William said.

'That's enough out of you,' Wendolin smirked clicking her fingers and making a huge leaf grow on the vines that muffled William's voice. 'Hurry let's change back before anyone else shows up,' Richard said to Bethany. 'What, no. What did you do to my overalls?'

'It's just a bit of tarter slop, here,' Richard said starting to unbutton the overalls, but he was quickly stopped by Bethany saying. 'That's okay you keep it,' and before he could argue she was rushing over to her new steed. All the others did the same seeing Jhona mount Fiona with Wasiz sat before him. While Bethany and Wendolin took a horse each Stephanie went to ride Caspian with Richard. Just as she was about to take Richard's hand to be pulled up Banbury stopped her and said. 'I ride with Richard girly, go on and get your own.'

'You can ride by yourself for a change Banbury, Caspian could do with a lighter load for a while,' Richard said.

'Bu-bu-but that's not how it's done and you know very well I can't control one of these things,' Banbury argued. 'Mount up or get left behind Banbury,' Wasiz yelled to him. 'Blasted, bloody Leaflins. Blasted bloody horses,' Banbury went on trying to pull himself on the black horse that was left. Roots spawned under his feet and lifted him from the floor, gently placing him into the saddle. Before he could thank Wendolin his horse reared up forcing him to cling on for dear life as they rode away from the cottage. Leaving Captain Slade and his men in a rather sorry state.

The Forgotten Hero

Chapter Five
The Lost King

'Balmoth, Balmoth. It's doing it again,' Banbury yelled as his horse who he'd quickly taken to calling Nobby was straying from the road to gorge himself on a tasty tuff of grass once again. 'Which Balmoth are you calling for?' Jhona replied.

'Whichever one will fix this daft pony. Go on, back on the road you stupid sod,' Banbury continued as Bethany rode beside him and took his reigns. 'You realise me nor Wendy have ridden a horse before,' she said leading them back on to the road. 'Yes well, your pony clearly isn't as vindictive as Nobby here. Got something against dwarves he has,' Banbury said making Nobby shake his mane and charge ahead. Thanks to the Elites providing the party with horses there was no longer any need to go to Lonas. Travelling on north west would see them miss it completely. Only the town of Inaka would they pass but Caspian saw fit to lead them around it at quite a distance. Over the hills that bordered the Fields of the Wearet they went. From their heights they found themselves close enough to see the white steeple and grey tiled roof of the speckled monks monastery peeking above the treetops that surrounded Inaka. The scenery was tranquil and once they went over the hills and down the other side the flat ground made their journey relatively easy for both mount and rider. As they travelled a noticeable gap had emerged between the Leaflins and the others. While Stephanie was content to chat with the Balmoths and listen to Wasiz jabbering on when the scenery around them sparked an interesting story her sisters had been keeping their distance and spoke little. Both now looked over their newly found friends in a new light after hearing about the events at the Afeun. This left both to wonder the same thing. 'What do you think it is? Jhona must have abilities like us to take on a whole group of those Elites with only the goblin,' Bethany finally asked her sister. 'Quiet,' Wendolin whispered to her. 'I think it's the air. When he rescued us I heard this whistling sound and then a rock struck the one guarding me and Stephanie. I think he's using the element to guide his arrows and things like that,' Wendolin said in a hushed tone. 'Hurry up and come see,' Stephanie shouted back to the pair. Ahead the group had stopped to quell Banbury's steed once more and beyond lay the Lavender Lake.

Few dare venture to the very edge of the gorge that the Lavender Lake runs through. A terrifying ten mile drop would meet any who took a misstep on the many loose rocks that covered the ledge. If they were lucky enough to avoid the countless jagged spires of rock that jetted out from the walls that is. Even if one was to fall into the lake at a relatively safe height the thrashing rapids beneath would soon pull even a very skilled swimmer to the bottom. There the swirling waters are strong enough to grind whatever is pulled beneath to a bloody pulp. Unfortunately the worst of these rapids lay directly beneath where our party hoped to find the cave Elidom had told them about. Two days of walking and riding, one night under the stars and one interruption from the Elites had brought them to the gorge's edge. Arriving around midday Banbury and Wasiz were quickly tasked with locating the cave's entrance while the others made camp. A task made considerably easier thanks to the Leaflins. Chores that would have taken the Balmoths hours now took minutes. The fire was quickly made and their canteens soon filled. Wendolin had even become civil enough to create them each a woven hut of vines of their own to sleep in. An uneasy tension though still upset the relative calm with Wendolin and Bethany taking every opportunity they could to pull Stephanie away from the others. She unlike them couldn't believe either of the brothers were murderous rogues, likewise concerning Wasiz and Banbury. A little rough around the edges maybe, but all made her feel safe in a way she hadn't known since her childhood.

'Is there any grub ready?' Banbury asked as he and Wasiz returned to the camp. 'Did you find it?' Jhona inquired. 'There's no cave down there, your Seer sent us for a golden goose,' Banbury said.

'I thought we were here for a weapon not a goose,' Stephanie asked.

'He means Elidom's tricked us, sent us here just to keep us out of the way,' Jhona said.

'No, that's not it. He was sincere when he said he wanted to help. They just didn't look hard enough,' Richard said. 'See for yourself, not even his map can find it,' Banbury said.

'It's true I fear he may be right Richard, there's no sign of any spectres or mythical weapon,' Wasiz said. 'I say we cut our losses. Head back to Inaka for supplies and get going to the Vale. It will take us weeks to reach the Grey Count's hold at this rate,' Jhona added. 'We will wait until night fall. One more night will change little,' Richard said.

'Listen to him Richard if me nor the rotter can find that cave in the daylight it's not there I'm telling you,' Banbury told him. A huge shadow then cast over their camp making all of them jump to their feet. 'Quickly, follow him,' Richard ordered assembling the group to follow the shape soaring in the sky back to the edge of the gorge. 'What is it?' Bethany asked. 'Charlemagne, he's the master of the sky,' Richard said as the griffin swooped down. Flapping his massive wings he climbed higher until with his outstretched wing he was able to block the sun. Casting his shadow over the gorge, letting Richard and his friends see a silvery blue mist covering a tiny opening in the chasm's wall. 'Ta, that's no cave not even Wasiz could fit through there,' Banbury blustered as Charlemagne disappeared in the sky. 'It's not like there's a path down to it either,' Wendolin said leading Richard to turn to his brother and say. 'Do you think you can manage it?' Reluctantly Jhona went to the edge and the whistling sound Wendolin had heard began to whizz about them.

'See I told you,' Wendolin whispered to Bethany as the wind flowed from Jhona down the gorge to the gap. Hitting the hole the rocks around began to shake making the loose ones fall away. As the force of the wind increased more followed until a hole large enough for them to walk through was left. 'That will do it, don't strain yourself,' Wasiz said taking a hanky from his bag to wipe the sweat from Jhona's brow. 'Don't fuss Wasiz, I'm fine,' Jhona said batting him back.

'Impressive, but you shouldn't be that worn out from a simple spell,' Bethany said holding his wrist to check his pulse. 'Most don't have the limitless strength you and your sisters seem to possess. That's about as much as I can handle at this distance,' Jhona said.

'It's lucky you have me here then,' Wendolin remarked making the trees bend and their branches grow to form a spiral staircase of wooden steps to the opening. 'Are you okay to go on?' Wasiz said to Jhona.

'Stop Wasiz, I'm alright. You don't have to fret every time,' Jhona said.

'Are you sure about this? Doesn't look very stable,' Banbury complained.

'That is why you're going first,' Richard said pushing Banbury onto the staircase forcing him to go down the first step. 'It's wobbling,' Banbury yelled. 'It's just your own legs wobbling Master Bale,' Wendolin said as she and her sisters went past him. Round and round they went, descending deeper into the gorge until they could hear the rapids crashing into rocks beneath them. When they found themselves before the opening all the Leaflins realised the confidence they'd previously possessed had left them. A bone chilling wail cast a freezing gust of wind over the sisters as they approached. 'What was that?' Stephanie said. 'Probably just the cave settling, right?' Wendolin said looking to Bethany. 'Of course, there's no such thing as ghosts or spectres. That's what father would say anyhow,' Bethany said. None though wished to be the first to enter causing them to wait for the others to catch up. 'Go on then Banbury, shouldn't you be used to caves like this.'

'Ta, didn't become a sailor because I love the underground lass. I rather hate it in fact. He's more suited to grim holes such as this,' Banbury said pushing Wasiz on. 'So be it. Once again it's left to the great thief to lead us through unspeakable peril,' Wasiz declared as he gingerly went into the cave. 'Here we go and do not fret or fear Leaflins, for my nose can sniff out any trap this trove has,' Wasiz boasted and like worried sheep they all followed him into the darkness.

Squeezing past the others Jhona went to Wasiz and took a rag from his bag and then asked. 'Do you have a flint?' As he wrapped the rag around an arrow.

'Silly me, completely forgot you lot can't see as well in the dark as I can,' Wasiz said stopping and using the fire striker he carried to set alight the rag. With their makeshift torch the others could now see the green slime oozing down the walls. 'Is it some sort of plant?' Wendolin said as she went to touch it.

'D...D... Leave it be,' Banbury stuttered. 'It's soul rot, touch it and your skin will blister for weeks.

The Forgotten Hero

Just one of the many awful things the underworld has to offer. Keep your water handy it will soften the sting slightly. Hurry and see us through here with our heads still on our shoulders rotter.'

'Relax Banbury, we shall have you free of here soon enough and besides…' Wasiz said abruptly stopping as he felt a flat rock he had just stood on sink, followed by a loud click. 'You said you could smell a trap,' Wendolin yelled.

'Don't worry,' Wasiz said as he waited for something to happen. 'There see, that was no trap. Just a loose stone,' but as Wasiz spoke the cave began to shake. Making rocks drop from the ceiling that allowed soul rot to rain down from the openings. Pouring down at such speed it soon pooled on the ground forcing them all on. The path went downward steeply and as they went all would end up yelping from the sting of the vile green goo. The walls around became thicker with it as they went on until it vanished from the walls and the path grew wider. The ceiling rose to such heights none could see the top, leaving just a carpet of black above their heads. Even Wasiz wasn't able to make out the ceiling above them.

'Quickly Wendy heal their stings,' Bethany ordered as she healed the burns on Stephanie's hands. As the sisters healed the others Wasiz began to look around, letting his eyes adjust to the darkness. A strange shape in the distance looked like it was wobbling causing him to begin inching closer to it. 'Wasiz, wait until your wounds are healed,' Jhona said as Wendolin healed a large burn on Jhona's neck from the soul rot splashing on the wall as it fell. 'Don't fret, it hardly got me and my skins used to such things,' Wasiz replied too enticed by the shape to stop. All of a sudden he did, stopping dead in his tracks and standing as still as a statue while the strange shapes rose before him. The sound of clinking iron followed and beneath the dark shapes a ghostly white mist grew. Rising from the floor the mist gave off a white light that revealed the shapes to be iron armour. Within the mist continued to increase until a spectre grew beneath. Forming arms and legs from the mist to fill the clanging chainmail that hung from the breastplate. In the slits of the helm silver eyes shone and as silvery teeth appeared the spectre spoke. 'Who dares enter the King's grave?' His voice was soft but filled them all with terror and rather than coming from its mouth the sound seemed to reverberate from the mist. 'Who dares walk on the sainted soil of his Highness?'

'Blasted ghouls, Richard we should turn back less we be cursed with this lot,' Banbury insisted. The mist was slowly surrounding them illuminating the cave around as it went, showing that all around decaying bodies of dwarven soldiers lay. Each slowly rising as the mist seeped into them. 'Who dares enter?' The voice bellowed once again, this time sending chills through all there. 'We meant not to intrude on any tomb,' Wasiz promptly replied. 'Simply lost in the underworld are we.'

'Lies, grave robbers,' the voice said and for a second it sounded as if it was grinding its ghostly teeth.

'Yes, for the weapon that cursed us do you come. To steal, to rob us of our eternal bodies.' The sound of spears and swords being lifted from the ground made them reach for their own weapons as the figure before Wasiz grew taller. Casting out its arms it declared. 'Death, a never ending death is the King's curse. Bound to his hold forever is his iron arm.' A great sword grew from the mist to rest in the spectre's hand as he spoke. 'Death and unending anguish upon any who dare seek his might.' With that the figure went to strike, but an arrow flew between the gap within its helm bringing a powerful gust of wind with it. Casting the spectre back and breaking apart what was left of the corpse within. 'I think we'd all heard enough of that,' Jhona said. Soft wails turned to fury filled screams and the spirits of King Lex Darum's iron arm used their decaying corpses to charge. 'Who has water?' Bethany yelled as Wasiz threw her the only canteen they had left. Most of their supply had been emptied in the tunnel in a vain attempts to wash off soul rot. 'This can't be it,' she complained as Wendolin retrieved a pair of swords from the ground. 'Call your leaves Leaflin,' Banbury yelled as a pair of rotting bodies came within range of his scythe. With a swing he hewed both of their heads off but the bodies still charged on regardless. Flailing their axes around until Wendolin cleaved an arm from one, kicking the rest of its body into the other. 'I can't call my leaves you idiot there's not even roots around here. Everything's dead,' Wendolin yelled as she threw her spare sword to Stephanie. 'What am I meant to do with this?' Stephanie yelled as she barely caught its handle. A spear then struck the ground beside her, distracting her from the corpse that leapt up from the ground, knocking her down it began to clamber over her. Its broken jaw started to fall away as its face rose to meet hers. Dropping rotten teeth onto Stephanie as its ghoulish hand tried to grip her throat. A boot soon cast this husk aside and Richard quickly pulled Stephanie up to her feet. 'Stay to my back,' Richard ordered and Stephanie was happy to do so. Banbury's scythe continued to slice bones from bodies until Banbury felt it jam into something. The blade had become trapped within the ribcage of a mangled corpse and before he was able to retrieve it the body violently spun. Snapping the blade from the pole before Banbury could retract. Spears and arrows fell all around as the raging screams grew. The little water Bethany had shot about like tiny cannon balls casting their foes aside as they flew, however the canteen was quickly running dry and the onslaught of corpses continued unabated. Richard stabbed through the breastplate of one before him only to have his blade pulled from his hand. Another swung a mace for him and using all her strength Stephanie lifted her sword to block the blow. Only an ounce of effort did it take for her sword to be batted aside by the mace. As the corpse drew back Richard caught its arm, pulling its humerus bone from its shoulder letting him retrieve the mace and crack it around its head. 'We can't keep this up Richard, every one we kill just finds a new vessel,' Wasiz cried out, the many harnesses he wore were empty. He was left with only the two daggers he held while Jhona's quiver was down to a handful of arrows. Reaching to Jhona's belt Richard took his sword yelling as he did. 'We need a path through.'

'I'll clear the way, but that will be all I have,' Bethany said. Jumping over a pair the little water that was left darted through the air after her. Shredding the pair of walking dead she passed as it went to her back. With another wave of her arm it darted past her, expanding to form frozen spears of ice that quickly grew in length as much as they were able before exploding. Sending out shattering glass like shards of ice that cleared the way of enemies. 'Hurry and regroup,' Richard ordered as he tossed the mace to shatter a skeleton and took Stephanie's hand. 'Then what?' Banbury said.

'Run,' Richard yelled. Releasing two arrows from his bow Jhona used what energy he had left to send a gust of wind with each buying them precious few seconds as they ran. The stumbling corpses soon started to encircle them once again as the path before them rose. Without knowing they had ran to the centre of this tomb. Here the ground rose up to a small plateau where a rusted blunt sword rested on top of a stone sarcophagus. 'It can't truly be,' Banbury said as the mist controlling the corpses of the iron arm rushed to them, their light illuminated the words carved over the stone. 'Here be King Lex Darum bound to eternal life, eternal suffering. Bound with his kin to guard his prize until it's claimed by the worthy and wise.'

'That's the sword you wanted,' Wendolin raged seeing the useless blade. 'They're charging again,'

Bethany shouted over. 'Jhona get the sword a blunt blade is better than none,' Wasiz said.

'No don't touch it,' Banbury yelled. 'You'll curse us same as him.' Ignoring Banbury Jhona reached for the sword and as soon as he held it the mist began to fade. The corpses fell back down dead and all our party froze as the crashing of steel faded and they were left in the pitch black.

The silence was abruptly broken by Jhona's cry followed by a beam of blood red light. It engulfed the sword he held making it vanish from his hand and then flow through the sarcophagus. The lid started to shake and then slowly slid away to let the hands of the one kept within reach for the sides and heave himself upright. 'King of Kings,' Banbury muttered as King Lex Darum sat up straight. Unlike the King's soldiers his body still held life, but only a little. 'Finally, finally,' he coughed and spluttered as he spoke. 'Finally someone has made it past the others.' He was almost jovial as he lifted his weak arms in a vain attempt to greet them. 'So it was true, your fable, your death,' Banbury said.

'I am not so dead yet young master,' the King said looking down to him. 'What clan do you hail from?' He asked looking over the faces around him. 'Quite odd faces you all have. Clear the gloom from them. Your trial is done.'

'Bale is my family name Highness,' Banbury told him. 'Bale I don't know this family, but you will make their name I'm sure young master. The King's breathing then became sharper as he spoke. 'Hurry now not long do I have left, the Kalarumba has kept us prisoner for so long and only a few minutes am I left with.' Reaching to his side he retrieved one of the five items that sat around him. Holding up a curved dagger he announced. 'The Kala was a weapon none should have ever have wielded. Its making was a mistake that saw all I held dear lost and the shadows who whispered in my ears as I crafted her lose their prize also. More power than even the almighty Norcea could wield did the Kala contain. A god fell in her making and with it the world could have been broken in two. So powerful was it the sword itself became a living thing. A living entity that saw the hatred in my heart and the evil I or anyone that would wield it could bring. So when the ambush came it saw its chance to be free of me. Saving my soul only to curse me and have me watch over what it became. Five it now is, separated so only those of the same just goal can wield it as one,' Holding out the dagger the King passed it to Banbury. 'Banbury Bale to you goes the Kala's dagger, plain and simple it may appear but care for it as you would your dear wives. Show it you have love within you and a great change in it you will find.' His hand raised again, this time shaking as he attempted to hold up a silver long sword. Its blade glimmered even in the dark and within the pommel on the hilt a red gem rested. 'Richard Balmoth of the rangers,' the King said making all begin to wonder how he already knew their names. 'The silver sword of the Kala. A blade sharper than any other and will grant that spark that lies within you some life.'

Taking hold of the sword Richard felt a rush of energy cascade up his arm, like small static shocks pinching their way up to his shoulder. A plain silver ring then followed, but King Darum looked perplexed as he looked to the Leaflins and said. 'Hmm, well this one just says Leaflins. Again and again, Leaflins, Leaflins.'

'We are the Leaflins sir,' Stephanie said.

'So you are and since you spoke first you shall take it for now,' and as Stephanie went to take it King Darum cupped her hands in his. 'For them this will make water flow even in the driest deserts and trees grow upon snowy peaks, but for you nothing will it do. For no aid do you need Stephanie Balmoth, no aid at all.' Pulling her close he whispered in her ear. 'They though will need you, know that this quest of yours will fail without you. Let not the woes of others slow you, nor push you from the path you wish to follow. For a loving heart as yours beats best when you let others hear it,' as she stepped back Stephanie said.

'Thank you sir, but I'm a Leaflin not a Balmoth.'

'Hmm, yes I suppose you still are. I am sorry, you see so much when you sleep I don't know if am here or there. What else have we here?' He said taking a hair clip from his lap. 'Yes, Jhona Balmoth, the son of steeds, the one who held the sword. The clip is yours, for one who travels so far you will never be too far with this close by.' Passing it to Jhona the hair clip instantly began to change shape to become a soaring eagle. One item remained in King Darum's sarcophagus and as he rolled it back and forth in his palm he glared to Wasiz, who stared back much the same. 'This one doesn't give your name as the others did theirs,' the King said.

'What name does it give you? I go by many, I doubt you've heard even half.' Wasiz boasted.

'It is not a name you're known by. Wasiz of the Red Water. The rotting thief from below the soil. The chain breaker of a titan's hold. From far deeper and darker places than any of my kin have dared go does cracked tooth come from,' the King said and held the item to his ear. 'I see. It does speak your name, but only in a faint whisper it is. The other though it roars, barks it in my ears like a raging beast fresh from the hunt. So be it, for now it is yours. To you the hourglass goes and safe from the true masters of power will it keep you. Best you keep it close thief for the rightful master of the glass will one day find you.'

'Let him, I may even let him take it,' Wasiz said looking at the hourglass pendant for a second before putting it in his bag. He was hoping for mighty arms or some incredible magic to help end the Grey Count. An hourglass pendant was the last thing he had expected. 'Hurry now, only seconds I have left. Go on from the head of where I rest, keep your path true and a way out will find you. Go on with you, it is time I finally sleep and with my men pass to the halls of our fathers and lost kin.' With that the King laid back and rested his head to the pillow. With one final breath his skin began to peel away and crumble to dust. The blood red light faded as the King did and in the darkness they stumbled their way to another tunnel where at the end a small ray of sunlight could be seen.

Chapter Six
Inaka

'Daylight at last and fresh air,' Banbury blustered as they climbed above ground. 'Aren't dwarves meant to like the underground,' Bethany said.

'Not Banbury, we're lucky he stayed down so long without freaking out,' Wasiz said as he helped pull her up. 'Lucky ta, was just so much going on I didn't even have time to think about how cramped it was. Or how dark and dismal and dark,' Banbury said as a mild panic started to take hold of him. 'It's okay Banbury we won't be going into any more cramped or dark places for some time now. I hope anyway,' Stephanie said.

'Seems we've come out a few miles from Inaka,' Richard said.

'Finally some luck,' Jhona said using the hair clip he been given to pin back his fringe. After Banbury had calmed down Wendolin almost cried when the others decided to call the horses once they arrived at Inaka, meaning they'd be walking there. Although all were weary and desperately in need of a decent meal each had a spring in their steps thanks to their recent success. For the Leaflins this victory softened even Wendolin's mood. To them it was as if they'd never accomplished anything in the past and this was their first true success. Rarely did any not achieve their goals, but until now all their feats had been at the

93

Countess of Accultian's request. 'Let me try the ring on,' Bethany said.

'Fine, but don't go mad or anything. We don't know what it will do to you,' Stephanie said passing it to her. Just holding it made Bethany's skin shine and water start to drip from the ends of her fingers. 'This is incredible,' Bethany said waving her hand so the water danced around her. 'Let me try,' Wendolin said taking Bethany's hand and snatching the ring from her. Once on Wendolin's finger her skin shone the same as her sisters had but instead of water dripping from her hands flowers with big red buds began to grow in her wake, leaving a trail of blossoming roses as she went. 'It's like my energy's doubled, tripled even. I feel like there's no limit to what I could do.'

'Don't hog it Wendy,' Bethany complained trying to wrestle the ring from her. Pushing her off Wendolin ran ahead of the others and found a dead willow whose branch's were broken and its trunk had been burnt. Placing her hands to it the burnt bark fell away, broken branches were fixed and in a minute leaves covered them. The plain ring seemed to work as a mage's staff would, increasing the power of the wielder and providing a huge boost to their energy. Leaving the sisters to argue over the ring the others wandered on, not as impressed with their items as they were. 'A tiny knife, after all that how can these be the only weapons we walk away with,' Banbury said.

'At least you got a blade,' Wasiz complained as he fiddled with the hourglass. 'Safe from masters of power, that's what he said wasn't it,' Wasiz went on as the King's riddles slowly became clear to him. 'Jhona cast a spell on me, quickly now.'

'What why?' Jhona asked.

'Just throw a gust of wind at me, go on,' Wasiz insisted. 'No I don't want to hurt you,' Jhona said.

'I'll do it,' Bethany laughed after getting the ring back from Wendolin. Water then pooled in her hands and darted through the air to Wasiz. Bethany was sure this was some sort of joke and expected Wasiz to flamboyantly leap aside, but he didn't and as the water darted to him she began to panic. Rising her hand she went to stop the spell but before she was able it struck what seemed to be an invisible wall around Wasiz and evaporated. 'I knew it,' Wasiz chuckled as in his hand a glow was slowly fading from the hourglass. 'There's more to these items, think about what he said to you.' Taking the silver sword from his belt Richard felt the shocks running up his arm once again. Closing his eyes he focused on it, making the sensation run from his arm and down his body. Sparks then covered his hand that soon went all about him, a blast of blinding light followed that engulfed him and shot into the sky. 'What happened?' Jhona yelled running to where Richard had been standing. 'He just exploded. Oh Richard whatever have you done,' Banbury cried.

'He can't have,' Stephanie mumbled. 'He can't have just exploded, how's that possible?' As the perplexed group scratched their heads the bolt of light that shot to the sky now plummeted back down. Striking the ground a few feet from where Richard had stood, a great ball of sparks and light exploded blinding them once more. When their eyes cleared they saw Richard stood there looking as confused as they were. 'Where did you go?' Banbury yelled shoving past Stephanie to reach Richard. 'Blasted woody, Had me worried you'd gone and blown yourself up.'

'What happened?' Stephanie asked.

'It was like I was this ball of energy. I could see but I had no body or much control at all. Next thing I knew I was falling and then here I am,' Richard said. 'Try again, but this time think of something that calms you,' Jhona said.

'What, he isn't doing that again,' Banbury insisted. Ignoring Banbury, Richard closed his eyes and once again let the tingle run up his arm. His mind raced as he wondered what calmed him, instantly though he relaxed when Stephanie took his hand. Her soft skin on his emptied his mind letting him think of only her. 'Look out Richard, it's happening again,' Banbury said while running to take cover behind a boulder. Opening his eyes Richard saw the sword he held now radiated sparks while lightening flashed over the blade. 'This is amazing,' Richard said as he and Stephanie stared on. 'Want to try it,' Bethany said adjusting the ring on her finger. Placing her hands to the ground water quickly pooled around her, two steams then ran off to form pools of their own. These rose from the ground turning to ice as they grew until two frozen soldiers stood before Bethany. 'This is g...G... Becoming a bit much isn't it,' Banbury stuttered.

'Fancy a bet,' Wasiz said sitting on top of the boulder and filling his pipe. 'Bet on what?' Banbury said. 'A barrel of crikal rum on the Leaflin,' Wasiz said. 'You're on there, Richard's never lost a duel. Hear that ranger you give her what for,' Banbury yelled.

'Go easy, please,' Stephanie said as she left Richard's side. 'Don't worry I'll play nicely,' Richard said. 'I wasn't talking to you,' she replied making Richard look to Bethany whose smile now stretched across her face like a laughing hyena. Without warning the ice soldiers ran to Richard. More water rose to each freezing as it reached their hands. Gifting the one on the left a sword while the other wielded an axe. Jumping back from the swing of the axe Richard flung his own blade upward, sticking the ice soldier in the side. The heat of the lightening running over the blade melted through the ice cleaving the soldier in two. Raising his sword he blocked the blade of the other sending chunks of ice and sparks flying. 'Look out Richard, that other one's up to something,' Banbury shouted over, his voice though was quickly muffled by the many daffodils growing over his beard. 'You're not allowed to help him,' Wendolin chuckled as the panicking dwarf desperately tried to pluck the flowers from his facial hair. He was right however for now the stricken body had melted and without Richard seeing had pooled behind him. With a mighty swing the remaining soldier knocked Richard's sword aside and lifted its frozen foot to kick him back into the trap that had been set. It succeeded and as Richard was shoved into the pool, spears of ice shot up creating a cage around him. 'Ready to give up?' Bethany teased.

'Not quite,' Richard muttered placing both hands to his sword making the beams running over it increase. Slamming the blade to the ground it sent a shockwave of sparks and blinding light cascading from him breaking the spears surrounding him. With another swing the lightening covering the blade grew in length doubling the reach of his sword letting him easily hew the head off the last ice soldier. With his adversary still blinded Richard went to advance but found he was stuck. Ice had frozen his feet in place and slowly crawled up his leg, making his blood freeze as it rose. Knowing he was close to losing he went to strike the ice to free himself but the headless soldier hadn't fallen and before he was able to it caught his hand and pulled his sword from it. 'Okay. I yield,' Richard said. He had used all his strength to carry on, but when Bethany approached he saw she'd barely broken a sweat. 'This ring really makes a difference. I could just about control one soldier without it,' Bethany said.

'It was strange, like the sword was telling me how to use it,' Richard told her and when his restraints were removed he fell back landing on his rear. 'You took it too far, I knew you would. Here fill this,' Stephanie ordered. Pushing an empty canteen into her sister's chest for her to fill. Taking the full canteen back she held it to Richard's lips so he could drink. 'Well that's a fine thing, lost your first duel and me a barrel of rum at that,' Banbury complained. While Stephanie fussed over Richard he took the Kala dagger from his belt. 'Treat her like a wife, is that what he said,' Banbury went on. 'That was the gist of it I think,'

Wasiz said. 'Well how am I meant to treat a knife like a lady. Won't be taking it to bed with me that's for sure,' Banbury said. 'What tosh, that's no knife,' Wasiz said snatching it from Banbury. 'It may seem plain but its blade is sharpened finer than any I've seen and here, look,' Wasiz said as he balanced the dagger on one finger. 'It's been perfectly weighted, grander than any dagger I've pinched is this and I've procured a fair few.'

'Want to swap?' Banbury asked.

'Oh no, I'll stick with what I was given. Besides how would I know how to treat a wife,' Wasiz giggled handing it back. 'I think we have played around enough don't you,' Wendolin said.

'Quite,' Richard replied. 'I doubt we're going to discover all their secrets here, let's get on to Inaka before night fall.'

Luckily even with their antics the party reached Inaka a few hours before sunset. Unfortunately as they wandered past the first few homes they noticed Elites patrolling the town. 'What are they doing here?' Jhona said. 'We won't get the supplies we need with them storming about,' Wasiz added.

'It might be alright, that Slade chap seemed determined to capture us himself. I don't think he'd have told many others, would be too much competition,' Richard hoped.

'Maybe so, but I'd say some disguises are in order,' Wasiz said.

The Forgotten Hero

'Not again I still haven't gotten my uniform back,' Richard complained while Wasiz slinked off. Leaving them to hide themselves in a farmer's field behind a pile of hay bales. It didn't take him long to return and when he did they all found themselves pleasantly surprised. 'I had to be quick so I only got enough to get you all out of your rangers get up,' he said as he handed out the garments. For Richard he'd returned with a crisp white shirt and black cotton trousers. He handed Jhona another white shirt but unlike Richards this had black buttons running up the centre. Some bright purple trousers followed and then each turned their capes inside out so the black lining showed rather than ranger's green. Lastly he gave a long blue dress to Bethany and once all had hidden away to change she filled an old bucket with water. Letting all attempt to wash off as much of the muck the King's tomb had coated them in as they were able. In hope of further aiding their attempt at hiding their identity both Balmoth's brothers put up the hoods of their capes, draping the cloth over their faces. Richard then decided it would be best to enter the town in smaller groups, so as to draw as few eyes as possible. A plan he soon regretted as Wendolin took Stephanie's arm and walked ahead with Bethany close behind. In their groups they made their way into Inaka hoping to meet back up with their steeds and gather all they would need for the long journey ahead.

Inaka was the busiest town the south of Alidor's mainland currently had to offer. Sitting in the shadow of Meceller had protected the settlement from the war and was now the only worthwhile market town to visit this side of the Lavender Lake. Two by two Richard and his friends entered the town while the Leaflins went together, leading the way past the fields and down the cobble path into Inaka. All three were quickly distracted by the many market stalls scattered around the town, as soon as they passed the tall stone houses that encircled the town the streets were awash with them. So many southern traders had flocked to the town that tables laden with stock filled every free space at the side of the road. Some residents had even taken to renting out their front gardens to traders. Greed however seemed to have gotten the better of these residents as the ones they rented space to jostled with one another for room in the tiny gardens. 'Head down Richard,' Banbury said as a pair of Elites marched past. Thankfully they didn't even give them a second glance likewise when they passed Jhona and Wasiz further down the road. 'Seems they're under the command of another Captain,' Wasiz said.

'Must be, or they're just used to strange couples here, they didn't even glare at you,' Jhona said.

'Let's grab the bits on this list your brother gave us and hurry to the pub before they do take notice,' Wasiz said.

'Wendolin look. These are just like the ones Miss Porter used to make,' Stephanie said making her sister look over a jewellery stall. 'Come on you two, we should find the stuff they wanted,' Bethany said.

'How much coin did the goblin give you?' Wendolin asked as a shop window caught her eye. 'A few pieces why?' Bethany said as her sister snatched the purse Wasiz had given her and rushed to the shop's door. 'What's she doing?' Stephanie asked.

'Don't worry I knew she'd do that so I took half out,' Bethany said showing Stephanie the gold coins in her hand. Opening Stephanie's purse she dropped the coins in. 'Come on let's get what we need and hurry back to the others. I don't like being in these crowds,' Bethany continued as people bustled past them. 'I know what you mean, I feel like they're all watching us,' Stephanie said.

'Don't worry we're just being paranoid, let's hurry along,' Bethany said. The Leaflins though were right to be weary. For a pair of watching eyes did spy the girls entering Inaka and now hurried back to their Captain. No Captain of the Elites did he run to but one who watched over a group who called themselves Thorns.

Inside the tailors Wendolin had rushed into she found it contained hundreds of suits and dresses, hats and bonnets. Only one drew her eye though and she went straight over to the window where a mannequin modelled a stunning red dress. 'Good day my lady,' a goblin said as he strolled into the room. To Wendolin's shock he was the total opposite of Wasiz. His face was clear of blemishes and he walked upright unlike Wasiz who walked hunched over like he was always half asleep. He strolled over placing a monocle over his right eye and said. 'Yes, suit you that will my lady. A mighty fine dress for any evening meal or important soirée. Let me get it down for you to try.'

'I don't think I could afford it. Do you have anything red that's, well, cheaper,' Wendolin said handing the purse to him. Peering in the goblin looked back rather displeased and then asked. 'What is it that brings you to Inaka?'

'I am travelling with my sisters, just stopping by for supplies,' Wendolin said.

'Well I'm sure I have something, wait here I'll go take a look,' he replied handing back her purse and lumbering over to an open trunk where he began rummaging through. 'I don't suppose, no it would be silly if you did,' Wendolin said.

'Did what?' the goblin asked. After thinking to herself for a few seconds Wendolin replied. 'Well we ran into this goblin on the way here, my sisters and I. Called himself the something thief, oh what was it?' This made the goblin slam his trunk closed. 'The Rotting Thief,' he snapped spinning to face Wendolin.

'Yes that was it,' she said.

'You met the rotter, yet you still carry gold. So he's here is he,' the goblin said.

'I wouldn't know about that,' Wendolin lied.

'Don't fib girl, falsehoods don't suit you. Go on take it from the mannequin, but you tell Wasiz that pays my debt to him,' the goblin said. Jumping at the opportunity Wendolin quickly began removing the dress from its mannequin before the goblin could change his mind asking as she did. 'How do you know him?'

'Wasiz is the reason I'm here now, my cousins and others also. Goiz is my name and without his bravery I'd still be stuck under the soil in dreary rags,' Goiz said gesturing to a fabric screen for her to change behind. 'That doesn't sound like the Wasiz I know,' Wendolin replied. 'He wasn't always just a cunning and quite irritating thief you know. Once he was a soldier, we all were,' Goiz said.

'A soldier, what like a proper one? Standing to attention and all,' Wendolin said.

'Oh yes, but goblin armies aren't as organised as others. Most of our kind are born in the dark and forever live in it. Wasiz though hated the life he'd been given so with others he plotted to overthrow our ruler and free our kind from the hold the god who ruled over us had. The plan he weaved saw one of our own take the throne, a tyrant was caged and those who wished were finally able to head above ground,' Goiz informed her. Wendolin then emerged from behind the screen. 'Oh yes, if you didn't come by I would have had to refuse to sell it to any other for it was made for you my lady.'

'You are sure we're both speaking of the same Wasiz, broken tooth, spotty nose,' Wendolin asked.

'The very same and you're to tell him that pays whatever debt he claims I owe him,' Goiz insisted.

Richard and Banbury were soon heading to the tavern to rejoin the others, both carrying a variety of goods.

Despite this Banbury's appetite would quickly see them waylaid. Every pastry or cake stall they passed caught his attention, leading to increasing lengthy reviews of each from Banbury. While Jhona and Wasiz had been delayed at the blacksmith. 'That much for some arrow heads,' Wasiz complained. 'Daylight robbery that's what it is. Bet they're not even good enough to craft green leaf arrows with.'

'They're the best arrow heads this town has and as it goes I'm the only smith, only one worth seeing anyhow. The price is the price, take it or get off with your woody,' the dwarven smith replied past his lint filled beard. 'It's fine we will take them,' Jhona said. 'He's robbing us blind, three pieces a head, the cheek. Think we were in Duniesa with those prices,' Wasiz continued complaining all the way to the shop's door and even as they went to join the others. Only a drunken man falling to the floor before a group of Elites stifled him. 'Please father, let me prove me worth,' the drunk man begged from the muddy cobbles. 'You have no worth Jofrin and have proved that many times. Move aside for I am done with putting up with your constant failure. Done also am I to have a son as useless as you. Go on back to your hovel, to that wench and your bastard boy,' the Elite leading the others replied. Lifting his foot he kicked Jofrin aside and marched past with his men following close behind. Leaving his son with his face to the floor. 'He's a funny sort of father,' Wasiz said holding out a hand to the scruffy man before him. 'I'm a funny sort of son,' Jofrin replied taking the hand.

The Forgotten Hero

'A tale worth telling I feel, come along one more drink will change little for you now,' Wasiz said patting his back and leading him to the tavern. 'Do you really think that's wise?' Jhona said as he watched Jofrin stumbling to his feet with Wasiz's aid. 'A story for a drink you have a deal there little fellow,' Jofrin said. It turned out he was already so pickled he was under the impression Wasiz was just a short wood elf, while he saw Jhona quite differently also. 'Don't fret dear pretty lady. Dear beautiful woody. For I have not reached my limit yet and if it's a tale your fella here wants, then a tale shall he have,' Jofrin slurred.

'With one more drink whatever tales you have to tell will be pure nonsense,' Jhona said.

'Don't fret dear lady,' Wasiz teased as they entered the tavern. The others had yet to return to The Old Roost. The tavern was one of six in the town of Inaka and easily the most decrepit of the bunch. Only the most deplorable dare enter but luckily for them this was the only tavern their new acquaintance had yet to be barred from. Going to the bar Wasiz left the others to find a table soon rejoining them with a sour faced man close by. 'Took a bit of doing, but I was able to convince this fine gentlemen to whip up an old favourite of mine,' Wasiz declared as the sour faced man placed the tray he was carrying before them. 'That's just coffee isn't it?' Jofrin scoffed at the mugs before them. 'Not quite. It has a few extras give it a go,' Wasiz fibbed. 'Long as it's booze like you promised,' Jofrin replied and then began drinking the hot drink before it even had time to cool. 'So why is it he hates you so, that father of yours?' Wasiz asked.

'My family name is Landon, that should tell you all you need know,' Jofrin remarked.

'So that was Lindow Landon, why's he with the Elites? Did he not command the guard of the north with his father?' Jhona said.

'Only the old remain in the guard must have been conscripted into the Elites. My grandfather and he were the first to be given the Elite blades they carry. They had hoped I would follow in their footsteps but useless as I am I ruined any hope of that,' Jofrin told them. 'If I could have just earned a sword I would be able to return to Tailor's Hope a worthy man, rather than the disgrace I am.'

'What did you do to upset him so?' Wasiz asked. 'I failed to pass the training, in fact they'd had enough of me after barely a day. Wasn't entirely my fault, I'd had a tad too much of the booze the night before. When I finally got to the training grounds the others had already begun. Leaving me to stumble behind until it was clear I wouldn't be getting any sword or golden suit of armour,' Jofrin said.

'Don't see why any want that armour anyhow makes them look just as the soldiers of the Crown did,' Jhona said as he stood up. 'What's wrong?' Wasiz asked. 'Don't be so jumpy, I'm only going to bog,' Jhona said leaving Wasiz to listen to Jofrin's drunken rambles. On the way he began to scratch his head as his mind drifted and as he reached for the door handle he thought of the Balmoth's farm and how many years it had been since he and Richard had returned to it. Going through the door Jhona kept this eyes down not wanting to see any of the foul sights a lavatory within an establishment such as this would possess. As he passed the threshold he noticed the colour of the floorboards change. Sunlight suddenly filled his eyes and when they adjusted he realised he was home. 'How, this doesn't make sense,' Jhona spluttered spinning to see the sour face barkeep looking through from the other side of the open door. Panicking Jhona slammed the door shut, something he quickly regretted when he opened it again to find not the Old Roost but his childhood bedroom on the other side. 'What sort of trick is this?' Jhona said to himself. Scratching his head once more he suddenly realised he had inadvertently been rubbing the hair clip. Taking it from his head he looked to it and said. 'It can't be, travel so far but never too far,' Jhona mumbled and while rubbing his thumb over the hair clip he thought about a room he'd spent many months in after Seer Avlor Tranem finally convinced the pair of brothers to let him train them. Opening the door it revealed no bedroom but a throne room. Before Jhona lay the grand hall of the Seer's golden tower in the city of Duniesa, quickly though Jhona moved the door so that it was open just enough to see through a crack. Unfortunately the Golden Tower was not as he remembered and the booming voices of the Seers made his anxiety grow even more. 'It must be done Elidom. The war was long and broke so many but with the absence of an enemy the elves are scattering. The people need an idol to bind them together, someone to hold up above others as your humans did with their King,' Seer Marlos La Sore spoke in a harsh tone to his former mentor. He and all others wore robes that bore the Seer's mark over the back. An embroidered watching eye, sewn with golden tread. Five Seers there are Eloise and Marlos La Sore were two. Avlor Tranem and Elidom Godborn made four and finally Seer Kuran Dune was the fifth. A bloated body did he have with a round bald head and even while discussing important matters he continued to stuff his fat face. 'You should just do as you're told Elidom, we have voted and you lost,' Seer Dune spat.

'You should know better boy,' Avlor shouted. 'We are not rulers and were never meant to be. The whole reason we are together is because one of our own was vying for power. We should do what Inkark never saw fit to and be content with what we have, not seek more. Making him a King risks the peace we fought for, the peace all of your mothers and fathers died for.'

'What of your peace Tranem? Young we were when we agreed to your plot. So young we didn't see the folly in it, but babes being manipulated by those who call themselves wise. Let us think what has the peace we paid so highly for brought us,' Marlos declared. Pushing Avlor aside he went to Elidom. 'Death, that is all your peace has given us. Death at the hands of your pets. Death at the hands of mortals on bloody dogs and before that orc scum plaguing our lands. The only benefit from your plotting was the Countess and her mages. A benefit you let your new toys jeopardise with foolish actions.' Taking hold of

109

Elidom's robe he pushed him towards the throne. 'We know your lie Elidom. You and Avlor tried so hard to hide it, but few are willing to keep your secrets anymore. So sit and as you sit think. Think how this all could've be avoided. Think how my hands, how Eloise's hands would be clean of blood and our minds safe from the horrors that war brings. Think of all those lives and all their deaths and then remember whose doing it was. Take the throne and with the Elites we will pull the elves back together as one. Be crowned and then sit here thinking while we fix your many mistakes.' Reluctantly Elidom Godborn walked up the steps to the golden throne that now rested in the hall. Looking to it he wavered, only for Marlos to command him on. 'Go sit down Godborn, this is how it must be.' Reaching the throne Elidom felt sick, no normal throne was this but solid gold. The seat was cushioned with red velvet, the seat though wasn't what made his stomach retch. The great golden shape of a griffin is what sickened him. Massive outstretched wings cast shadows over the hall while its head looked down to forever spy on whoever sits upon the throne. Once seated the main doors of the throne room opened and in marched the La Sore's Elites to witness the crowning of their new King. 'Madness, those bastard La Sores,' Jhona snapped. Unfortunately he had spoken aloud and the sound made a pair of Elites turn their attention to the door he hid behind. Both heard the door click closed as they approached, but when they opened it only a mop and broom did they find. As a golden crown was placed on the head of the first King of all elves,

Seer Marlos La Sore's voice drowned out all others. 'Let it be known that in this place, that at this time Elidom Godborn is no Seer. For he is King of all, King of the lands, King of the seas and skies. King of all elves, of any creed and place. Peace is his only goal and with his blessing I will bring it. For the Seer's Elite will bring peace to all we see fit and once it is taken ensure it is kept.'

Idiots Jhona thought. *I have to get back to the others, tell them what's happening here in the north.* Suddenly the reason he'd left the table in the first place came to him. Rushing to the door he ran out of the farmhouse hurrying to the outhouse. Noticing as he went the farm wasn't as overgrown as he'd imagined it would be, but was in too much of a rush to notice who slept in the cornfield across from him. Slamming the outhouse door shut Jhona began doing what any would in such a space. Now dear reader I don't know about you, but a fear both myself and our dear Jhona share is a worry that when one is mid stream so to speak, someone else would suddenly pull open the lavatory door. This fear for Jhona at least was hugely overshadowed when not just the door to the outhouse was removed but the walls and roof also. It was lifted up to leave Jhona totally exposed. As he scrambled to make himself decent he noticed two huge feet before him, then heard what had been the outhouse crashing down to the ground behind him. 'Who's this then, some troublemaker trespassing on my farm. Hmm there's not much of ya is there,' the giant said poking a terrified Jhona with his enormous finger. 'Barely get a mouthful out of you. Best grind you up and use you to season a nice roast. Yes that would be it I think, what you say to that troublemaker,' A shadow then cast over Jhona and he looked up to see a female giant towering over him. 'Stop that Herbert, you're terrifying him. Little thing was just using the little house,' she said.

'He shouldn't be in the little house, nor the big house, he's trespassing he is,' Herbert replied.

'Excuse me, but I'm not trespassing. This is mine and my brother's farm,' Jhona said once his fear had began to subside a little. 'No it's not. It's my farm, been so past few years and I've never seen you or your brother 'ere before,' Herbert said.

'We have been away and sadly our work has kept us from here,' Jhona said.

'Hmm well suppose you could've been, but I won't be moving. We like it 'ere, me and my wife. I'll just eat you up and they'll be no need for us to leave then,' Herbert chuckled.

'Stop that you fool, we won't do anything of the sort,' his wife Beverly snapped.

'Well we won't be going either, we have giant squatter's rights we do,' Herbert said.

'There's no need to fret, perhaps there is an agreement we can come to,' Jhona said.

'What sort of agreement?' Herbert asked.

'Well you seem to have been taking fine care of the place, aside from the outhouse that is. There's even corn in the field. That's something both me and my brother never managed, so hows this sound. In return for land to farm and a place to live you will keep the farmhouse in good order the other buildings also. I will leave again soon, but me and brother will wish to return here one day,' Jhona said.

'That sounds extremely fair to me,' Beverly said. 'He's only offering such a good deal because he knows he'd lose in giant court,' Herbert said.

'Stop it you silly man. All these stupid threats, you know very well we don't eat wood folk, nor is there any giant court,' Beverly said clipping her husband around the ear. 'We are in agreement little one, we will keep the farm well kept and have it ready for whenever you or this brother of yours wish to return.' Leaning down she held out her finger for Jhona to shake. 'Excellent, Jhona is my name and Richard is my brother. I'm sorry to cut our meeting short but I must get back to him.'

'How is it you trespassed anyway? I didn't see you walking up the lane,' Herbert said.

'We've worked out he wasn't trespassing and I bet you were sleeping on the job once again,' Beverly complained as another clip around Herbert's sore ear followed. 'I didn't come up the lane, still trying to work out how I got here myself,' Jhona said. Going back to the farmhouse door he held the hair clip the same as he'd done when imagining the golden tower. Running his fingers over it as he did, but thinking of The Old Roost. Opening the door he revealed the tavern and the sour faced man looking back perplexed.

The Forgotten Hero

After Jhona left to use the facilities Jofrin's drunken wallowing went on as Richard and Banbury joined them, shortly followed by Bethany and Stephanie. All arrived quietly and drew few eyes as they rejoined the others. Wendolin though drew the attention of all within The Old Roost as she cast the door aside and strolled across the tavern. She was stunning in her red dress and Goiz had even cut her hair. Long crimson locks had been shortened to rest just above her shoulders and over her left ear three red roses now rested, their petals fluttering as she went. Not only gifts for herself did she return with. A lengthy conversation had gone along with Wendolin's makeover, leading her to tell Goiz about much of their journey. 'All that questing and not even a pair of boots for it. Cracked Tooth be damned. The bugger never did think things through.' Much more blustering regarding his old comrade followed as he began sauntering about his shop collecting an arm full of equipment. An old scabbard Goiz had handy fit Richard's new blade perfectly. Followed by some slightly worn but still perfectly usable boots for each of the Leaflins, something all hoped would ease their aching feet from the miles they'd been walking. 'The tailor Goiz says his debt to you is paid,' Wendolin shouted over to Wasiz unaware she'd been followed into the tavern by commander Lindow Landon and his Elites. After glaring over his son and the strangers about him he sent one of his men to pin a poster to the wall while he spoke, reciting the words upon the poster almost verbatim. 'The La Sore's seek men, elves of any family may apply but two generations of family history must be provided. The Elites will grow and soon all of Alidor will be under their guard, their banner.'

'Why only elves? Are wood folk not good enough for your tacky armour?' Wendolin said interrupting Lindow. 'Don't antagonise them,' Stephanie said trying to stop her sister. Before she or the Commander were able to speak further a wood elf burst in, covered in sweat and clearly incredibly panicked he shouted as he entered. 'A horde, a horde has been seen.' Seeing the Commander the man ran to him and grabbed his arm. 'A caravan left for Meceller but a day ago, they will be at their mercy my lord.'

'No orcs roam these lands,' Lindow said shrugging him off and with his men he left The Old Roost leaving the man to chase after them. 'They do my lord I've seen them, riding on hogs they are. You must ride to them,' the man begged.

'I shall do no such thing, it is on them to guard their wears not I,' Lindow replied.

'It is a caravan of people sir not wears. Please my lord they believed the countryside safe with so many Elites marching,' the man said but he wasn't helped, simply batted away again making him trip and begin to fall. The falling man though didn't hit the floor, instead he was pushed back up by Wendolin. 'What is the point of you Elites?' She snapped to Lindow making all those passing by look to them. Sadly the pair of eyes who spied the girls arriving at the town had returned with their Captain. 'We all see you prancing about but now you're needed all you can do is brush off your own.'

'These people are not my own woman, nor are you,' Lindow scoffed.

'Cowards are all any who wear your armour are,' Wendolin said. 'Incredible, she's truly incredible,' the Captain of the Thorns said to the scout who had fetched him, both hid in the crowd concealed under dark red hooded capes. 'Like a beautiful flower that should only be encouraged to grow and flourish.'

'What's the plan Captain, there's no chance of taking them here, not quietly anyhow,' the scout said.

'Take them, oh yes I suppose that is our task,' the Captain said eyes still fixed to Wendolin. 'Maybe there's another way, yes there must be.'

'So brave she thinks she is, why don't you go running to their aid? I'm sure a woman like you would put up quite a fight,' Lindow laughed encouraging his men to join him not noticing Wendolin didn't flinch at this suggestion. 'Fine where is this caravan?' She said snapping to the exhausted man. 'She's truly serious,' the Elite mocked. A bustling could then be heard spreading through the crowd as Fiona and Caspian lead the other horses to them. The others slowly rejoined Wendolin leaving Lindow to realise those of Inaka were now far less impressed with him and his Elites. He ended up in such a fluster he didn't notice until leaving the town and riding away that he'd lost his sword. Sitting before the tavern Jofrin was finishing another bottle as his new acquaintances prepared to leave. 'Here,' Wasiz said to him dropping Lindow Landon's sword to his lap. 'How, how did you get this?' Jofrin slurred. 'Your father was too preoccupied, he didn't notice me sneak it away,' Wasiz said. 'Head back to your family Jofrin. Tell them you became an Elite but soon realised the folly in it and wished to return to their embrace. Go home and become a father your son will never gaze upon as you do yours.' Jofrin watched Wasiz and the others leave Inaka along with much of the town's folk. Once their steeds faded in the distance he began his own journey home, but this journey would be the only one Jofrin would go on with the sword to his belt. Such vigour did he feel wearing it, before even returning to his family's home in the town of Tailor's Hope he found himself marching before the town's mayor. Hours of arguing and petty bickering followed but by the time he finally left they had both agreed to reform the guard of the north. After Jofrin was able to convince the mayor the Elites would never care for their interests and were even less likely to do anything meaningful to protect them. Sober and clear headed he went from the mayor's office to his home not noticing the worried faces of all who recognised him. For they already knew what Jofrin would discover upon his return home. Shortly after he'd left to train as an Elite his wife Vera had been taken gravely ill. A sickness struck her that no cure could be found for and only two days after Jofrin left she passed. Leaving their son in the care of their neighbours. When Jofrin learnt this news he was broken once more and the sober headed man who'd returned to Tailor's Hope sought the comfort of booze once again. His father's sword was hidden beneath his bed and there it stayed for years. Gathering dust until the day it would be needed.

'Wendolin wait,' Richard yelled as he and the others tried to keep up with her. 'We don't have time to wait, you heard that man,' Wendolin said.

'I agree, but even with my new sword we are no match for an entire horde,' Richard said riding before Wendolin Caspian stopped her steed. 'Move aside or me and Comet will run through you,' Wendolin said referring to the dark brown Meceller horse she rode. 'That's a poor name for a mount,' Richard remarked making Comet flare her nostrils and shake her mane, threatening Caspian as Wendolin had Richard. The others all crowded around saying much the same as Richard did, but Wendolin would not be deterred. Sadly those the Countess had sent for the Leaflins had soon caught up with them, and in the bushes and bracken around the path they watched as their targets began dismounting from their steeds. While Wendolin argued with her party they prepared a plan.

The Captain of Thorns Thrimore Embalem and his right hand man Ducker Krosh now hid in the foliage. After leaving Inaka they had been rejoined by the mage who the Countess had sent to bring the Leaflins back to Accultian. Galger Santouren, eyes of pure white did she have for an awful ability she possessed. 'There she is,' Thrimore said.

'Perfect, just draw off the others until I can turn them, can your rabble handle that?' Galger said.

'My men can handle rangers and a thief easily. Never much liked dwarves though, tricky little sods they are,' Krosh said.

'I was speaking to your Captain cretin,' Galger snapped. Thrimore continued to ignore her however, for bright red hair now shone in his eyes. 'What beauty is this, for each glance of her makes my heart swell. Never have I seen such a woman before. Not one so fair or so full of fire,' Thrimore said.

'What's wrong with him?' Galger said.

'You wish for my input now,' Krosh replied.

'Krosh, away to the others. Prepare the cult grip,' Thrimore ordered.

'The what?' Galger said.

'A trap, a handy one for mages. We shall draw them in, make them think we are friends and then strike before any of them know what's happening,' Thrimore said. 'That's stupid and it will take too long,' Galger replied. 'Not at all it can be done with just a simple order,' Thrimore told her as a smile crept over his face, a smile the vile mage didn't see completed. Before she could react a blindfold was thrown over her eyes and tied tight by Krosh while two others bound each of her hands. Tying each finger together before chaining them behind her back. 'See it is as easy as that,' Thrimore said. 'Dead, you're all dead, the Countess will kill you all,' she yelled before her mouth was quickly gagged.

'She makes a good point, why we turning on easy coin all of a sudden?' Krosh asked.

'You saw her also, how could we raise our hands against such beauty. We shall speak with her, we must,' Thrimore said.

'Oh dear Jhona for I went to the trees to get you a flower but only thorns and pricks did I find,' Wasiz said. 'I know Wasiz, how many do you suppose there are?' Jhona asked. Both he and Wasiz had noticed what the others had yet to. 'A fair few pricks I'd say,' Wasiz said. 'Get the others ready quietly we don't want them to notice,' Jhona said but before the pair could prepare Thrimore walked from the foliage and to the side of the road where the others argued. Hands raised he said. 'For the Leaflins I was sent, but a foul thing is the Countess so a deal I wish to make with you red lady.'

'Shoot him, go on Jhona pop one in this bugger's head,' Banbury ordered.

'What sort of deal could we make, you don't seem to have anything we want,' Wasiz shouted over. Waving to Krosh, Galger was bought forward and dropped before Thrimore. 'You,' Wendolin said as rage filled her. Roots rose and instantly took Galger into the air. 'Wait my lady we will need her yet,' Thrimore said.

'If you have her then you know her deeds,' Wendolin said as the roots retracted into the earth pulling Galger down with them. 'This is the witch that stole us away and killed our parents.'

'Please my lady your kin live still, for they were there the day you were taken and she can free them from the stone as she did you,' Thrimore said.

'You're lying,' Wendolin said.

'I swear it, they wait for you in the Humtees,' Thrimore insisted as the roots stopped pulling Galger down. 'And what is it you want in return? Betraying the Countess must come at quite a cost,' Wasiz said.

'Nothing but a minute or a few seconds if that's all you will grant me,' Thrimore said to Wendolin. 'For I shall be at your command forever more if you would promise me but a mere moment alone in your presence.' None too impressed with the man she turned from him to the others and said. 'We must travel to the Humtees to find out for ourselves.'

'A quest you can go on when we part, this lad can hold the mage until then,' Banbury said.

'She's right if they're alive we have to free them,' Bethany argued.

'You don't even know if she will free them,' Jhona said. 'She will or she will suffer for it,' Wendolin threatened as cries came from Galger, roots beneath the ground had continued to stab at her legs. 'Richard please if he's telling the truth we can't just leave them encased in stone,' Stephanie begged.

'We don't have time to deal with this now if you wish to ride to aid the caravan also,' Richard told them. 'Then let us ride with you, my men will take good care of our mage here,' Thrimore insisted.

'You're assassins are you not, won't be any good in an open fight that lot Richard,' Banbury said. 'We weren't always in the sorry employment we find ourselves today. You'd need forty of your dwarf there to match one of my Thorns,' Thrimore boasted.

121

'Little does this twat know of the Bales. Let me down Nobby. I'll give this woody a hiding he won't soon forget,' Banbury said. Nobby though had other ideas and had began walking up the road, completely oblivious to the situation unfolding around him. Going to Wendolin, Thrimore reached up and took her hand. 'Let us ride together my lady and allow me to clear your path of foes.'

'There's clearly something very wrong with you,' Wendolin said. 'So be it. Follow if you must and if you speak the truth you'll have a minute but not a second more. If you lie however you'll be joining her,' Wendolin threatened as Galger was pulled from the ground.

Chapter Seven
To Meceller We Go

Simeon Harcord had not expected any trouble when he agreed to lead a caravan of families from Inaka to Meceller. Now though as caravans and wagons rushed to form a circle he feared he'd soon meet his death at the hands of the Blooded Spike's horde. A tribe of orcs famed for riding upon ferocious buffalo hogs. Wagons were encircled and arms handed out, just as the first spear scored a defender and about the carriages and wagons snorting hogs ran. While their riders continued to harass the meek force of defenders within with volleys of arrows and spears. All hope of living faded as an orc leapt over the wagons cleaving heads as he bounded on. Stopped only when Simeon's sword hewed his arm off and then drove into his chest. Killing one crazed orc though would help little, but as others were posed to invade their defences another roar drowned out that of the snorting hogs. A fair clear cry it was, one that sent a chill through the attackers making even their bone's shake as the sound echoed over the horde. The crackle of thunder followed and then to the north east Simeon saw a white horse and its rider. To the sky the rider held a silver blade as sparks flew from it. Little encouragement did the bulk of the Blooded Spike's horde need to forget about their attack on the wagons. Most knew that steed well and the glory taking its head and that of its rider would bring.

'You were right, that certainly got their attention,' Richard said. 'Too right it did, help me up now and I'll give them what for I will,' Banbury said as he waved Stephanie down and then began trying to jump up onto Caspian's back. 'This is a bigger fight than we expected my lady,' Thrimore said.

'If this is too much for you and your men feel free to flee, I won't be,' Wendolin replied. With a grin to her Thrimore then turned to Krosh. 'Divide the men only the battle hardened will join the charge, set a guard on the mage and have the rest break through to support the wagons.'

'As you say Captain,' Krosh replied feeling more vigour than he'd felt in months. 'To blood boys, to blood and battle, a real challenge at last. A feat only the Thorns can face, draw swords and ready arrows,' he cried as Thorns made ready. 'What should I do?' Stephanie asked Bethany. 'Just stay clear of the fighting Steph, we can handle this,' Bethany declared, tapping her steed's side she span forward and down the slope. Frost is what she had called to her mount, a name that referred to the many speckles of white fur that pierced through her brown coat. Chunks of grass were thrown in her wake and instantly Wendolin followed, not wanting to be outdone her and Comet quickly charged on. 'To the red lady Thorns, for with her we shall see our victory,' Thrimore cried as he and the Thorns followed blowing on horns and hollering as they charged. 'Awfully excitable bunch ain't they?' Wasiz said. With the Thorns he and Jhona rode, ahead went Richard and Banbury. The sound of snorting hogs and raging orcs grew louder until the bulk of the Blooded Spikes were before Bethany and Frost. Spears and arrows flew but all broke upon shields of ice that surrounded her. Leaping from Frost's back allowed her steed to flee as Bethany was catapulted to the head of a charging hog. One swing of her arm sent forth a blade of ice cutting down the orc riding it, another swing ended the hog leaving her on the ground with orcs charging to her. The Thorns then rushed past her and she was taken up by Wendolin and pulled to Comet's back as the two forces collided.

What started as a large melee soon broke apart as great vines and soldiers of ice tore into the Blooded Spike's horde. The Thorns were greatly outnumbered but to only describe them as skilled would be an understatement. For each wielded a blade as if they were born holding one. Every arrow they released found its target and even their steeds showed no fear as hogs grunted before them. 'There's one. Richard look out,' Banbury yelled as a spear was thrown to them. Leaning back to dodge it Banbury slipped and fell from Caspian's back before he could compose himself. Pulling himself up he went to retrieve his scythe but his empty harness quickly reminded him he no longer had it. 'B-b-b-bugger it all,' he yelled and then ran to retrieve a spear from the ground. Knocked down though Banbury was before he could reach it. A drooling hog had bounded into him and now his rider readied a spear to kill the dwarf before it. Taking the dagger from his belt Banbury yelled. 'Come on then you bugger.' Friends were thankfully close by for an arrow passed through the orc's neck before he could throw the spear. 'Stop mucking about Banbury,' Jhona shouted to him as he and Wasiz rode past upon Fiona. 'I'm not mucking about,' Banbury shouted back as hot breath engulfed the back of his head. 'Balmoth get back here,' Banbury yelled as the hog bit into the back of his shirt and tossed him over the ground. 'Get away from me bacon,' Banbury ordered flaying his dagger at the ravenous beast. Not sharp are the teeth of a buffalo hog, flat they are and made for grinding their prey. A fact Banbury learnt when the hog bit down on his left leg. Lunging forward Banbury grappled the hog's ear and drove the dagger into its head as the beast gnawed on his leg. The skulls of these hogs are incredibly tough and little to nothing did this do to deter it. The hog gnawed on him even with the dagger embedded in its head. Thoughts began to flood Banbury's mind and he worried he'd never see his charming home or loving wives again. 'Just die you blasted devil,' Banbury let out the frantic cry as he slammed the base of the dagger's handle, hoping to drive the blade deeper into the hog's skull. What happened though Banbury and certainly not the hog could have expected. A blood red light shot from the blade as soon as Banbury's hand hit it. A light that increased in size, morphing the dagger as it grew into a battle axe that tore apart the hog as it formed. 'That's more like it,' Banbury beamed using the axe to pull himself up past the fallen hog's corpse.

'Up there, it's their commander,' Wasiz said. Fiona turned and ran up a bank to the east, to where eight heavily armoured orcs surrounded a tall grey hog and its rider. 'What's Jhona doing?' Wendolin yelled seeing him and Wasiz ride away. 'They have the leader in their sights, they mean to end this. Join me and let us make sure their way is clear my lady,' Thrimore said riding alongside her and holding out his hand. Taking the ring from Bethany Wendolin took his arm and was pulled from Comet to his steed. A group had peeled away to charge Jhona and Wasiz but vines suddenly rose before them forcing them to turn and attack their source. 'Nasty, stinking mages,' Tartiss roared from his slope. He was too distracted by the battle to see a white steed charging to him. Wendolin and Thrimore quickly dismounted sending his steed clear as orcs on foot and in the saddle of hogs bounded to them. 'Ready to run yet Captain?' Wendolin asked.

'From you my lady, I fear it would take more than this world has,' Thrimore replied and to one another's backs they faced the onslaught. Vines pulled Thrimore from strikes as his blade guarded her from the tusks of hogs and around them their bodies piled. For only a second did the Captain of the Thorns and the red lady fight alone before others joined them. Richard's sword and Bethany's ice blade were with them as Banbury hobbled his way over desperate to show his new might. 'Who are they? Who? Who?' Tartiss raged as he watched his horde fail. A yelp from one of his guards then distracted him from the battle. An arrow had pierced the eye of one of his warriors, passing through the thin slit in his helm. An impossible feat for any archer but one. Leaving Tartiss bewildered as another of his warriors fell and a white horse darted past dropping a figure in black as it went. 'I give you one chance warlord as I have with others of your ilk before,' Wasiz declared walking before them. 'Leave here and never return or I shall steal your life from you.'

'Steal my life,' Tartiss mocked, but when Wasiz removed his hood his mocking tone vanished and he ground his teeth. For years his kind had traded a tale of a goblin with one protruding tooth, who alone had routed a horde sent forth from the Blood Works. As another of his guard fell with an arrow in his guts Tartiss felt a dread creep over him. 'Rotter,' he bellowed. 'No Rotting Thief orders me. I'll have your head and let my hog feast on the rest of ya,' he bellowed raising his arm. Sending his guards on to face the Rotting Thief he went to instruct his hog to follow but before he was able an arm wrapped around his neck. Pulling him from the back of his steed, sending him and Jhona rolling across the ground. He had leapt from Fiona's back and pulled Tartiss down with him. Enraged his hog soon forgot about its rider and bounded off after Fiona, leaving Tartiss to draw two crooked swords from his belt and face Jhona. Stolen daggers were soon removed from Wasiz's harness as Tartiss's guards swung halberds and claymores at him.

Thankfully he was no fool as many say, knowing they would flee once their leader was slain he kept his distance. Letting the heavily armoured orcs wear themselves out as Jhona duelled their leader. 'Give in and save what you have left,' Jhona ordered, readying his bow. 'We don't give in, cowardly wood folk. I'll chop you up and then your rotting runt,' Tartiss spat. An arrow soared from Jhona's bow, but to his surprise Tartiss swung his sword knocking down the arrow and rushing to Jhona readying his other as he ran. Barely a second did Jhona have to react, raising his bow just in time to block the sword. Embedding his sword in Jhona's bow Tartiss tossed it aside and used his remaining weapon to swipe at Jhona forcing him back. Drawing the blade on his belt Jhona blocked the next blow as Tartiss growled. 'Lay down ya mouldy maggot, lay down and let me spill them guts.'

'You should have taken his deal,' Jhona said sliding his blade to the base of Tartiss's sword to force him to his knee. Quickly pulling an arrow from his quiver Jhona jammed it into Tartiss's leg making him fall just as Fiona charged to his back. Tartiss covered his face and prepared himself to be trampled but Fiona simply leapt over him retrieving Jhona as she went. Thinking he was safe Tartiss began to sit up forgetting what chased Jhona's steed. The grey hog hadn't even seen its rider, too content to chase the white horse it was until its tusks tore through Tartiss and it was blinded by his blood. Riding on Wasiz was soon upon Fiona and the orcs that remained began to flee when the sight of their leader scored on his steed's tusks found them.

'Krosh get the injured in the wagons and send me eight others to give chase,' Thrimore ordered.

'There's no need, the Blooded Spike is what this rabble call themselves. They were once of the Blood Works, with their chief gone the rest will return to the island,' Richard said.

'How can you be so sure they will not regroup?' Thrimore asked.

'This isn't the first horde we've broken up, don't worry they will scatter. I shouldn't fret for the injured either,' Richard said making him turn to see Bethany and Wendolin had already began lining up Thorns along with the wagon's defenders to have their wounds healed. Bethany then ran from the line to Jhona who stood over a bleeding orc. 'Woody filth,' the orc spluttered. 'Stay still I can stop the bleeding,' Bethany said. 'No, they'll send me back, back to him,' the orc began panicking as Bethany tried to help him, opening his wounds further. 'Send you to who?' Jhona asked.

'Think he's dead. You elves, woodys don't see him. They think he's dead and gone but he's not. He's always there, always watching. All but orc don't see.' Sitting up the orc grabbed Bethany's arm. 'The shadows, the creeping darkness comes for us all. None will be spared from the wars it will bring,' the panicking orc then choked and succumbed to his wounds without any understanding his words.

'My lords, how are we to show our thanks?' Simeon Harcord asked as the wagons were lined up and prepared to hurry on to Meceller. 'Rangers that is what you are, am I right my lord?' He continued vigorously shaking Richard's hand. 'Myself yes, but he and the others, well they are here on work experience you could say,' Richard smirked. Glancing around Thrimore saw his Thorns being thanked much the same as Richard was. 'Hear this,' Thrimore yelled standing up on a fallen creature. 'My Thorns need no thanks, nor gifts of flowers or booze,' he said throwing a glare to Krosh who already held two bottles of fine wine. 'Only your silence is what we ask in return. For in Meceller we are not liked, swear this to us and friends to the Thorns you will always be.' Simeon nodded and shook on Thrimore's hand as he stepped down, but then asked. 'I lost most able fighters in the attack. I know I ask much my lords, but Meceller is still a day and a half's ride and your aid would be much appreciated. I'd see you and your men are well paid also and I have a sturdy caravan you're welcome to.'

'It can't be done, Meceller's council would make you share our fate if they see you riding with us,' Thrimore said. 'Only if they know my lord. Travel with us to the Arizun Stream before we pass to the stream there is a patch of trees your men can hide themselves within. Wait there and it will take me but a few hours to return with a King's ransom to reward you with. We are carrying some cargo that the council of Meceller will part with a great deal of coin for when we arrive. An

131

award of sorts that will see you paid well for your time.'

Looking over the line of wagons Jhona and Wasiz noticed a man running around the carriages looking rather panicked. 'Where have you ran off to?' He said to himself as he looked under wagons. 'What have you lost?' Wasiz asked.

'A boy, an irritating boy who doesn't sit still. Stay in the carriage that's all he had to do, dearie me where has he gotten to,' the man said but beamed as he saw Bethany leading the boy he looked for to them. 'Is this who you're searching for?' Bethany asked. Unlike the man the boy was remarkably well dressed. His shoes were perfectly polished and over his tailored white shirt and black trousers he wore a jacket with white embroidery that ran from the tip of the jacket's tails to swirl up the length into rather pleasing patterns. 'Where have you been Sire? I told you to stay put,' the man said running to him. 'I'm fine Anderson, I wasn't scared at all,' the boy lied. For in fact Bethany had found him hidden in a wagon hiding under many blankets almost as pale as a ghost from fright. 'I see you have met my most valued customer,' Simeon said walking over with Richard. Thrimore though made sure neither Anderson nor his young charge saw his face. 'Allow me to introduce Richard Balmoth we have him and his band to thank for rescuing us and this here is our precious cargo. Prince Anwayes Roian,' staring to Richard the Prince then asked. 'Are you one of my father's men?'

'Far from it. I'm a ranger,' Richard said.

'There is no such thing as rangers. My mother says they died out years ago, fled their posts to die in the wilds,' Anwayes said.

'Do they look dead to you?' Wasiz snapped over the Princes' shoulder making him jump. 'Come along let's get you settled for the rest of the trip,' Anderson said ushering his charge away. 'The council in Meceller holds all the power there these days. His father is but a puppet to his wife's whims,' Simeon said. 'They keep the city so tightly sealed little news gets through that the council hasn't been able to manipulate. I may have heard many a tale of your deeds over the years ranger, but don't think others in Meceller will have heard.'

'Is it true the trees there are as tall as mountains?' Bethany asked.

'Almost, have you never seen the Evertree good lady?' Simeon asked.

'No, myself and my sisters have seen little of anything,' Bethany replied.

'Then it is settled, you must join us the rest of the way and see it for yourself,' Simeon insisted.

'I don't know if we can, the Humtees is our next destination,' Bethany said.

'What luck, Meceller is on the way there and seeing the city would barely add a day to your journey,' Simeon told her. 'It probably is about time we meet this council and their King,' Richard said turning to Jhona.

'Seems the Leaflins have made the decision for us,' Jhona replied as Simeon lead the girls to a wagon.

The Forgotten Hero

Krosh and a pair of others soon heaved Galger into the caravan Simeon had gifted them. Banbury took so long to return to the others partly down to his injured leg, but mostly thanks to the fact he'd been dragging a dead hog along with him. 'Whatever are you playing at,' Wendolin said stopping him to heal his gnawed leg. 'Be a sorry sight to leave all this fine bacon behind. Get a few grand gammon joints out of this I will. Trouble I am having is how to turn my axe here back into a dagger, it's awfully cumbersome like this.' Banbury though wasn't able to change it back, but found it fit nicely in the harness that used to hold his father's scythe. Wasiz quickly joined Banbury and helped him get the slain hog into the caravan for them to butcher as they travelled much to the disgust of Galger. With the Thorns riding around them even if more orcs lay in hiding none dared show themselves as they travelled on.

Caspian lead the convoy and after a day the Arizun Stream was on the horizon, leading to a rumour to grow around the wagons that the zatifas can lend their great speed to other horses about them. For every horse, pony and even an old mule who'd normally need a constant supply of carrots to move managed to keep pace with him. When they reached the edge of the stream boats waited to ferry the young Prince home. Of white oak they were made with sails of flowing green that held the King of Meceller's mark. A white crown sat at the base with the tips of the crown leaching up to form a blossoming white tree. Before coming into sight of the those around the boats the Thorns peeled away with the caravan. When they arrived at the patch of trees Simeon had told them about they were as appalled by the state Banbury and Wasiz had left it in as Galger was. 'I'm a bit concerned Captain,' Krosh said as he and Thrimore looked to Galger who the pair of amateur butchers had left in a puddle of blood and entrails. 'About what?' Thrimore asked reaching for a bucket to fill with water. 'Concerned about you,' Krosh huffed as the pair walked to a pond that sat close by. 'There's no need to be,' Thrimore said.

'I'd say there is. This woman has cast some spell on you. Has you as I have never seen in all our years,' Krosh complained . 'Don't get me wrong. I'd have not left Simeon's lot back there to feed the crows, but how far do you intend to follow this red lady?' Krosh said. 'Do you not see it? Do you not see the shine that follows her. It's like a star rests behind her eyes, while her hair burns like the sun. Perhaps she is a witch and I'm under some terrible curse, but it is one I'm happy to be afflicted with,' Thrimore said. The shine of Caspian's and Fiona's coats then drew his eyes to them drinking from the pond. 'These Balmoths though, what do you make of them? Their steeds are unlike any I've seen.'

'Zatifas,' Krosh huffed rather miffed all his worries were so easily shrugged off. 'It is not their steeds that concern me. These Balmoth, the Leaflins. They have more enemies than we can handle. Forget the Countess, the Balmoths even have the La Sores placing bounty's on their heads and that's to say nothing of the goblin who rides with that Jhona.'

'Just trust me Krosh, as you have before. I feel we are being given a way off the ledge we've been clinging to ever since my mistake. A way for not just us to get home but the others as well,' Thrimore told him before taking the full bucket to wash out the vile within the caravan.

Richard's party all shared the same boat aside from him and Jhona who Anderson had called over to the Prince's boat. Seeing them set off Simeon hurried along the bank yelling after them as they sailed away. 'Find the Toppled Dwarf once in the city. I shall seek you out there with your reward.'

'See you do,' Wasiz yelled back before slinking down beside Banbury. 'Take the helm would you, my arms are not what they used to be and there's a strong current up ahead,' Anderson asked Richard. Changing places Richard took the rudder's pole and said. 'You didn't ask us here just to have me steer. What is it you wish to say?' Glancing over his shoulder to be sure Anwayes couldn't hear he then whispered. 'The King is mad Richard, served him for years and a more loyal servant he does not have than I, but he is sick. His madness grows and the council do nothing but line their pockets. Thing is, I saw your healers back there and I also know who the ones in red you ride with truly are.'

'Make your point,' Richard said.

'Nothing shall I say of the Evertree's own, but your healers could they help him, cure his sickness,'

Anderson asked. 'Ask them as you have me and I'm sure they will help if they're able, but what's this about the Evertree's own?' Richard wondered.

'Those men you ride with, Thorns is that what they call themselves these days. Once they were the King's own guard. Their banishment is another symptom of his sickness.' Seeing Richard wanted to know more he leaned in further. 'Ask any in the city and they'll spew the same tripe the council comes out with. Plotted to kill the King they'd say, planned to take power by spilling the blood of the royal family is what they'd tell you.'

'So what is the truth?' Richard asked.

'Plotted they did, but not against the King but his council. During the human's war and even after many sought safety in Meceller. Not just wood folk like you and I, but centaurs and beasts of the west lands, even displaced dwarves rushed to its walls for safety. From the south hundreds of elves fled along with all others who feared the fangs of wolves. The city was overrun, none had enough, but then overnight the hordes of people began to thin and as the weeks passed few but wood folk would remain,' Anderson said.

'Where did they go?' Richard asked.

'The Evertree's roots go deep as does the greed of those who rule there. Gold, it is a sickness worse than what troubles the King. See there,' Anderson went on, gesturing to two snow covered peaks far in the distance. 'Within those hills is the realm of Entos, the brothers Kupert and Koroast Entos rule there. Within their hills they mine and forge jewels beyond wonder.

Incredible works they make and no others can forge weapons as they do. It is there they were sent and some say still work their mines to this day. A fair amount of coin was the council paid for this unwilling workforce, something a young Captain discovered. Doing what any would in such a situation he went to someone he believed he could trust with this information. Not knowing the one he had confided in had been at the heart of the bargain made with the Entos brothers.'

'Who was it?' Richard asked making Anderson double check the young Prince wasn't listening. 'The boy's mother Queen Amelia Roian. The young Captain barely made it from the Evertree with his life and rather than just seeking him out the Queen demanded the heads of all the Evertree's own to hide her deeds. She then sent her sheriff's searching, not only the men were punished. Parents were tortured to give up their young and those who didn't replaced them on the gallows. Since that day the sheriff's have grown bolder and only those with deep enough pockets are able to stay on their good side.'

'So what are you really?' Anwayes asked Jhona.

'It is as we said, we are rangers,' Jhona replied. 'And as I said they don't exist, not anymore the rangers of Meceller are just a fable,' Anwayes said in a fairly snobby fashion. 'It's just as well me and my brother are not from Meceller then isn't it,' Jhona said.

'Then how did you become rangers? My mother said the rangers were bandits, who used to prey upon the people before the Evertree named my father King and they fled to the wilds,' Anwayes announced.

'I would not put much weight into whatever fable this mother of yours may have told. For the story my friend told me and my brother of them is far grander than any she may have sullied your ears with,' Jhona said. 'What friend?' Anwayes wondered.

'Funny that you have so many questions for someone you're so sure is a myth,' Jhona chuckled.

'Fine, perhaps you are rangers. Now will you tell me,' Anwayes scoffed as he folded his arms. Jhona then went on to tell him how he and his brother had ended up in their green uniforms. 'Me and my brother had gone to be trained and educated by a Seer. He taught us to read and write and became quite insistent that we would both become bookkeepers. Little did we know about the high elf's vault and cared even less to be bookkeepers. One day when the pair of us were studying me and my brother came across a book. Not just any book was this but one that held the history of Meceller's rangers. Only slim, barely a chapters worth of pages thick. That was enough to intrigue us and we quickly gained all the knowledge we could have them from Seer Tranem. Men and woman of valour they were and before your parents ruled Meceller they were the people's guard. From Meceller they rode when the orcs of the Blood Works were set upon the lands. North this great horde went aiming to pillage the forest city, not expecting their path to be blocked by any until the rangers cries reached their twisted ears and ahead they rode. A great charge of soaring arrows and thundering hooves followed and lead to a skirmish the orc call the battle of the waking wood. This act scared many of their like from the trees of Meceller, sparing the city from their wrath. For the orcs believed hundreds of warriors such as these waited beneath his tress, ready to pounce on any who dare try and pass. Luckily they didn't know the truth of it. Unfortunately no more lay in wait and of those who rode from the city none ever did return from battle. Then when the human's purge began our mentor Seer Avlor Tranem made us sit in the Seer's tower while the south burnt. Until the night me and Richard could stay idle no longer. We snuck from the tower, had our uniforms made and crossed to the south before he'd noticed we'd left. With that the rangers had returned and in their uniforms we hoped to spread the same fear among the humans and wolves as others had the orcs before.'

'That's nothing like the story my mother told. What happened next, after you and your brother rode south?' Anwayes inquired.

'Oh no, but one sorry story will you get from me. You'll have to pester Wasiz for more. He's a far greater story teller than me and hundreds of fables he's found over the years,' Jhona told the young Prince.

'Look there, those statues,' Bethany said pointing to two stone sculptures on the west bank of the stream. The figure of a woman held the other in her arms as if he was dying. 'It is a monument to the first high elves, marking the war amongst their own. A stream didn't always flow here and back when the trees of Meceller had yet to even become shrubs the high elves vied for control of it. Some wanted the lands for their own, to clear it for their ilk. Others like them wished to protect it and they died trying to do so, Martha and Santra Dune are their names. Founders of Duniesa and bringers of the Seer's light,' Wasiz said.

'Do all goblins possess such a talent at telling tales as you do Wasiz?' Bethany asked.

'I'm afraid not my lady, it is a talent I alone wield,' Wasiz boasted.

'Look trees,' Stephanie declared.

'I've seen trees Steph,' Wendolin snapped.

'Not like this, look,' Stephanie said making her look ahead. There past wooden walls and the gates to Meceller's dock great oaks stretched into the sky. No trees taller does Alidor have to offer, four hundred foot tall the greatest of these lush green towers of bark are and even from the boat the Leaflins could make out tree houses and walkways going between them. Over the great canopy of green these trees created another towers higher than any other. Sat in Meceller's very centre was the Evertree, the white oak that lore says birthed the wood elves themselves and whose acorns fell to create the forest city of Meceller. Sailing closer the sight of the city beyond was blocked by the wooden wall that ran around the entirety of the forest city. Construction of which began when orcs first marched forth from the Blood Work and made taller still when the humans of the Crown City began their revolt. Ahead gates that blocked their boats opened and

141

The Forgotten Hero

beneath the walls our party went to receive a far more hostile greeting than any had expected.

Chapter Eight
The Royalty in the Evertree

'Step out, the lot of ya. Step out and get checked,' a sheriff ordered. After passing beneath the wooden wall and into Meceller men wearing grey uniforms and fur hats who called themselves sheriffs had directed their boats from the shore. Sending them to a dock that was surprisingly sparse given the size of the city. Only two other boats floated alongside the dock, both of which had a group of these menacing looking folk in fur hats rummaging through or simply tipping out whatever containers the small boats possessed. The sight of the King's insignia making its way along the Arizun Stream had drawn a sizeable crowd, but their chattering quickly fell silent as more sheriffs arrived. 'Get away, Berkus,' Anderson barked back as he hopped to shore. 'These here are the Prince's guard, they won't be conforming to any of your checks.'

'They must be inspected like all others. It's the council's orders, had word there's mercenaries about they have,' Berkus said.

'My friends are here on important business after rescuing me from a horde of orcs on our journey. Are you and your men not meant to guard the road?' Anwayes said. 'It's the Elite's road to guard now little Prince, best you remember that next time you go running off,' Berkus scoffed. 'Who are they then these

143

guards of yours?' He went on looking over Anderson's shoulder to Richard. Before any others could reply the young Prince shouted. 'They're rangers, rangers from the north. Sent by the Seers.'

'Enough now lad, let's not be shouting about other people's business,' Anderson said pulling him back. 'No such thing, there ain't no rangers,' Berkus spat as the crowd mumbled around him. 'That is a statement I am done hearing. We are just as your Prince tells you. Jhona Balmoth is my name and I am a ranger, let no others tell you different. Move yourself aside for I quickly tire of looking upon foul shapes such as yours.' Pushing an increasingly frustrated Berkus aside Jhona then waved his arm to Anwayes to lead the way. As they marched on Berkus grabbed the collar of another sheriff, almost spitting in his face as he ordered. 'Get to the tree, tell her people who call themselves rangers are here.'

'I've no interest in ailing Kings, where's this tavern the wagon chap said about, I'll meet you there. Got a fine bit of cooking to do,' Banbury said. Their visit to Meceller couldn't have drawn more attention. For round every corner and down all the streets crowds lined up to see their Prince return, but more importantly get a glimpse of who he'd returned with. 'Who are they?' Some mumbled.

'Soldiers of fortune I'd say,' others said. All chattered amongst themselves until before the steps that lead to the Evertree's entrance, where the largest crowd had gathered one dared to yell past sheriffs to them. 'Who be your guard my Prince?'

'They're rangers,' Anwayes shouted back as he ascended the steps. 'No,' the great booming voice of his mother silenced the crowd. 'The Rangers are lost, who are you truly?' Wasiz then stepped forward to take on the greatest test his abilities had yet to see. For only a few lines did he need to speak to hold a whole city's attention. His nostrils flared as his hood fell back and his arm's rose. 'The rangers return Meceller, for lost they were. Lost to the wilds. Fell in a bloody battle did the first who guarded these great trees, so no these are not them. A new breed you have here. The Balmoth brothers reformed the forgotten rangers and while you hid behind wooden walls they fought. Take up a seat and fill my pipe and I shall tell you their tale.' As Wasiz spoke Anwayes sat upon the steps of the Evertree wanting to hear. The crowd though only murmured to one other. 'Perhaps the tale of valiant steeds and dastardly gnomes is not fit for these fine trees to hear. A shame, a pity even.'

'Do tell us Wasiz, if you'd please. Ranger Balmoth did say you know tales from even the forgotten age. Fables few others have ever heard,' Anwayes begged. Within the crowd the murmur faded until a voice from up high yelled to them. 'So who be this ranger and what does a stray of the red water know of valiant deeds?' With a slip of his heel and flick of his cape Wasiz declared. 'Piqued your interests have we. Settle down and listen intently and you'll soon see.' To him all eyes went and silent was the crowd before the

Evertree. Making his mother rage as Wasiz's tale began and Anderson lead the others to her. 'You were meant to retrieve the boy, not bring whoever this is to the Evertree. They sully it with their lies,' Amelia said.

'Your highness please hear me, they have healers with them. I beg you let them try and help our King,' Anderson begged.

'You expect me to let some strays tend to my King,' Amelia snapped.

'I beg your highness I have seen their work with my own eyes,' Anderson went on. After numerous attempts to persuade his Queen, Amelia simply snapped her fingers in his face to silence him. 'It matters little. Even if these healers of yours could help he is too weak to see any, he can barely lift himself up in bed,' Amelia claimed, but this was soon disproven. Wasiz's tale had not only enticed a city but its King also. Just past a point in his tale where the great Caspian had splattered an extremely unpleasant gnome a great laugh came from high up the Evertree. 'What a story, I should like to meet these Balmoth brothers.' Leaning from his window totally nude, wearing only his crown was King Lousras Roian. A huge scraggly grey beard covered his face while his bushy grey hair was frizzed up into a huge wiry ball. 'And you shall meet them your Highness, for they wait by your Evertree's doors. Do make yourself decent though my grand King of white oak. For fair woman follow us and I fear they may faint upon the sight of your magnificent self,' Wasiz yelled up to him. 'It is settled then, a feast. A feast for the

146

Balmoths and a robe for myself. All have heard it, so it must be,' the King said.

'You go on, I don't like this place I'll go with the dwarf and wait there,' Wendolin said.

'Are you sure? I'd imagined you'd love it here,' Stephanie replied.

'These trees, they're not natural,' Wendolin said. 'And the things you can do are,' Stephanie scoffed. 'It's not like that, it's something else, something evil rests here. Trees remember the things elves forget and these trees talk of foul things.' As Wendolin spoke the branches of the Evertree seemed to her at least as if they shuddered. 'Never mind best you hurry on or your ranger will leave you behind.'

'Do you think they would?' Stephanie muttered. 'Just leave us I mean. I feel as we are part of the band now,' she went on letting her voice raise as Wasiz's arms flayed before a sniggering crowd. 'Do you not feel as such?'

'No, it's safe to assume I understand little about your feelings sister.'

'I feel as I am being seen for the first time in my life Wendolin. Around them I feel at home even when miles from a warm fire or cozy bed,' Stephanie said turning to look over her strange friends. They were undergoing a rather brisk search by the sheriffs after having their weapon's confiscated. 'Hurry on to your ranger and save your feelings for him,' Wendolin huffed leaving her sister. Most entered the Evertree while Banbury and Wendolin went in search of the

The Forgotten Hero

Toppled Dwarf and Wasiz continued to enthral hundreds with his stolen tales.

Inside the Evertree the Queen's mood grew increasingly worse, even more so when her husband began descending the wooden steps of the white oak yelling as he went. 'Fetch the food, get the wine and set some seats out for our guests. A fine feast we will have I say.' He'd put a robe of fallen autumn leaves over himself to hide his modesty and while he hopped down the steps servants hurried to make the table in the hall below. Leaping over the final few steps like an exuberant child would, the King then looked straight at his wife and said. 'There you are nanny, go fetch the boy. Is he back from his adventures?'

'I'm not the boy's nanny. I am your wife,' she snapped back. Comically rubbing his eyes the King then stared at her with wide eyes. 'So you are, my mistake my darling. The Balmoths,' he then yelped and ran past his wife. 'These must be the Balmoths,' he grabbed both Richard and Jhona's hand and began walking them towards the table. 'We get so few interesting guests these days. Hurry and sit down you must tell me of your journeys.' Towards a long table in the centre of the Evertree's hollowed oak they were lead, noticing as they went another table to their left. A small round table that had four portly men sat around it counting the contents of the many bags of coins that surrounded them. Reaching the table the King sat at the head after seating the Balmoths to his left and the Leaflins on his right. 'Get your King his tea Berkus,'

Amelia ordered the sheriff who'd followed them from the dock into the Evertree whilst Anderson went to King Roain's side and said. 'My King forget the Balmoths for the time, speak with the others. These are the Leaflins, I believe they could help cure what ails you.'

'Silly Anderson nothing ails me,' King Roian said as his tea was placed before him and Amelia took her seat at his side. 'How could they possibly help him, see sense. Your King simply needs rest and no unwelcome visitors claiming to be rangers,' Amelia snapped as the Prince's nanny walked past on her way to fetch the boy from the Evertree's steps. 'There's my wife come and say hello my dear,' the King shouted waving her over to the table. 'She's not your wife, that is the nanny,' Amelia stated.

'Then who are you?' the King replied.

'I'm your wife,' Amelia said.

'So you are, I'm sorry my dear I do get mixed up these days,' King Roian said as the nanny approached. 'Can I be of help your Highness?' the Prince's nanny asked and the King seemed to completely forget what his wife had just told him. 'Here's my darling wife, Amelia let me introduce you to the Balmoths my dear,' King Roian declared.

'That's the nanny,' his wife sighed placing her head in her hands. 'Ah yes, terribly sorry nanny, but you two must stop trading places. It's cruel to play tricks you know,' the King said.

'Just drink your tea my dear, it will help you think clearly,' Amelia said pushing the cup into her husband's hand as she threw a glare to the Prince's nanny. 'Do your job and get the boy to his room. I'm sure he's heard enough of that goblin's rambling.' Noticing his guests all looked rather awkward around the table made the King raise his cup. 'Please excuse my son's snappy nanny,' he said gesturing to his wife.

'Hurry and fill your glasses, break open the wine and let us have a jolly time. I can't imagine your journey has been an easy one thus far, but here you can at least fill your bellies and rest for the night.' All their glasses were filled, but when the waiter reached Stephanie she stopped him and asked. 'I don't suppose I could get some tea also? I don't really like wine.' A question that made the waiter look nervously to the Queen. Before she was able to respond King Roian lunged forward and lifted up the teapot for the waiter to fetch. 'Of course you can dear lady, she always makes too much for just myself anyhow. Terribly good for the skin they say it is. Can't remember who it was that said it though. Probably a clever chap whoever it was.' Reluctantly the waiter took it from him as he wittered on and went to pour Stephanie's drink. Letting the Leaflin's notice the Queen's glaring had moved from the nanny to them as he did. 'Tell me of your travels then. Are the plains of my beloved Wearet as fair as they ever were? Still as lush as ever I hope,' King Roian asked.

'The plains are still scarred by the war your Highness. Many of the towns and villages still lay in ruins. The ones that remain habitable sit empty and only house ghosts,' Richard said.

'Empty, scarred. What is this about war?' The King replied. 'Do you not know what's been happening past your forest?' Jhona asked.

'The King does not need to worry himself with the Seer's wars,' the Queen said.

'Perhaps he should be concerned, since it was his people who suffered most. Have you not seen the Wearet since the Crown City marched through?' Jhona wondered. 'What is this they're talking about?' The King asked. 'It is nothing, the council have your affairs well in hand,' Amelia said.

'Maybe I should speak with them. See about all this war,' the King said with a slight slurring tone in his voice. 'No,' Amelia snapped putting her hand to his shoulder. 'Just drink your tea my King. Don't let the strangers worry you.' She went on forcing a calmer tone into her voice. 'If you say so my dear,' the King replied as he sipped on his cup. The same tea that Stephanie wafted under her nose letting her recognise a scent coming from the cup. Nudging her sister Stephanie let Bethany smell it and after a quick glance at the King whose eyes had began to slowly close both she and Bethany knew what ailed the King of the woods. Fentis leaf, a plant only found growing within dormant volcanos. Once picked and boiled it let out a scent both sisters knew well. With it one can make a potion that will make the consumer incredibly sleepy and easy to manage and was something the Countess had used on them many times. 'Dearie me all this excitement has taken its toll,' the King said through a yawn. 'Yes, best you be back off to bed,' his wife insisted. 'Anderson help him to his room would you.'

'Are you sure you don't want me to take a look at him?' Bethany asked. 'I'm fairly certain I can help him.'

'As I said there's nothing you can do for him. He has the best healers there is and there is no cure for his madness,' the Queen said as Anderson helped King Roian from his seat. 'Did they tell him to stop drinking your tea? I'd hope they would, you do realise drinking it in large doses will rot your insides and cause a rather horrible death. Not even the Countess used it in tea,' Bethany replied glaring to the Queen as she did.

'What's she saying?' Anderson asked as he helped the King pass. 'Just do as you are ordered footman, this girl seems to have yet to learn her place,' Amelia said. 'Quite right, I'm sure Bethany didn't mean anything by it,' Richard interjected noticing that while they'd been distracted by the ailing King the Evertree had slowly filled up with sheriffs. Once Anderson had begun ascending the stairs with King Roian all started inching closer to the table. Strolling over to the table the council members surrounded, Amelia retrieved a pair of letters from it, saying as she did. 'Little news passes this forest without me hearing and few things transpire beyond I don't get word of.' Holding up the letters she went on. 'So which bounty do you suppose I should claim? The one the La Sore's Elites have placed on the heads of the Balmoths, or do you think it would be best to claim the one the Countess of that sordid island has placed on her runaway mages?' Amelia chuckled dropping the letters down as the sheriffs encircled the table. 'This is all one big misunderstanding, I can assure you,' Richard insisted as the gruff hand of Berkus grabbed his shoulder. 'I don't think she's listening Richard,' Jhona quipped. 'Please my Queen, don't do this. Whatever promise the Countess or La Sores have made will be a lie,' Richard told her but was ignored and as Stephanie was pulled from her seat all realised they had to act. Grabbing Berkus's hand Richard pulled him forward as he shot up from his seat, breaking the sheriff's nose on the back of his head as Jhona jumped from his seat and kicked it into another pair of sheriffs. The water from the jugs on the table soon froze the arms of the one trying to restrain Bethany while Richard leapt over the table to grapple with the sheriff trying to pull Stephanie away. Doors were slammed open as more of the Queen's grunts rushed into the brawl. After punching down a sheriff Richard then felt water flick his face. To him and Jhona a stream of flowing water carried their confiscated weapons to their hands after knocking down the sheriff who took them. Reaching for his sword Richard yelled to his companions as he drew it. 'Close your eyes.' As the blade was revealed it sparked until the sparks covering it exploded into a blinding light that filled the Evertree. Once it faded Queen Amelia saw her men had been blinded and her unwanted guests now ran to the Evertree's doors. 'After them you idiot,' she yelled to Berkus who could only clench his broken nose in response.

Beyond the Evertree's grand doors Wasiz was still keeping the attention of the Prince and all others who crowded the streets or watched on from balconies or branches. Until Jhona ran to his back and said. 'Enough showing off, it's time to leave.'

'Leave so soon, but I've barely told a handful of stories,' Wasiz complained before he noticed the sheriffs chasing them. The girls soon rushed past Wasiz as Jhona had, followed by Richard. 'Wrap it up Wasiz we have to go,' he shouted and grabbed Wasiz's cape pulling him along with him. Each disappeared into the crowd as the sheriffs bolted past the Prince whose nanny quickly took his hand to lead him away while the sheriffs began dispersing the crowd that had gathered.

'Finally a bit of luck,' Banbury said running into the Toppled Dwarf's kitchen. To Banbury's relief the cooking facilities sat at the base of the tree that the Toppled Dwarf ascended. A rickety fence circled the base and the furniture scattered about within. While up the length of the tree many winches took drinks and food to each of the platforms that increased in size the higher they got. The stove was hot and Banbury was soon frying slices of sizzling bacon, to the disgust of the owner. 'You can't cook that muck here,' the barkeep stated and as he and Banbury argued Wendolin looked around the tables. All about were terribly gloomy, like most she past who hadn't been taken up in the mass following the Prince. A lone old wood elf then caught her eye, he was staring into space and had barely touched the drink before him. His face reminded her of someone and she found herself wandering over to him. 'You look lost,' Wendolin said to him. 'Oh, I am sorry ducky. Did not mean too. I'm just waiting I suppose,' the man said.

'For what?' Wendolin asked.

'It is silly, do not bother with me my duck,' he said. 'Budge up,' Wendolin ordered pushing the man along the bench he sat on, realising as she did his legs had been broken beyond repair. Both his feet had been twisted and the bones shattered, making each foot face the wrong direction. 'Seems I am bothering, Norcea knows why. Nor am I a duck. Wendolin Leaflin,' she said holding out a hand to him. 'Phieus, Phieus Krosh,' he replied quite taken aback. It had been many years since any woman had shown an interest in him, especially one as stunning as her. 'So Krosh is his last name,' Wendolin said.

'Sorry,' Phieus replied.

'Never mind, what happened here?' Wendolin asked placing a hand to his stump. 'My son,' Phieus said. 'Your son did this?' Wendolin asked in shock.

'No no, of course not ducky. He was one of the Evertree's own you see. When the sheriffs couldn't find my boy they came for me. Took my legs the buggers did, but I didn't tell them nothing. Bastard sheriffs, I'd cut them up myself if I had but one working toe,' Phieus said. 'What of your son?' Wendolin asked.

'I don't know, he's alive, I hope. This was his favourite tavern you know. Find him and his Captain here most nights I would, carried each home more than once. I think maybe they'll just come back one day and it will be as it was again,' Phieus sighed. 'I'm sorry my duck, please don't believe all in Meceller are as miserable as myself and others here, but with the Evertree's own to the wind this city has become a grim place.' Phieus then looked to Wendolin and saw her grin. 'Your son is safe Phieus Krosh,' she whispered. 'To a patch of trees on the west side of the Arizun. There he waits. You best run master Krosh for he will leave soon,' Wendolin said.

'How, how do you know this and I can't run anywhere my duck,' Phieus said as Wendolin stood up and left him. 'You should try master Krosh,' Wendolin replied and took the ring from her finger, placing it back into her pocket. Phieus's hands went to his lap and then ran down until he yelled and jumped up throwing the table over as he did. 'My legs, I have my legs,' he was amazed, astonished even. No word could accurately describe the feelings the once impaired man felt. Running to Wendolin he embraced her and said. 'My lady you have saved me, freed me to find my boy. How ever can I thank you?' Wendolin then saw her sisters along with the others running towards the tavern. 'Just be ready to run master Krosh. It seems our time in Meceller will be short,' she said as the others leapt over the fence and rushed to her. 'What did you do?' Wendolin yelled to Wasiz. 'I did nothing, seems your Countess has eyes here and we have to leave,' Wasiz replied. 'There they are, get them by order of the council, the Balmoths and their company are to be put in chains,' a sheriff yelled.

'Follow me,' Jhona ordered rubbing his hair clip and going to a door that rested in the trunk of the Toppled Dwarf. Opening it he revealed it went to the wagon Simeon had gifted them. Beyond the door Krosh stared back wondering what was happening. Before any could go through Phieus was almost kicking his way past others as he rushed through to embrace his son not even caring to question how it was possible. 'Hurry and go, everyone,' Jhona ordered. Banbury was just able to get a handful of bacon as Richard pulled him along with him and all left Meceller. Leaving the sheriffs to open the door they passed through only to find a ladder to the higher levels of the Toppled Dwarf.

Few realised the impact they'd had on the city and its young Prince as they left it behind. Wasiz though saw his eyes as he rattled off one after another of the Balmoth's exploits. For his tales are not just to create a giggle among friends, or to praise worthy deeds. Just a few who hear them will find it and best you think yourself lucky if you do. Inspired was Prince Roian and running up the great heights of Meceller's wall he charged along it to the highest point, the Hammerfall. Keen eyes he has like all his kind, so past sheriffs he barged to watch along the Arizun Stream until he saw white horses ever so faintly in the distance. As he watched their shapes fade Anderson joined him. 'That's what I will be Anderson, I shall be a ranger.'

Chapter Nine
The Humtees

'Why not just use your clip to get on to the Forgotten Vale?' Banbury said.

'Because I have never been to the Forgotten Vale. It can only take us places I know, I think,' Jhona replied. He now sat behind Wasiz on Fiona's back. Using the hair clip to escape Meceller had been a good idea at the time, but had drained Jhona of all his strength. He could hardly muster the energy to keep his head up. 'What about the Humtees?' Bethany went on. 'Could I use it to take us there?'

'Maybe, but to send us all would leave you in the same sorry state as I,' Jhona said resting his head on Wasiz's back. 'Then just us and the mage will go,' Thrimore declared. 'It may be worth trying Richard, would certainly speed us along to Vurcun. That way myself and the rest of these Thorns can keep going and the caravan will be free for Jhona to rest,' Wasiz said.

'He's right and we can use its door. Travel to the Humtees, free our parents and be back before Jhona even wakes,' Bethany announced.

'Here, it's no use to me in this state anyhow,' Jhona said removing his hair clip and handing it to Bethany. In her hands the hair clip changed shape transforming from the soaring eagle to a teardrop stone that held a stunning blue light. 'Just think of where you wish to go and reach for a door.' With that the little will Jhona had left to stay awake left him and he fell fast asleep lent on Wasiz. 'Come along madam, time for you to make up for all your wrongdoing,' Krosh said.

'Easy with her. You know I'm none too impressed with this ducky. I didn't raise you to be going around nabbing young ladies,' his father said.

'Believe me if you know only a tenth of what this woman's done you'd understand,' Krosh told him as he heard Thrimore giggle. 'Come along ducky, can't keep the Leaflins waiting,' he mocked as they took Galger from the caravan. 'It's settled then, the three of us will go with Thrimore and the mage,' Wendolin said.

'Richard also,' Stephanie blurted out and then quickly went on trying to justify him coming along. 'Even if you share the load you both may end up in the same state as Jhona there,' she said pointing to Wasiz and Banbury who now helped him into the caravan. 'If she tries something we'd need more than just Thrimore.' With the door of the caravan closed Bethany did as Jhona said. Thinking about her home she reached for the door, but when she opened it only the sight of Jhona sleeping greeted her. 'It doesn't matter who comes if it doesn't work,' Bethany muttered. Closing the door she tried again, this time thinking about the town of the Humtees itself. Focusing on the grocers she reached for the door again and sighed in relief when she saw full shelves of leafy greens beyond. 'It worked,' she yelped. Running ahead of the others Wendolin went through first, closely followed by Thrimore dragging Galger along with him. 'We shall find a camp and rest a bit before going on. Be sure not to dally Richard the skies grow darker before their time. The Grey Count won't wait forever,' Wasiz said.

'Don't fret we will be back before you have time to miss us,' Richard said following Stephanie to the door. 'Are you okay?' Stephanie asked Bethany before going on. 'I'm fine just go,' Bethany ordered and her sister along with Richard went through, that though was all Bethany could manage. Sweat poured from her forehead as she fell to her knees. Thinking quickly she took off the hair clip and tossed it through the doorway sending it to land at Stephanie's feet. A second later only Jhona lay behind the door and Bethany soon joined him passed out from exhaustion same as he.

'See, she's not as invincible as she acts,' Wendolin smirked. 'Don't be like that, do you think she's okay?' Stephanie said as she went to retrieve the hair clip. Once again it changed, going from a shining stone to a blossoming white rose. Taking it from her Richard put it in her hair and said. 'Don't worry Wasiz and Banbury will take care of her and we shall see how tough you are when we return red lady.' Leaving the green grocers the group found the isolated town of Humtees quiet. When the locals looked through their windows and saw them shutters and curtains were slammed closed. 'This is not as I remember,' Wendolin said.

'Where is everyone?' Stephanie wondered. Going up Peacock Lane to the Leaflin's cottage they still saw nobody. Even Miss Steward who rarely left her porch had vanished. 'Look Miss Porter's jewellery stand is even gone.'

'They must be hiding somewhere,' Wendolin said. When they reached the Leaflin's cottage all thoughts of where the other occupants of the village had gotten to were forgotten. There they found their parent's cottage burnt, little of their childhood home wasn't scarred by the fire and in the doorway two stone sculptures rested. Frozen in stone Terence and Sophia Leaflin had been and there they had stayed since the day the Countess had sent Galger to kidnap their daughters. Taking Galger before the statues Thrimore said. 'Do as we wish and you can go on free of us and the Countess if you choose.' Taking the gag from her mouth Galger replied. 'Get stuffed, she'll find you. You and all of your woody scum.' Roots then pushed the stones in the path aside. Running over the ground they found Galger's feet and pierced her left sole. Her cries were soon stifled by Wendolin pulling her head back. 'You should stop fearing her mage, instead fear me. For whatever trials she has made you endure I have seen a hundred times and in my torment I developed many unspeakable acts of my own I wish to test.' Menacing and positively ghoulish was Wendolin's voice leaving Galger only one option when Thrimore removed her blindfold to reveal her pure white eyes. Looking upon the statues blood dripped from her eye sockets. Followed by grit that poured from her tear ducts and the stone shapes in the doorway slowly became flesh once more. The last bits of stone crumpled away and the Leaflin's parents drew breath for the first time in

161

years. Putting the blindfold back over Galger's eyes Thrimore moved her aside as the sisters rushed to their freed parents. 'What, whatever is this? What happened to the cottage? Dearie me Mrs Leaflin this is quite a thing.' Mr Leaflin said patting his chest and looking around their ruined home, his wife however only saw them. Just babes they were when she last saw the pair. Now in the blink of an eye they were grown, but both balled as a lost child would as their mother reached for them. 'I thought we'd lost you,' Stephanie cried as her mother's arms went around her and Wendolin. 'What has happened? You're both so tall,' Mrs Leaflin said. 'Wait Bethany, where is Bethany?'

'Don't worry she is with friends,' Stephanie told her as she felt her father's hand tussle her hair and two long bulky arms around them all. 'It's truly them, my tiny Stephanie and little Wendolin, dearie me Mrs Leaflin how much have we missed?' He said then he saw Thrimore retying the blindfold over Galger's eyes. 'You,' he barked leaving his family. 'Last thing I saw was you. What did you do?'

'She turned you to stone, her eyes let her seal away whoever she pleases. Rumours say the Countess stole the ability from a witch who dwelled in some remote cave,' Thrimore said.

'And who's this?' Mr Leaflin said storming before Thrimore. 'They're the ones who saved us father,' Wendolin said grabbing her father's arm, worrying he was about to thump Thrimore. 'Not them both,' Stephanie protested. Running to Richard she pulled him forward proudly stating as she did. 'This is

Richard Balmoth, he's a ranger. With his brother and their friends they saved us from Accultian and brought us home.'

'Did they now?' Mr Leaflin said. 'Why?' He asked eyes fixed to Richards. 'We needed their help sir,' Richard replied.

'I bet you did, boy as skinny as you are, doubt you'd last a week in the wilds. What about him then?' Mr Leaflin said turning back to Thrimore. 'Never mind him,' Wendolin scoffed. Going into the house she found an old mug that hadn't been broken. As she headed back to Galger's side Stephanie asked. 'What are you doing?'

'Fixing this one. We can hardy just send her off as she is,' Wendolin replied. 'Step back from her,' she then ordered Thrimore and he left Galger be. 'I did what you asked, let me go as you promised,' Galger snapped as she heard Wendolin stepping closer. 'You can go, once I'm sure you won't put another through the hell you made for us,' Wendolin said putting the cup to the ground between the pair. She then gripped Galger's head between her hands. 'What are you doing?' Stephanie said.

'While you and Bethany ignored all you could at Accultian I learnt her cursed skill,' Wendolin said.

'Wait you can't, you can't. I'll be blind again you can't,' Galger begged, but black roots had already held her in place. Wendolin then spoke words her sister had only heard the Countess utter. Ancient words from a language only a few who still lived knew. 'She speaks as the first did,' Thrimore said as roots shrouded in

163

shadows sprung from the ground. 'It can't be, a Seer taught me and I know their words. This is something else,' Richard shuddered as the roots grew. 'It's shadow magic. A twisted form of sorcery even my mentor feared.' The shadows wrapped over Galger, crawling up her legs and over her chest until they reached her white eyes where they consumed her eye balls. Galger screamed as a black goo oozed from them and dripped down her cheeks, filling the mug between the pair. 'How are you doing that?' Stephanie spluttered.

'Enough Wendolin you're hurting the girl,' Mrs Leaflin complained, but Wendolin didn't stop. She continued until Galger's pale eyes turned back to green. Her pupils were as they had been before the Countess injected her with the ooze that now filled the mug, but just as she was before she was blind. Taking the mug from the ground Wendolin left Galger to cry on the floor and then ordered Thrimore to find fire. Pulling an old lantern from the ruins he removed the candle and used his flint and steel to light the wick. 'Seems you girls have learnt a lot since we lost you,' Mr Leaflin said. Using the flame Wendolin lit the ooze alight and left it to burn away to nothing. Turning back to her parents Wendolin took a deep breath. 'You didn't lose us, we lost you. It was all my fault. If I'd never have fallen for her lies you'd never have gotten hurt and nothing would have changed, but I'm stronger now, stronger than her. I promise the Countess or her mages won't ever bother you again,' Wendolin declared. The sound of someone slowly clapping then began to echo about them followed by a sarcastic voice. 'Oh how very touching, truly it is heart warming to see a family reunited,' the voice said. Spinning Richard saw men in black emerging from the trees around Peacock Lane and sat on the fence opposite the Leaflin's cottage an elven woman in black leather sat. 'That voice, Trussa is that you, why are you here?' Galger snapped.

'Did you really think our mistress would leave retrieving such a valuable asset to only you, and now it's clear you've failed quite incredibly,' Trussa said.

'Wait. I haven't failed, I was betrayed. Those Thorns tricked me,' Galger protested.

'Sounds like failure to me and we both know she cannot bear disappointment. You're so predictably stupid Galger. I'd knew you'd lead them back here soon enough,' Trussa said as fire slowly consumed her hand. A ball of flames then leapt from her palm and engulfed Galger before any could react. 'Kill the men, the women are mine,' she then bellowed as the flames covered her arms and she span from the gate to advance on Wendolin. 'Get them into the cottage,' Wendolin yelled as vines went up. Grabbing her parents Stephanie ran to get them clear of the fighting while the fire tore through Wendolin's vines and she desperately tried to retrieve the ring from her pocket. 'They're Crows of the Wilds,' Richard announced drawing his sword, readying both he and Thrimore for the fight to come. 'Blasted slavers, no wonder the town's folk are all hiding away with this lot about,' Thrimore said. Trussa's goons charged to the pair, but what they hadn't expected was an old bull to bound through them trampling most of their number and forcing the rest to

165

flee. 'That's my boy Gladys, you give them what for,' Mr Leaflin yelled over from the ruined cottage. Flames continued to turn the vines Wendolin summoned to ash, until all of a sudden the fires faded. Not all those of the Humtees had been cowering behind closed windows or locked doors. Mr Barracroft the towns unofficial peacekeeper had snuck up on the cottage after Gladys had rushed to retrieve him. When he was able he'd crept up behind Trussa and cracked her round the back of the head with his staff. 'We've had more than enough of you mages around these parts, be away with you,' he ordered.

'You stupid man,' Trussa yelled as flames covered her once again. She rose to strike the man, but as she did a branch swooped down from a nearby tree, spearing her through the chest. The ground quickly opened up swallowing Trussa's screaming body beneath the soil to hide what Wendolin had done from her parents. Leaving only a small patch of Trussa's blood behind along with a rather perplexed and a slightly terrified Mr Barracroft.

The fires faded and calm slowly returned to Peacock Lane as a bewildered Mr Barracroft embraced his old friends. 'Unbelievable,' he declared grabbing hold of Mr and Mrs Leaflin. 'It's truly unbelievable, I must tell everyone. A feast, yes we must have a grand meal to celebrate this day. Not only are you freed but the girls return also. What a day, what a mighty fine day.'

'Stifle yourself Mr Barracroft, you'll explode if you carry on like this,' Mr Leaflin said. The silent town soon began to bustle with life once more after Mr Barracroft ran about knocking on every door he could find. Before they knew it a small celebration had begun. For ever since the Countess came to the Humtees a darkness had covered it. As if the shadows that followed her that day remained watching over the sleepy town, filling its people with dread and despair. Thankfully the realisation the curse placed on the Leaflins was broken by none other than their own daughters seemed to help cast this anguish aside. Peacock Lane was soon awash with villagers and as the sun set they praised the Leaflins long into the night.

The people of the Humtees crowded around Richard plying him with delicacies. From home made cheeses to scrumptious leek and carrot pies, ensuring Richard's plate was rarely left empty. While Mr Barracroft happily filled his and Thrimore's wine glasses time and time again, providing extremely in depth stories about how he'd made each. The night went on and wine and stories flowed until Richard saw Stephanie leave the table and wander off up the lane. Making an excuse he quickly followed as Wendolin tugged on Thrimore's collar. 'Come with me,' she whispered. Both left the table discreetly and Wendolin lead him away.

Before him Wendolin walked along an overgrown path thats bracken parted before her. Deeper into the woven trees they went, silence surrounded them and only the bending bracken made a sound, until she stopped and turned to face him. Concealed now the pair were, hidden from the world in the mist of great tangled trees and vines, but their whereabouts mattered little to Thrimore. His eyes never left her and as they travelled and fought beside one another she found hers rarely leaving his. She raised her hand to the clasp on her shoulder and released it speaking in a nervous voice she didn't know as it began to fall from her. 'You have done what you promised, my parents are free and you may have your prize, your minute.' Before the dress fell past her waist Thrimore caught it and held it back to her shoulder. 'No. For no prize to be won are you. In your eyes I find a love that seems endless. Seeing your smile I feel myself at home, together in happiness we should dwell. Let me not just be a winner claiming a prize, but the man who would love you in any light. Who would follow you as if you were a queen and love you more than any king or other being. For if you offer but one night alone as my reward I reject it, but the chance to make your heart beat together with mine is all I truly wish for,' Hearing his words as his eyes pierced hers her body quivered. Never had Wendolin felt such a sensation. She wanted to speak, tried to even, but no words came to her. To slowly brush his hand from her shoulder was all she could manage. Her dress fell away leaving her bare before him. 'One night or more will be your choice Thrimore, but after one you will see I am just a weapon and can never be more.' Her voice crackled as she spoke. The cold of the night began to sting her skin until his hands went around her. 'Not to me, never did I see such and never would one night or more make that so.' Like it was instinct her hands began unbuttoning his uniform. Finding one another's lips they fell upon the ground as moss grew from the forest floor, creating a bed about the pair. With each kiss their desire increased, both were like beasts in heat, rolling in the moss in a fit of passion the pair were. Until on top of Thrimore Wendolin climbed realising her true feelings she spoke without thinking. Any thought to tease or scold the rogue was gone, replaced by a love for him she would never share with another. 'My love you will be forever more my dear brave Thrimore.' With that she took him into her and together they were made one beneath a blanket of stars and tangled trees. Writhing upon her new found love she was until collapsing on top of him both in ecstasy. A mixture of joy and wonder filled Thrimore's mind but as his heavy breaths faded he heard her cry. 'Why cry now?' He asked as he held her close. Taking his hand Wendolin ran it over her until it rested over her stomach. 'No matter how many times, no matter how many ways we try I could never be a woman for you.' The strong sister Wendolin was, the tough rock that held her sisters together even through their torment, but now little of that rock remained as she spoke past tears. 'She couldn't take it. She wanted our abilities for herself but nothing she did let her take my skills from me. So she cut out my womb, believed it would make me weaker, like it had others she'd done the same to. It didn't. Just left me as broken on the inside as on the out. I'd have died that night if not for Bethany, but it was so soon after we'd been taken. We were still so young. She couldn't repair the damage they'd done and struggled to keep me breathing. Even the ring's power could never make me what I was. If only I could be more to you Thrimore, for over these last days I have felt anew beside you. I host such feelings for you, more than I have ever had for another but I can never give you a family. Never give you a life to be proud of where we can grow in love.' As Wendolin spoke Thrimore's hand rose to her cheek and wiped away her tears. 'Stop this talk, for I do not care and never will. My life is not so simple itself and far past broken am I. Forget these thoughts for no greater woman have I ever known and any life with you I would be proud to share.' Together they laid there until Wendolin's eyes dried and both smiled to one another as if they would never stop.

As Stephanie walked away from the festivities she heard sticks breaking behind her. Knowing what followed she went on until she came to a large spring that was hidden behind a bed of reeds. Into the reeds she went as the following footsteps drew closer. Richard had never been far since she left the lane, entering the reeds shortly after her he soon found the pond's edge but had lost sight of Stephanie until her voice came from his back. 'Why are you following me?' She asked startling the ranger.

'I am sorry, I did think you wanted me to,' Richard replied. 'And what did I do to make you think that?' Stephanie snapped.

'My mistake I shall return to the others and leave you be,' Richard said and went to take his leave trying to hide his glowing cheeks. Before he could though Stephanie blurted out. 'I'm not like them you know. I'm not a mage, not a fighter like them. I'm just me Richard and I can't be anything more,' as her eyes began to fill his hand cupped her head. 'I would not want you to be more, for everything you are is why I see you. No one with more caring hands have I seen and never have I met a woman so strong. Powerful you are lady from the stars. For even without the magic your sister's wield you stand taller with a face more fair than any can bear.' Interrupting Richard before he could say more her lips found his. Even she hadn't expected it but now she had done it she didn't wish to stop. His stubble stung her but didn't deter her nor his hands that gripped tighter as their tongues met. Dress and tunic removed she was carried into the warm water. Washing one another's body in the spring Richard soon noticed the many scars that covered Stephanie's back. Before he could ask Stephanie answered the question on his mind. 'The show she put on for you and Jhona wasn't the first. She soon realised how worthless I really was, so she used me to test the other two. She would cut me, force them to heal me and try to take their power as she did.'

'She'll never take you back Stephanie, I promise you,' Richard said.

'She won't stop sending her mages. Trussa won't be the last and when your quest's done, so will we be,' Stephanie said.

'You know I didn't much like Wasiz when I met him or Banbury for that. I was trying to create the rangers and then Jhona found the Rotting Thief and everything got even more complicated,' Richard said.

'What's your point?' Stephanie asked.

'Even though they vex me we became a family, of sorts. A strange one I grant you but one I was hoping you'd want to be a part of.' As Richard spoke a smile creeped over his love's lips. Hands to her hips he lifted her from the water and declared. 'So what say you Leaflin? Do you dare travel on past this quest to the next? Whether it's to fight the great titans of the deep, or flee from vipers up high. The Forgotten Vale will soon be our past and on we should go into the future together.'

'Then to the future we go. With rangers, rotters and sailors in tow,' Stephanie said as they laughed and danced in the waters together for as long as their tired eyes would allow them.

Chapter Ten
A Surprising Arrival

It didn't take long for Krosh to lead the caravan to a fairly out of the way spot to make camp. Thorns were hurrying about making fires and pitching tents when Jhona woke with Bethany's foot inches from his nose. 'What happened?' He asked Wasiz stepping out of the caravan. 'Sun's set, don't think they'll be back until morning now, hopefully that's good news. Best keep the door closed though, never know what may occur,' Wasiz replied. 'What's with Bethany?' Jhona asked.

'Your hair clip took a toll. Same as it did with you, hopefully Wendolin will have it in her to bring them all back,' Wasiz told him.

'And Banbury, where's he gotten off to?' Jhona said. 'With those Krosh fellows, been drinking up a storm since we made camp, the lot of them have. Seems that Simeon's lot gave away far more bottles than we noticed,' Wasiz said. Both then heard a faint sound in the distance. 'What's that then?'

'Sounds like singing,' Jhona said retrieving his bow and finding an arrow. Going away from the fires and drinking Thorns they began to hear the song more clearly. 'Beasts and birds and bugs and grubs, too many to count, so many to love. Whether above the ground or under the soil I see you there and your constant toil.'

173

'Who goes there?' Jhona shouted startling whoever it was singing, making them stumble and fall onto the ground in front of the pair. Lying before them was a man wearing a tatty suit covered in dirt and carrying a lute. 'Well hello there who is this? Odd pair about on a dark night such as this one is,' he sang as he rolled onto his back and plucked the strings of his lute revealing a huge muck filled beard. His hair was golden blonde but you'd never have known given how much mud covered him. A group of red squirrels then hurried around him and started trying to help pull him up. 'What are you suppose to be?' Wasiz said.

'He's a high elf Wasiz,' Jhona said nervously. 'Well yes I am, one of the very few left, but no friend I am with any of those in towers hidden in cities of stone. To the beasts I do go, to meet the other creatures of this world. I care for them that I do and would rather sit beside them than any of you.' As the squirrels pulled him onto his feet he strummed his lute and went on. 'But talk I do with one of the old, one who unlike the others shares fine stories that are worth being told. Tales about brothers and thieves and so much more. Oh yes he drops many scripts to my door.' All of a sudden he sprang up before Jhona and smiled as he sang. 'Balmoth he said, small they were but with his help they all grew quite tall. Thieves who rot he speaks of too. One who steals more souls than gold or jewels.'

'He's talking about Avlor, I think?' Jhona said.

'Who is this fellow? He stinks of dung,' Banbury said joining them. 'And Banbury Bale a dwarf of renown. One of the very few who dreads the underground.' The man's singing went on as Banbury asked again. 'W-w-who is he to know us?'

'Don't fret master Bale for I mean no harm. A scent I was following one that caused me some alarm,' the man replied. Sauntering past them as he played his lute he started looking over the steeds until he saw Fiona trying to hide herself at the back of the herd. 'There you are, come on out poor thing,' he said waving her to him. 'Leave her alone, she doesn't need you pestering her,' Jhona said.

'I'm afraid she does for a difficult birth it will be.' Saying this the man stopped playing his lute and the wood it was made from started to morph into a tall wooden staff with the head of a sleeping bear on the hilt. 'Wait, she's not pregnant. What even are you? Some sort of mystic,' Jhona snapped.

'Hide it well the zatifas do, stops them being plucked from the herd but bearing she is and in pain also. Step aside and do not worry for any spell,' the man said. 'Even if she is you're going nowhere near her,' Jhona insisted making the man slam his staff to the ground and stop his singing. 'Step aside boy,' he bellowed and appeared to grow in height, casting a bright light over the camp that made the trees around them shudder. 'For I am the master of the beasts, I am the hand that guards them. The founder of their council is I and care for them as no other could do,' the master of the beasts declared. Before Jhona or any other could respond Fiona fell to the ground making Caspian charge over. Jhona quickly stood aside letting the master of the beasts drop to Fiona's side as Caspian

175

nuzzled her. 'Dearie me, you hid it too well, her legs are twisted and will need help to get free,' the master said. 'How can she be pregnant?' Jhona said.

'How do you think?' Wasiz mocked looking to Caspian. With a valiant shake of his mane Caspian made it clear he was as unaware of Fiona's pregnancy as they were. 'Here we are, let's just move you a little more,' the master said running his hands over her belly. 'I'm so sorry I should have known,' Jhona said.

'As loyal as a wolf is she and would not have left your side until she wasn't able,' the master said. Fiona's wails grew as Thorns lit fires around her to keep the expectant mother warm as her labour went on long into the night. Finally just as most had lost the will to stop their eyes closing from exhaustion her cries stopped and another took their place. Gentle but loud neighs rang out from the pure white foal as she was placed beside her mother and licked clean. 'She is gorgeous Fiona,' Jhona said.

'Silly old sod ain't you Caspian,' Banbury said as the proud father laid down with Fiona. Within minutes the foal was up and after timidly taking her first steps she was soon hopping about. Wobbling on she landed upon sleeping Thorns as she learnt to walk. Leading to the Thorns to quickly nickname her jumpy Jenna, after she jumped about the camp landing on most. All quickly fell in love with the new arrival, but Jhona soon realised Fiona wouldn't be going any further with them, not that she was prepared to admit that herself. 'With me she can stay and with the beasts will be safe,' the master said.

'You swear it, they will be cared for as if me and my brother were with them,' Jhona asked.

'I swear they will be, fear not Jhona Balmoth for I see you as you do I and only caring souls will they see until you arrive,' the master said.

'Come along, we should eat. Leave them to rest,' Wasiz said. While the master of the beasts sat playing his lute, surrounded by Thorns who enjoyed his songs more than he expected they would, the newborn settled down with her parents. 'Here we are, leaves and beans for the woody and gammon steaks for us,' Banbury said handing out plates. Wasiz and Banbury were soon eating but Jhona drifted off gazing into the fire before them. He had so many feelings running through his head, seeing Jenna's birth had made him think about so much. He began to think about what Richard and Stephanie's fling could become and when their quest was done. Banbury would return home to his wives and now even Caspian was a father. What of him though, hidden well under rosey cheeks and fluttering lashes a deep depression hid. When young he had found his place with Richard and Caspian, but whenever Richard would call him brother it made him feel strange, like it didn't fit. Years passed and these feelings of being out of place grew, until he met Wasiz. Never had another looked to him the way Wasiz did, none others saw him as he was but in truth even Jhona didn't know what would truly end this lull. Like his brothers had before Wasiz halted these grim feelings but in times of great stress, emotions such as these have a way of compounding themselves. Seeing Jhona's face drop Wasiz kicked Banbury's leg and said. 'Go get some more wood, the fire's fading,' Wasiz said.

'What you g… G… Pestering me for, it's fine,' Banbury said but after receiving another kick and a glare from Wasiz he dropped his plate and went off in a huff. 'What has you looking so furlong?' Wasiz asked.

'It is nothing,' Jhona said, but needed little more persuasion to break. Tears fell from his eyes and dropped to his plate before it fell from his lap. 'I don't know why Wasiz, I truly don't. I should be happy but I'm not and I don't know why,' Jhona said. 'Richard, Caspian, even Banbury have found their love and they're happy so why aren't I?'

'My dear Jhona, love like they share is not meant for all in this world. Some will find it on their own path as our friends have done, others will never find it at all, but we are neither I feel. Bent we are,' Wasiz said moving before Jhona with a cunning grin painted across his face. 'Yes, bent on a different path. A road that makes our desires far more refined than those around us. I see the dark cloud that follows you, let it not stay for good, let me bat it away and find us a clear sky to dwell under.' Placing his hand to the goblin's cheek Jhona said. 'I worry it is not as simple as you would wish it to be.'

'Then let us make it simple, for I never wish to see you taken by sorrow again. Just tell me what the world you seek is and I shall steal it for you,' Wasiz said. 'I'm sorry Wasiz I see no world where I'm happy as I am. There is no heist or scheme that will part the clouds that follow me,' Jhona said. With his hand to

Jhona's Wasiz laughed and said. 'Dear Jhona you underestimate how truly cunning and delightfully devious your Rotting Thief can be.' With a glint in his eyes Wasiz went back to his seat as Banbury returned with his arms full of kindling. 'Here we are. C-c-cruel you two are sending an old sailor such as me to get fuel for the fire,' he said dumping his arm full of wet wood onto the campfire sending a plume of black smoke into the sky. 'You idiot Bale, now everyone in ten miles will know where we're camping,' Jhona said.

'Hurry and get your Thorns up Krosh, we have to move,' Wasiz ordered. So used to moving in a hurry were the Thorns their tents fell and got packed up in almost an instant and their steeds were ready to march just as quickly. 'You and Caspian must take your little one and go with the master there,' Jhona said making Fiona rub her nose on his cheek. She didn't want to leave but knew well the Forgotten Vale would have no safe places for her or Jenna to hide. Caspian though had other ideas, a brother he was to Richard and Jhona. More importantly he believed both would soon get lost without him. Running his mane over Fiona he conveyed these feelings to her and with loving eyes she bowed her head to him. All were ready to leave but thankfully whilst hitching up the cargo Banbury noticed someone was missing. 'Blasted girl. Bethany, Bethany. By my conkers where's she got to?' He shouted.

When Bethany woke her head was still spinning from passing out. While all others were falling over the new arrival she had taken herself off for a walk to clear her head. Unfortunately for her she wasn't alone and as the trees cleared she saw a hunched over man who looked to be a dwarf. He used a cane to walk and wore a poncho that dragged along the floor, with a tatty hood that rose to a sharp peak. Nothing about the man made Bethany worry until his eyes met hers. When they did the hairs on the back of her neck jumped up, goosebumps covered her arms and her heart raced. 'What are you then?' The man said edging closer as he spoke. 'You look like one of those from Meceller a wood elf, yes that's it, but you're not that are you. There's something else there am I right.' Bethany didn't reply, her anxiety had grown so that her lips were only able to tremble as the stranger got closer and looked over her. Suddenly the man grabbed her hand and ran his thumb over her palm. 'Starborn,' the man then declared with a wicked grin. 'Yes, fell from the skies to a world you were not meant to find. What, what's this? So there are three, three sisters.' An arrow landing before the man's feet forced their hands apart and Jhona's voice cast away whatever grip he had over Bethany. 'Stay away from her, or the next shall pluck out your eye,' Jhona threatened running between the pair with an arrow ready in his bow. 'How dare you raise arms to me,' the man yelled slamming his cane to the ground making even the grass about them shudder. 'We will not fall for your tricks deceiver, begone. There is nothing for you here. Return to whatever hole you dared crawl out of,' Jhona said. The same anxiety that had stunned Bethany now rushed over him making his arm tremble as he tried to hold up his bow. 'I know dwarves,' a voice to the man's back said making him spin to see Wasiz stood there with a dagger ready to poke him in the belly. 'I know them well, after living in shackles and serving their god, you have little choice but to. You especially learn their stink,' he said and then took a big sniff of the man. 'So what is that smell that follows you, is it the scent of the Wizard June or someone else?' As Banbury arrived Thorns soon surrounded the clearing Bethany had wandered into, but alike Bethany and Jhona they were all stunned upon seeing the Wizard June. All aside from Wasiz and Banbury that is. 'Who's this old tuffer and what's he want with our Leaflin?' Banbury blurted out as he retrieved his axe. 'Leaflin that's an interesting name,' the Wizard said as both he and Wasiz had held one another's gaze. 'Not as interesting as the story you have to tell, who is it behind those eyes?' Wasiz asked.

'That is a tale you shall never be smart enough to steal chain breaker,' the Wizard said and waved his hand turning the dagger Wasiz held to ash. 'Stand away Wasiz, I'll have him,' Banbury declared but Wasiz's voice stopped him before he drew close. 'Don't,' he yelled as the Wizard smirked. 'Do you know what stops them?' The Wizard said gesturing to the wood elves around them. 'It's something the inferior races of this world don't possess. An instinct that tells you when you're in the presence of your betters. When in an audience with one who could take your life in an instant. An instinct that yells to them, telling them to run. You cave dwellers and underworld monsters may not feel it but that doesn't mean I can't send you on to

181

the Nexus all the same.' Using his cane the Wizard batted Wasiz aside and went to take his leave but not before turning back to Bethany as he went. 'Be safe Leaflin, be safe and survive this quest of yours and we shall speak once more.'

'Who is he?' Bethany asked as the man faded past trees and all began feeling themselves once more. 'What did he say to you?' Wasiz asked rushing to her. 'Not much, he took my hand and seemed to know me. Who was he?' Bethany asked again.

'The Wizard June, a man we had hoped was lost to this world,' Wasiz said.

'Hurry back to the caravan we can talk as we go,' Jhona ordered.

The Thorns all found themselves on edge as they returned to the caravan and even Phieus was feeling rather uneasy after they returned and he was informed of the goings on. Wasiz though wasn't as flustered as the rest instead an intense look of irritation covered his face making his long nose twitch as they walked. Finally Bethany plucked up the courage to ask. 'Was that the Wizard you spoke of when we passed the Plains of Nore?'

'That would be him,' Wasiz replied. 'The deceiver is what Elidom called him and after seeing those eyes I think I believe I may know why. Don't get me wrong it's not like I haven't been known to tell the odd mistruth from time to time but there, that Wizard. His eyes were like window's through which you can only see lies.'

'Where did this June even come from, he didn't look like I was expecting?' Bethany said.

'You expected him to be elf did you?' Banbury said. 'Not an elf but perhaps a bit taller, is he one of your people Banbury?' Bethany asked.

'No he's no dwarf and that is all I know of him for sure. Stories say he wandered the world as the titans did before Norcea's own,' Banbury said.

'The lore surrounding the Wizard is vast but sudden was the change within him,' Wasiz said.

'What change?' Bethany asked.

'He would speak for hours with trees and rocks, that's what they would say of him in the titan's age. Days he would spend having rather in depth conversations with whatever creature or intriguing root he would come across. Tales such as this is all you would ever hear of him. After a great many years more stories started to emerge of a Wizard, but cruel this man was. Evil beyond any other some said of him. It seemed the Wizard's tastes had changed, no longer passive and dorsal was he but menacing and bloodthirsty is the man he became.'

'What was it that changed him so?' Bethany wondered. 'None know. Forget that fool though for I have made him sound more fearsome than he truly is,' Wasiz said seeing how pale Bethany had become. 'You have at that. Don't you worry Leaflin I'll see he keeps his d-d-distance far from you,' Banbury said and took her wobbling hand in his, popping it onto his shoulder to lead her on. 'What is it?' Jhona asked as the others walked on. 'Just as I said,' Wasiz replied.

'Then why's your nose still twitching,' Jhona quipped giving Wasiz's quivering nose a gentle flick. 'How long have we been travelling together?' Wasiz asked once he was positive Bethany couldn't hear. 'Long enough for me to know most of your tricks and see when something's bothering you,' Jhona said.

'Exactly, we've been together since Fandisco was a boy. Never though in all our travels have we come by him. Never has he sought us out before. Nor have we ever wished him too,' Wasiz said.

'You think he was looking for the Leaflins? Why though?' Jhona asked.

'Maybe. I don't know, but it would explain why he showed up all of a sudden. We can't know for sure and I worry we may never figure out his true intentions,' Wasiz said. More questions did Jhona have but too close the pair had gotten to the others and all were now even more eager to move on than before. Fiona watched with the master of the beasts and her newborn as Thorns mounted their steeds and began charging on. Knowing all that lay ahead of them now was Vurcun and the Forgotten Vale.

Chapter Eleven
The Envoy's Marked Men

Within the Forgotten Vale little life can be found, only those the Grey Count allow to pass make it through unharmed. Those who aren't there by his request would normally find themselves taken away by bats of tremendous size. To have every drop of blood drained from their bodies within halls built for that sole purpose. Times though are far from normal within the Forgotten Vale. For in the twisted dead trees no bats rested and over the sloping barren lands only black sheep with dead white eyes grazed the thin ashy grass. Never fair or green was the Vale, barren and untouched was this land before the Grey Count built his home upon it. His presence alone caused trees to grow, but of black bark were they. Bent branches twisted together blocking out all light, while their trunks contorted into fearsome images. Above black clouds seep into the sky from the Paratis. Three tall spires of smooth black stone, flashes of blood red veins cascade up their length to pour out the dreaded night from their peaks. To the centre of the three formidable towers lays the Grey Count's hold. A fortress with black walls to match the towers they sit between and past the coal iron door of the keep the Count's warlocks spill the blood needed to sustain the darkness their master must dwell in. Up in its rafters they work, scurrying like rats around a bubbling pot of spitting blood. Casting out the eternal darkness that hangs over the Vale, shrouding them forever in the night so his kind can roam freely within his realm. Enchantments and sorcery of the Count's own making did these warlocks normally use to spread his deeds. Now though as the blood boiled the warlocks read from a book their master had put out of his mind long ago.

Such a tight grip did the Grey Count usually have over the Vale that even his own daughter would have to go to extraordinary lengths to avoid screeching bats or patrolling soldiers of the Night's Scar as she went. Now though all was quiet and only the sound of her footsteps could she hear. Past dead trees Calenir walked as a handful of bats flew high above watching the skies and the ground, ready to warn her if any others followed. Going along a path the ones she stalked had created after their countless secret meetings. Finally after months of watching from shadows and well placed threats she had found where they meet. An old cabin that rested between two dead oaks, thats rotten branches breached the cone shaped and gap filled thatched roof. This is where one after another of the Grey Count's generals and most trusted advisers piled in to plot their master's downfall. All vampires have an affinity with bats, but most would soon chatter to the Grey Count about the plot they devise. Making all who snuck there come alone leaving the bats that followed Calenir the only ones fluttering in the sky. Going far enough away from the cabin so she wasn't noticed. Calenir sat to the base of a tree and bit her thumb, making blood drip from the tip. Using the blood she painted three diagonal wavy lines over her forehead and closed her eyes as she crossed her legs. With her hands clenched closed on top of her knees she began to utter words only her kind could. To the bats that followed above she spoke and once her eyes opened she saw what they did. Sending the group of bats over the cabin they were able to sneak their way beneath the thatch so Calenir could spy on the meeting that was beginning inside.

'Time grows short, only a little longer can we keep the Count ignorant of our deeds,' General Hervass Hunfor said. He was one of the Grey Count's generals who commanded the legions of warriors of the Vale he ruled over. One of two generals who now crammed into the cabin. Crathore Blaffer was the other's name, while the remaining two who joined them had been chosen by their host because of their positions within the Paratis. Salvia Wiggins was a close adviser to the Grey Count while the last Sallow Dunkworth was the Paratis Quartermaster. Their host had been long at work planning and finally the last piece he needed to complete his long awaited plot would soon be in his hands. 'His daughter is already asking questions of us regarding the third legion's whereabouts and the Count himself will notice if you keep using the Night's Scar to carry out your deliveries,' Salvia said.

'The Night's Scar serves the true master of the dark, as they always have. They will do as commanded and stay silent,' Crathore snapped.

'Yes, but others will not,' Salvia said. 'Not just his daughter skulks about, but the general of the fifth also. Together they could sway the Count from the path he must follow. If the gate is to open…,' Salvia's sentence was quickly cut off by their host's hand slapping the rest of his chair to silence her. Calenir hadn't yet noticed him, sitting in the corner upon a chair strewn with black fur he was. A thick black robe covered him, with a drooping hood that concealed his face so only his pale white hands and long cracked finger nails could be seen by the bats in the rafters. 'The gate shall open,' he hissed from beneath his hood. 'The gate will open onto this world and the eternal darkness will rain down upon all who oppose our Master's will. No interference will now be tolerated, deviation from my works will be met with only death. The Night's Scar soon return with the artefact, with its power we will open the gate and his reign will then be eternal.'

'What of this artefact? You send legions into hiding, risk all our necks and will not even tell us what for,' Sallow said.

'He speaks true Envoy, what is it the Night's Scar bear?' Salvia asked.

'They carry the tool for the elves undoing and you need not know more. Thinking to question me is seeking to question him. Each of you are to devote all your measly efforts to ensuring their safe passage. Two of the elf's nights will pass before they reach the Vale. See they go unhindered by any,' the Envoy ordered.

'But what is it that could replace the blood and souls the gate would need to open?' Sallow said.

'Enough, your task is given,' the Envoy snapped. A thudding sound then came from beyond the cabin. Followed by the toe crawling snort of a hog from past the door that soon opened letting an orc step in. 'About time, where is Tartiss?' Crathore said to him. 'Dead boss, killed in battle he was,' the orc said.

'Then who are you?' Crathore replied.

'Duca, Duca Wynn boss, killed by the rangers the boss was,' Duca replied.

'Your mission is done though, yes?' Salvia said. 'No. The Prince had aid before we could slice him, bloody rangers and a woman in red they were,' Duca said. 'So the Prince lives, he's failed us. The one thing we sought is now lost to us. That boy's head should be being served to us, but we're served nothing but broken promises,' Sallow complained. Without warning shadows spun around Sallow crawling over him until they forced open his lips and started to seep into his mouth. 'I have heard enough from you and since you don't need your voice to complete your task it will be lost to you until you learn to only speak for the Master,' the Envoy said as the shadows choked Sallow. Falling from his seat Sallow desperately tried to speak, but not even a whine was he able to muster. 'You,' the Envoy then snapped to Duca, who was watching on in horror and beginning to wish he had fled to the Blood Works rather than return. 'Take what horde you have left, be ready to attack on my order as your Master would have been.'

'Yes boss right away,' but as Duca turned to leave he was blocked by the snarling fangs of a wolf. The huge wolf could barely squeeze its head through the door of the cabin. Wielding shoulders so broad they could span two doorways. A dark coat of deep brown fur covered him, while his teeth were bent and jagged. 'You didn't say there would be others,' the wolf growled. Rutter was his name, one of the few of his creed who still hungered for elf flesh. With the Crown City cast to the sea many wolves joined together for safety's sake, some though alike Rutter fled alone and grew almost feral in their hatred. Remaining bitter with an endless lust for revenge had made it fairly easy for the Envoy to add him to his list of marked men. 'He's a replacement,' Salvia said of Duca.

'I don't mean the orc worm,' the wolf barked and sniffed the air. 'There's another about,' his sniffing increased until he saw a bat in the rafters. 'Your noses are weak blood suckers, you've been watched,' the wolf roared and shadows quickly spun from the Envoy's hands killing the bat before he could flee. 'It must be her,' Salvia said.

'Find her Rutter. Find her and kill her before she ruins everything,' the Envoy yelled making the wolf dart into the woods as orcs and hungry hogs mustered behind.

In a flash Calenir's eyes were her own once more and she quickly rose to run. Lifting her bleeding thumb she went to transform herself into a bat. A skill all of her kind can master after years of vigorous training. Sadly even vampires can't out run a hunting wolf who has their scent. Before she was able to speak one word of the spell she was thrown down and cut across the chest by the wolf's claws, which left three deep wounds over her and blood pouring down her front. She tried to reach for the sword on her belt but Rutter had already pounced, landing upon her. He was poised to devour her. Bloody jaws dropped drool onto open wounds as the beast savoured his kill before making the final blow. Before he was able to eat his fill a flash of blood red came from the wolf's back and a black blade sliced at his hide. Leaping up Rutter howled as Calenir used her remaining strength to draw her sword and slice at the beast's throat. 'Hurry my lady drink this,' Kenthor said rushing to her. He was the youngest of all the Count's generals and the one the Envoy's marked men worried for. He uncorked the vial he held and poured the liquid within down Calenir's throat. It contained the blood of an elf and drinking it made Calenir's wounds heal at a greater rate. The war horns of the Blooded Spike sounded in the distance and their hogs would soon be upon them. Rutter rose before them once more as Kenthor ordered Calenir. 'Go, the blood will have given you the strength to change.'

'You can't change though, what about you?' Calenir said. 'Don't worry for me I can outwit a few orcs. You must find your allies. We can wait no longer. I found the third legion hidden in Amunden Trench. They have been readying for war and will march in the coming days. Find your Balmoth tell them the elves have only hours left to delay their end.' More horns blasted out as a rider spied the pair and the beast pounced. 'Hurry or our rebellion will die here with us.' Running to the charging wolf Kenthor threw his sword embedding itself into one of Rutter's broad shoulders. Black blades the warriors of the Vale wield, made from coal iron. A resource that can be found only within the Forgotten Vale. Once refined even the slightest cut from these blades would send a poison rushing through veins that turns skin black as organs sizzle. Rutter though seemed to not feel this poison as he span at Kenthor. Leaping aside at a great speed Kenthor drew the remaining blade from his belt and shouted. 'Get going,' to Calenir as he blocked Rutter's jaws.

'Don't you dare die again for I could hardly bear it the first time,' Calenir said as she reluctantly ran blood over her forehead and a flash of blood red covered her. When it faded only a bat remained that quickly took to the sky and fluttered away. Leaving Kenthor to grab hold of his sword embedded in Rutter's shoulder and drive it deeper, twisting the blade until finally after his jaws flayed and claws swiped the beast died. Unfortunately the Blooded Spike's hogs would soon charge through dead trees stopping Kenthor from resting for even a second. Spears were flung and into the bent bark he ran as spears fell to his feet and the tusks of the Blooded Spike's snorting hogs drew close.

Flying above the Forgotten Vale Calenir could see the Paratis. Past walls of bleeding black thorns within the centre of the three pulsing pillars her father's warlocks cast out the black clouds that keep the Vale in a constant darkness. Since the day the Paratis was built never have the clouds that hung above crossed the sky, but now they had began to stretch out to the north. The darkness created in the shadow had already spread over Vurcun. Towards the town she flew but as she went a shadow covered her from above. There flew a bat of great size. No bat of the Vale was it, for monstrous was its face. Contorted and covered in tears that showed the flesh beneath was the being's body. With wings that looked to be sewn together by thick black thread. Wondering about its origins was soon pushed far from Calenir's mind as it dove through the air to her. Viciously slapping her wings Calenir used all her might to fly away. Her wounds slowed her but Vurcun wasn't far and if she could only make it the buildings would conceal her. Darting into the trees she ducked and weaved her way past dead branches the foul creature couldn't follow through until the trees thinned and the walls of Vurcun were in sight. Over the walls she rushed and flew straight to the Tapped Toad. Where she burst through the window of the tavern as the giant bat climbed higher to circle the town as the few archers Vurcun had rushed to their posts. Screeching as it dived down and collided with a tower sending rubble along with the ones within plummeting to the ground, as arrows flew to no avail. Multiple pierced its flesh, but its will to fight on wasn't abated. Its screech forced bowmen to clench their ears as the creature's great frame lumbered over the wall. Leaving mangled bodies and the weeping wounded in its wake. Finally with arrows scarring its body and a spear in its gut it fell.

Not before casting out one last blood curdling roar, letting all there know the Grey Count's war had begun and his legions were preparing to march.

Chapter Twelve
The Growing Darkness

None of the people within the Humtees could know what was happening over the Tancoter Mountains and vampires couldn't have been further from their minds, especially the mind of Richard Balmoth. Who woke with the morning's sun warming both he and Stephanie. Together they had fallen asleep in one another's arms beside the pond. Not just the warm morn greeted the pair when they woke, but Gladys also. Who looked down on them as they stirred. 'Thank goodness, I worried that was your breath,' Richard joked as Stephanie looked in his eyes, both regretting the fact they'd soon have to return to the others. Making themselves as presentable as they were able they followed Gladys back to Peacock Lane. There Stephanie was quickly hurried away by her mother to Miss Porter's kitchen to help prepare breakfast. While Richard joined Thrimore who sat at a table in the front garden drinking a large mug of hot cocoa, after much insistence from Mr Leaflin to try the beverage. Approaching Richard noticed Thrimore was smiling to himself, in fact he had been ever since returning with Wendolin the night before. 'Good night?' Richard asked breaking him out of his daydream. 'Ow, well yes I suppose it was,' Thrimore replied. 'Yourself?'

'It was, amazing,' Richard said as he joined him at the table. 'I don't wish to sound vulgar,' Thrimore said leaning in to Richard. 'But have you, well you know. Done it before so to speak.'

'Have I been with a woman before is that what you're getting at?' Richard asked.

'Well yes, but I was trying to not be so blunt,' Thrimore said. 'I'm just wondering if it's normal to feel this way after.'

'How do you feel?' Richard asked.

'That is it, I don't know myself. My mind has never been so busy, but not with thoughts of different things. Only her crowds it, making me wish to do nothing but look upon her,' Thrimore said glaring through the window of Miss Porter's kitchen to see Wendolin doing very little as others rushed around her. 'I don't wish to sound vulgar as you say either, but I have known many women. Never though have I felt the things I do now for her. Stephanie is unlike any other, but one feeling pushes itself above others. I wish to protect her Thrimore and if you feel the same for Wendolin I would ask you to help me,' Richard said.

'How could I be of any help? The red lady's mind is her own and I feel will always be. Even love wouldn't sway her from something she has her mind set on,' Thrimore said.

'She will agree, I'm sure of it. Tell Wendolin we will leave using the door we came by at noon and make sure she says nothing to Stephanie,' Richard said sliding the hair clip he'd taken from Stephanie over the table to him. In Richard's hands the clip had become a green leaf and as it went to Thrimore it morphed taking the shape of an acorn. 'You mean to leave her behind,' Thrimore said. 'Once we pass the mountains we will find lands even me and my brother have never gone. Places the Seer who trained us said we should never travel to. I don't know what lies in the Vale Thrimore. This whole quest could end up being a trap or something much worse. Even if it's not and something else goes wrong I don't know if I can keep her safe,' Richard said. 'She won't bloody stay lad,' Mr Leaflin announced, for such a large man he had done a fine job of sneaking up on the pair as they spoke. Slamming a mug of hot cocoa down before Richard he went on. 'I know the call of the eternal love. It is a song that rang in my ears when the stone fell away and I saw I hadn't lost Mrs Leaflin there. They won't stay put in this little town now. Both are smitten with whatever it is you two are. Didn't need no fancy uniform to get a lady back in my day mind you. A big belly that's what they were after,' Mr Leaflin chuckled as the door opened and Mrs Leaflin strolled out with a tray laden with food. Quickly Richard whispered to Thrimore as he pushed the hair clip into his hand. 'Are we agreed?' Thrimore knocked the table twice to show he did as Wendolin and Stephanie were close behind their mother. 'Here we go, there's a bit of soup to start you off. Bit bland, Miss Porter's pantry is awfully under stocked I'm afraid,' Mrs Leaflin said and cleared her tray of soup bowls and crusty bread. She then hurried back in to prepare the next course, ignoring her husband who was insisting she sit and eat. 'Enough fussing over everyone Mrs

Leaflin. You will make these boys think I am some sort of slave master,' Mr Leaflin joked.

'I can't just sit down, there's far too much to do. You must get off your rear also and get about fixing my cottage Mr Leaflin,' Mrs Leaflin demanded.

'Our cottage,' Mr Leaflin replied.

'Mine, ours. What does it matter if it has no roof?' Mrs Leaflin said.

'Are meals always like this?' Thrimore asked Wendolin. 'Most of the time,' she giggled back as Mr Barracroft joined them. 'I do hope I'm not intruding, but I was looking to bend the ears of these lads for a moment.'

'They don't need to hear more about your wine,' Wendolin said.

'It's not that, there's something else I was hoping they'd turn an eye to,' Mr Barracroft said and both the ranger and Thorn wondered what the old man could have to show them.

Following him from the garden they went down Peacock Lane, leaving it Mr Barracroft lead them up a hill and from its peak the lands about were clear. 'Is a lovely view but why show us?' Thrimore asked.

'Look over the south, to the clouds past the Tancoter,' Mr Barracroft said. There dark clouds spread over the sky, darker than any rain clouds and every once in a while a flash of blood red could be seen cascading within. 'It is the Vale. For years I have watched the sky and over the years the clouds have never grown, until now. What was a patch of black in the sky that only covered the Forgotten Vale now seeps north blocking the sun's light. In but four days has it grown to this size, in another four it will be past the mountains. Another four and Meceller itself will be darkened by it and so on, until all is night and forever will we be in the darkness.'

'We have to get back, the others will be approaching the mountains by now,' Richard said.

'How can you be so sure they aren't rain clouds? How is it you know so much about the Grey Count?' Thrimore asked Mr Barracroft.

'I have watched these mountains for years boy, believe me when I say there's evil in them clouds. An evil this world hasn't seem since the orc hordes first formed to spread their terrible deeds.'

'You speak of the Dark Seer,' Richard said.

'The man's a myth,' Thrimore scoffed.

'He's no myth, nor any sort of man. For I was there when they say he fell. I fought before the Ash Caves as the hordes poured out. Beside wolves and humans of the Crown I did bloody my blade as Seer Marlos La Sore lead his greatest fighters into the chasm to do battle and defeat the man you call a myth.'

'What makes you think he still lives?' Richard said. 'I don't know he does. Those clouds though, they are the same that rested in the sky that day and only death will any find within the darkness they create. The age of the elf grows short. The Seers have squandered too much time warring amongst themselves and those they created to enslave. They have given our enemy all he needed to finish the war he started centuries ago.'

Mr Barracroft turned from the clouds to look over the pair. 'No armies do they have left to send it would seem. Just lads in fancy get ups and women from the stars left to hold the endless night at bay. To the apprentice of a Seer, to the guard of a King and healers with more bravery than sense do our hopes now rest with, quite a sorry thing.'

'Hurry and get Wendolin. I shall meet you at the grocers. We must hurry back to the others I never expected things in the Vale to escalate so quickly,' Richard said. 'What of the pale lady that Banbury told me of?' Thrimore asked.

'We must be swift and hope she still lives. Without her this quest will be nothing but a long journey before suicide,' Richard replied as both rushed away leaving Mr Barracroft to return his gaze to the spreading clouds.

Stephanie returned to the garden after washing up and receiving a rather lengthy interrogation from Miss Porter regarding the young man she'd returned home with to find only her mother was there. 'Where is everyone?' Stephanie asked.

'Your father is finding some help to fix the cottage,' Mrs Leaflin said.

'Not him, Wendolin and the boys,' Stephanie asked now worried they had left without her, a feeling that was soon proven correct when her mother looked back. 'Sit down, let's speak for a second before you do anything irresponsible,' her mother said. Taking Stephanie's hand she pulled her down to sit with her.

'Here, poor Miss Porter was up all night making these so you and your sisters best wear them,' she went on putting a hair clip that held a green gem into Stephanie's hair and handed her two others. One held a blue gem, the other red. 'I still remember your father coming home with your first ones. I know years have passed for you and you're all grown up and ready to fly the nest with no need of a nagging mother, but would staying here with us really be so bad.'

'It's not like that. I know you all think I'm weak, that I'm not as tough as Wendolin or as smart as Bethany, but I am. I can make a difference even without their abilities I just know I can. Besides how could I just wait here and hope they'll return when I can go and make sure that they do,' Stephanie said. Holding the hair clips tight in her hand she got up as her mother reached for her. 'You can't do the things they can Stephanie, you just can't. Let's stay put,' her mother insisted. 'Staying put,' Mr Leaflin blasted out as he strolled into the garden adjusting his suspenders as he went. 'Too right she should stay here with us old farts. Maybe she can get a job rubbing Miss Steward's feet and I suppose you'd marry her off to that nephew of Mr Barracroft.'

'What are on about you stupid man?' Mrs Leaflin snapped. 'If I'd have stayed put I'd never have found you and you would have never found me. To think how awful your life would be now without your handsome husband gives me chills,' Mr Leaflin laughed. 'Stop being so silly, ignore your stupid father,' Mrs Leaflin said. Brushing off his wife Mr Leaflin patted her hand from Stephanie's and said. 'You best hurry I just saw your Richard running down the lane to the grocer, if you're quick you'll make it before they leave.' With that his daughter's arms went around him. His wife's followed and then with a confident smile to both Stephanie ran to the gate where Gladys waited to ferry her into the village. 'You silly man,' Mrs Leaflin snapped as she was spirited away. 'Don't fret my love, I'd worry more if they were parted. At least together our babes from the stars will be,' Mr Leaflin beamed.

Once he'd arrived at the grocer's Richard waited until Wendolin and Thrimore joined him. 'She's not going to forgive you for this,' Wendolin said.

'Then why are you going along with it,' Richard asked. 'I'm her sister she can't stay mad at me,' Wendolin said.

'I wouldn't be so sure about that,' Stephanie declared as Gladys charged to Wendolin and Thrimore's back. She jumped from Gladys and handed the hair clip holding the red stone to Wendolin and then stormed before Richard. 'Was last night so meaningless you can just leave without even saying so, without even telling me how you feel,' Stephanie snapped.

'It's not like that, you know it isn't,' he replied.

'Then why go, why leave me behind?' Stephanie asked. 'I don't need you to protect me Richard, or you,' she went on turning to snap at Wendolin. 'Maybe you don't need me to, but that won't stop me wanting to. There are things happening that I don't yet understand. We don't know what to expect in

205

the Vale and from what that Mr Barracroft has shown us things are getting worse quickly,' Richard said.

'See sense Stephanie,' Wendolin said.

'I was in Accultian too you know, I suffered just as much as you,' Stephanie said.

'You faired far worse than us, they cut you, broke your bones just for us to fix and I'm done having to heal you past tears,' Wendolin begged her sister but nothing any could say would deter her. 'We started this together and it will end the same, I'm not going anywhere. Not until our contract is complete and we all come home. Not until we have a future past this,' Stephanie insisted. 'It's as I said the mind of a Leaflin is not easily swayed,' Thrimore joked.

'So be it, I can only warn you so much and have little time left to argue about it,' Richard said.

'That's more like it,' Stephanie announced. 'That sort of winning attitude will take you far Balmoth.' Upon Wendolin's head Jhona's hair clip had turned into a red rose and as she reached for the door Wendolin was happier than she imagined she would be when she saw the interior of the caravan past the door frame of the grocers.

Stepping through the door each were still amazed to find themselves back at the caravan. Richard's arm was quickly grabbed by Jhona as they hurried out, who soon told him about the new arrival and their unexpected encounter with the Wizard June. While Krosh went to his Captain. 'Welcome back Captain, nice night away?' Krosh said.

'Tease me later, I need you to gather the men I must speak with them before we go on any further,' Thrimore said. It didn't take long for the Thorns to gather around and standing before them Thrimore spoke. 'I have seen the clouds we will soon ride under, the south has always been hostile but now, they have become something else, something worse. I don't know what the Grey Count is planning, but like Richard and his band I agree he must be stopped. I would not ask any here to follow for I don't know what trials we may face. Alone I will go on with the red lady, Krosh will lead you to our old hideout within the Crimson Grove. If I don't return he will be your Captain.' This speech caused the Thorns to mumble to each other until Krosh eventually said. 'I don't much like that plan Captain.' Making all nod and murmur in agreement. 'We followed you from the Evertree, not because we had no choice, but because you are our Captain. You could have just ran from the city when the Queen sought our heads. You didn't though, you came for each of us first to save us from the sheriff's hands and since then you have seen us through trials no other could. So no Captain it is time we helped you. I'd say we'd have ourselves a mutiny of sorts if you try and send this lot packing anyhow.' A comment that caused a cheer amongst the Thorns. 'See, whatever trials we face you and the red lady won't be facing them without us.'

'To the red lady and the Thorn who found her,' Phieus cheered with others. 'So be it, together we will see how fearsome this Grey Count and his legions truly are. Forget the Evertree today. Today the red lady and her Thorns ride to break black clouds,' Thrimore said.

'What did you see that has him trying to send his men away?' Wasiz asked.

'Everything Calenir said was true. The darkness over the Vale is spreading fast. If we leave the caravan behind we should reach the mountains before night fall and be in Vurcun as the sunrises,' Richard said. Orders were given and Phieus Krosh was left to travel with the caravan to the Humtees where he and a couple of other Thorns who were around his age and older would wait for them to return.

The sun dipped below the horizon shortly after the hooves of their steeds tore up the ground of the Erauss Woods. Riding south west through its trees lead them around the base of the Tancoter. This made easy going for the horses but took far longer than Richard had hoped. Around the mountains they went and as the lush trees that bordered its south faded they crossed onto lands wood elves such as they would rarely ever dare to pass. This was the far south and here dwarves still rule over large swathes of the land to the west. While beneath the ground they fought constant wars against goblins and whatever else they found living upon the gold and precious stones they endlessly sought after. The drastic change in the landscape made most of their heart's sink. Few trees or green grass lay about once the Erauss faded in the distance. The most common sight was pile after pile of mined rock and quarried ground. Finally trees came into sight, but not fair and leafy were they. Before the outskirts of the dense forest of dead trees that filled the Forgotten Vale Vurcun stood. Of dwarven make were the buildings but long ago their kind had abandoned the town leaving it empty until a band of elves found it. Unaware of what dwelled in the forest beyond they made it their home and the town quickly filled. Rather than exterminating the population as others had wished the Grey Count was convinced to leave them be. Letting the town grow so when they did begin taking victims few noticed. Slowly a blood market grew in the dark of night until the Grey Count had a town on his doorstep that could provide him blood from all over Alidor as well as a continuous supply for his armies. Tall grey rectangular houses with flat roofs fill the town while the wall that encircles Vurcun was made from chiselled grey slate stone.

'It's all as grim as I expected,' Jhona said as they passed under the wall. 'Hold it, hold it right there,' a man wearing chainmail said as he stormed out of the guard tower beside the wall. 'What's all this then? We don't get large parties just turning up here. What's your business?' He asked while he looked over the many heavily armed men in red uniforms riding into the town. 'We come to meet friends for a reunion of sorts,' Richard said. 'Would you tell us where to find the stable master?' Staring up to Richard the man realised these must be the people the one waiting at the Tapped Toad had ordered him to let by. 'The stables you say. I'll see you right to its door sir. Straight down there and off to the left it's the Tapped Toad you'll be looking for, you'll soon find it. Has a sign bigger than your steed's noggin it does sir. Guniss is what they call me sir, anything you need sir you let me know.'

'He soon changed his tune,' Wasiz said as Guniss waved them on. 'Richard's pale lady must already be here.' Jhona said as he noticed the damaged wall and ruined guard tower. 'This town has seen better days.'

'The damage seems recent and look there. Blood still coats the slate,' Wasiz added. Going on before the tavern Thrimore and Wendolin went with his Thorns to take the horses to the stables while the others hurried inside. Once within things went as they normally would do when they came across a homely tavern with a warm fire. The Tapped Toad though was far from homely. The cobwebs covering the rafters and sticky tables didn't stop Banbury pushing his way into the kitchen or Wasiz filling his pipe after finding a suitable chair to sink down into. Richard though was soon ushered upstairs by the owner and with Stephanie close behind were lead to a room on the top floor that had no windows. An important feature given who usually occupies the room but thanks to the heavy clouds above sunlight was currently the least of her worries. 'It's about time you showed yourself,' Calenir snapped to the pair as they walked in. 'We have not taken so long, if anything we are early,' Richard said going to her and looking over the cuts to her chest. 'What happened?'

'Things are far more complex than I believed. I was right my father isn't the problem, it's this Envoy.

He's corrupted the Vale and has more than just mine working with him. A wolf found me, but Kenthor stopped it from killing me. Orcs upon hogs have also flocked to fight for him,' Calenir said.

'How did your father make a wolf aid him?' Richard said. 'Not my father, listen you cloth eared woody. It's the Envoy. He and his Marked Men are the ones plotting to open the builder's gate,' Calenir then saw Stephanie and snapped. 'Who's she?'

'Never mind that. What's this builder's gate?' Richard said. 'A relic from the high elf's day, something that requires great power to use. A power this Envoy claims is being brought here before this day ends. We have to take it before he can use it,' Calenir said and went to stand but her wounds were still too deep and she fell back. 'I don't think you'll be moving for some time,' Stephanie said.

'She's right, you must rest,' Richard added.

'I have rested long enough, Kenthor is still out there alone he should be back by now,' Calenir said. In fact Kenthor had returned. Not only had he been able to lose the ones hunting him he had also taken a prisoner while doing so. Barging into the tavern he dropped his prisoner to the floor and yelled. 'My lady, where is she?

'Calm down there fella, she's upstairs I believe,' Wasiz said making Kenthor stare to him and say. 'What sort of jester are you meant to be?'

'Wasiz the Rotting Thief at your service. There's something I'd never dreamt I'd say to one of the undead,' Wasiz replied with a sarcastic bow. 'Kenthor,' Calenir exclaimed as Richard helped her down the stairs. 'Thank the stars, I believed I'd lost you,' Calenir said as the pair embraced.

'I told you not to worry and I even returned with a gift,' Kenthor said helping Calenir sit down. He then pulled the woman he'd stolen to her feet and removed the bag that had been tied around her head. 'You bastard General Argal, the Count will see you roasted in the sun for this,' Salvia spat as the gag was removed from her mouth. Forcing her into a chair Kenthor bound her hands to it as she continued to threaten them. 'Enough, I heard you plotting Salvia. You are the only one here who should worry about being turned to ash. Especially since my friend here has found himself a silver blade,' Calenir said gesturing for Richard to partly draw the new sword she had noticed hanging on his belt. 'What is it he's bringing to the Vale and who even is this Envoy?'

'I don't know my lady you must believe me. He sought me out, forced me to join him. He only ever told me what I needed to know to do as he wanted,' Salvia whimpered. 'I don't believe you and your fake tears don't fool me Salvia. Who is he and what's he bringing to the Vale?' Calenir shouted to her making Salvia's cries turn to crackling laughs. 'The everlasting darkness will consume all. There's nothing, nothing your father or any can do to stay your fate,' she sniggered. 'The builder's gate opening is inevitable and onto this world his warriors will march to join our legions. The end of the first's war is nigh and the fall of the Seers will follow. The eternal darkness is destined to reign forever more and only shadows will be free to roam the world that remains.' Her laughs suddenly changed to chokes, she then started to splutter and convulse as her skin began to turn grey and peel away from her body as black slime spewed from her every orifice. 'Get back from her,' Calenir yelled as the slime covered her body and consumed her. 'The final curse,' Kenthor said. 'Who but your father knows of shadow magic as ancient as this?'

'None but him. He was the only one of Inkark's chosen to survive, there is no other. Only one who wields the shadow scripts could cast such a curse,' Calenir said as Salvia's body slowly fell to the floor in chunks of dissolving slime. The stench of the decaying body filled the Tapped Toad as Wendolin and Thrimore entered. 'Who are these chosen?' Stephanie asked. 'Where did you even find these girls Richard?' Calenir scoffed. 'They're the help we sought, they are the Leaflins,' Richard announced.

'And what good are they?' Kenthor said looking over the sisters. Pushing past the others Bethany went to Calenir and began to heal her wounds. For a second nothing happened but after summoning the strength of the Kala ring she was able to seal Calenir's cuts if only slightly. 'How, how is that possible? I've heard of high elves healing one another but for a wood elf to heal one of our kind, it's not possible,' Kenthor said. Calenir only looked back with anger filled eyes. 'Mages, that's all we need.'

'Seems we are exactly what you need,' Bethany said. 'I've never worked on someone like you before so that's the best I can do I'm afraid. Now answer my sister's question would you.'

'Inkark's chosen were high elves who wished to colonise the south. Others, namely Richard's Seers wanted to stop them,' Calenir said. 'That lead to the first war this world had seen, one that scarred the land and broke apart mountains in its wake. In order to gain greater power Inkark and his followers devoted themselves to the god of shadows, Kasseon. He gifted them with incredible skills along with a great tome of knowledge they named the shadow scripts, but even with this aid they failed. Defeated by Seer Godborn, their leader cursed all those he believed had failed him. My father only survived because he fled. He ran from the final battle far to the south and hid himself within the Vale, but even he couldn't escape Inkark forever. He placed the curse that created our people upon him making my father and the Forgotten Vale what it is today.'

'Is there a chance another of his chosen survived?' Bethany asked.

'It's possible, but unlikely. What we must worry for now is this relic the Envoy is bringing to the Vale. If we can take it their plans will be scuppered and will buy myself and Kenthor the time we need to take control of Paratis,' Calenir said.

'What sort of relic could power a builder's gate?' Wasiz said.

'Why do they need a relic to open a gate?' Stephanie asked. 'It's not a regular garden gate, legends say the World Builders themselves used them to cultivate the world. Not only this world does the lore say the gates will take you to though,' Wasiz said.

'Gates? There's more than one of these things,' Wendolin said. 'The stories say there were two,' Wasiz said. 'I believe they found one within Amunden Trench. They have been digging there for months under the pretence of mining for coal iron. It is there he has hidden the third legion,' Kenthor said.

'No others but the builders could command the power needed to open it,' Wasiz said.

'The Envoy claims to have something that will,' Calenir insisted as a bat flew through the window to chatter to her. 'We can't wait any longer the convoy is close and we must act now. Thanks to the man power you've brought we will be able to take them head on before they reach the Vale.'

'My lady we must not be involved, we should return to Paratis before the Envoy's Marked Men make their next move,' Kenthor said.

'Let us handle their cargo. We can take it quietly, without Thrimore here losing all his Thorns to a heavily armoured convoy,' Richard said.

'We can't risk it, if they make it past you that's it for us all,' Calenir said.

'Don't worry my lady there is not a prize in this world I cannot steal,' Wasiz insisted.

'I do hope you're right thief, because if you fail all will have been for nothing and no one will be able to stop the Envoy. I'll seek out what warriors I can. When this happens it will happen quick, be ready for anything. If this Envoy can wield the shadows as my

215

father does he will not be worth facing without me,' Calenir said. 'I shall find us steeds' Kenthor added leaving Richard to help Calenir to the door. 'So who's this Stephanie?' Calenir whispered once he was away.

'I could ask you the same of that Kenthor,' Richard replied. Her eyes then fixed with his and her voice became timid as they went. 'I don't want to lose Richard. I don't want to lose the Vale and I don't want to lose him. I told Kenthor there's a life for us when this is over and I desperately want it to be true,' Calenir said. Looking back to Stephanie Richard sighed and asked. 'Will it ever be over. I've made a promise quite alike that myself, but every second since the world has only grown darker,' Richard said. The rest of Richard's party passed the pair and it seemed Bethany had elected herself to go along also. 'I w…W… Shan't hear it,' Banbury stuttered as they passed. 'It's far too perilous a place to have you tagging along.'

'Perilous, such a big word for such a small man,' Bethany chuckled with Jhona and Wasiz.

'I won't hear any slight on my height lady, especially from one so skinny. Get snapped like a twig in the Vale you..' Banbury was suddenly interrupted by ice forming around his feet. Raising him up from the floor it lifted him to the back of Nobby letting Bethany climb up behind him after. 'Don't worry master Bale I shall ensure nobody snaps you in two,' Bethany said. Caspian had followed Comet along with Kenthor and all readied to leave, bickering as they did like only friends could while Richard and Calenir watched on until she said. 'There is some light left Richard. Even in the darkest hole in the most dreary places. As long as there's a few who seek it there's always a path from it. We must just find it and together create the days to come. Make a world that together we can be as we are and not what they wish us to be.'

'My lady, your horse is ready,' Kenthor said. Taking her arm he helped her onto their steed before sitting behind her. 'Go swiftly Balmoth and think only of our promises,' Calenir said as she held Kenthor's cold hands and the black stallion charged to Vurcun's gate. 'Seems we're riding together,' Jhona said reaching down to pull Richard onto Caspian's back leaving Wasiz to take Comet.

Soon they followed the pale lady under Vurcun's walls leaving Stephanie and Wendolin watching as the others left the town. Leaving them to wonder what they should do while waiting. Although neither had to worry for long.

Shortly after their companions left the Tapped Toad a group of extremely foul looking elves had began to crowd around the tavern where the Thorns had done little to hide their presence. 'Go easy the lot of you,' Thrimore yelled as his Thorns drank the tavern dry. It had been quite some time since most had been to a well stocked establishment and all were taking full advantage of a stocked bar and full pantry. Even more so after the barkeep had let slip the pale lady would cover their bill. 'Give me that,' Thrimore said taking a bottle of whiskey from Krosh's lips. 'Sorry Captain, little carried away I got,' Krosh slurred as Thrimore spun him to look out of the window and see the many grim faces before the tavern. 'Sort yourself and the others out. We may have to worry about more than just the Grey Count here,' Thrimore said. Leaving him he went to the door where Wendolin sat on the porch with Stephanie. 'I think we should go in,' Stephanie said to her sister. 'No, they'll think we're scared of them if we do,' Wendolin replied referring to the ever growing group across from them. 'Are we not scared of them, even a little?' Stephanie said. An elf man then strutted down the street towards them. Walking as if he had a pole shoved down one of his trouser's leg that went up the length of his back. Almost comical was his appearance but as he approached the men around stood to attention. 'What's this commotion, the Mayor don't like it he don't. Where are they then?' He said waving the dirty hanky he held about until one pointed to Wendolin and Stephanie. 'That's it? Where's the rest?' He asked. 'In the tavern Collector,' a member of the crowd replied. 'Right I'll see about this,' he spat as he stormed to the Tapped Toad's porch. 'You there, wench. Is it your doing? Well is it? Is it you who brought this cult of bandits here to my Vurcun? Is it not?' The man said blowing his nose as he spoke. 'They're not my men, who even are you?' Wendolin said just as a pair of Thorns fell out of the tavern in a drunken stupor and upon seeing her both cried. 'For our red lady,' in a childish giggle. 'They seem to think they are. Either way it's the Mayor's dungeon for the lot of you. Mayor

218

Pompson doesn't take unexpected guests well especially such large groups of ne'er de wells and as the town's Chief Coin Collector I'm to see to keeping the peace.' Waving his hand and filthy cloth about the people who had gathered before the tavern advanced on the pair. Mr Guniss however had other ideas. Storming before the lot as Thrimore left the tavern he barked and batted the Collector's minions back. 'Be off with your damned dogs Collector Brevoll. These here are guests of the pale lady, see you leave them be or you'll soon have to fear far more than the Mayor's fat hand around your chops.'

'The Mayor knows nothing about any guests of the pale ones. Quit your bluster Guniss and step aside or you'll be joining them in a bag,' Brevoll snapped back, but few of his followers seemed content to continue after Guniss's threat. A series of snide comments and rude remarks followed from both men until after violently blowing his nose Collector Brevoll and his unsavoury entourage dispersed letting Guniss return to the Leaflins and say. 'Sorry about all that there, some don't know what side of their bread is buttered best.'

'What was he on about? Why would he put you in a bag?' Stephanie asked.

'I did think you'd know my lady, being you're guests of hers that is,' Guniss said.

'Treat us as we're not and explain it then,' Wendolin snapped rather enjoying how nervously he looked to her. 'If you say so my lady, but I feel you will know most of what I do. The bag the Collector spoke of was a blood bag, long has he and the Mayor collected victims for their masters within the Vale. Deep in his dungeons rumours say they take them and there they're wrapped in large bags. Like massive potato sacks big enough to hold an elf if you can believe such a thing.'

'Why would they do that?' Stephanie asked.

'For their blood,' Thrimore said.

'That's it sir, a very valuable thing it is in these parts and Mayor Pompson has seen the Count's own well supplied in the stuff,' Guniss said.

'Seems we best stay clear of this Mayor and his Collectors,' Thrimore suggested.

Chapter Thirteen
The Stone of Seeds

The convoy carrying the Envoy's precious cargo was as
heavily guarded as Richard had feared. He and his
party had reached the edge of the Vale and had time to
prepare, but the size of the force still made Richard
nervous. 'Are you sure about this? He will be alone and
we won't be able to help if they spot him,' Richard said
looking up to Wasiz who now hid in the black branches
that created a canopy above the road. 'He's the only
one who can use the skeleton key and not retch. I'm no
happier about this but he was right it's the only way.
We just need to distract the others,' Jhona said. They all
concealed themselves around dead bark as the
armoured carriage and its guard drew close.

The iron carriage charged beneath the trees clanging
and crashing past branches. Even the bumpy road
didn't slow its pace nor did it hinder the heavily armed
guard that rode ahead. As it went beneath Wasiz's perch
he dropped onto it and quickly opened the roof hatch
and snuck in before the driver saw. Rummaging
through the cargo Wasiz emptied box after box until he
removed the lid from one to find a small locked metal
chest within. Retrieving his skeleton key he unlocked
the box to reveal it contained a glowing red stone big
enough to fill his palm. Wasiz couldn't stop himself

from reaching for it and as his fingers touched it his eyes glazed over as the stone showed him a thousand different tales. His mind raced as multiple visions rushed past his eyes. Blissful images these were, showing him tranquil scenes where he and all those around him flourished. Sinking further into this trance tears started to fall from his glazed eyes as the visions turned sour. 'No, not like this. It doesn't end like this, it won't. It can't,' Wasiz mumbled. Back to the tranquil scene he was taken but once again death soon tainted it. 'There must be a way. I can find it, I can. Just show me. Just a little more.' Tears turned to blood that ran from his eye sockets, but still Wasiz held the stone. His grip never loosened for even a second as each vision of loss drove him on further. Hundreds of times was he forced to witness this display. Thousands even for after the one hundredth and twenty sixth time of watching his love pass he stopped counting. Spluttering whelps forced past his lips as he drew close to giving in and letting the stone take him. A spark then bounced around his mind, the blood from his eyes slowed and he felt in control once more. 'I have it,' he spat as a glint returned to his eyes and the carriage was struck.

'He's taking too long,' Jhona said as they struggled to keep up to the carriages on foot. His worry that they'd soon speed away with Wasiz in tow was soon drowned out by an ear piercing howl. Ringing out it made all there drop to their knees and grab their ears. The riders of the Night's Scar fell from their steeds as they clenched their ears and their mounts charged off. Then out of nowhere a beast twice the size of a wolf, with hair so long and wiry it cut through skin like a knife bounded into the side of the carriage. Knocking it onto its side and freeing Wasiz from the stone's hold over him. 'What is that?' Bethany yelled.

'I haven't a clue. Get to Wasiz,' Jhona yelled as the ringing in their ears faded and they drew their weapons. The Night's Scar all charged for the beast leaving the others free to pull Wasiz from the overturned carriage. 'Are you okay?' Jhona said.

'Yes I'm fine and I have it, at least I believe I do,' Wasiz said showing him the chest.

'We need to run,' Banbury yelled as the beast tore the head from the last of the Night's Scar and turned its attention to them. With another great howl it bounded to them, even with a coal iron sword in its side it wasn't deterred. With a swing of its paw the carriage was cast aside and it sprang on Richard. He blocked the beast's bite with his sword but its huge paw then cast his arm aside and went to strike. It stopped as a bemused look came over it and it began to sniff them. Realising none were vampires its gaze softened, after sniffing each in turn quickly it soon lost interest and bounded off to tend to its wounds. 'What was that thing?' Bethany said.

'A long as it doesn't care about us I don't about it. Let's get out of here,' Richard ordered something all were happy to agree with. Banbury lead the way back to where Caspian and the others waited, but none had noticed how far they had to run after the carriage and the beast's sudden ambush had disorientated them even further.

'He's gotten us lost, curse me for letting him lead the way,' Richard said as the path grew thinner as they went. 'How are you so s-s-su…Positive I'm wrong,' Banbury blustered back. 'I don't know about you but I don't remember passing anything like that,' Bethany said, pointing to what appeared to be cobwebs woven between multiple trees. 'There aren't massive spiders in the Vale are there?'

'It's not spiders,' Jhona said readying his bow.

'Above you, look out,' Wasiz cried and looked up to see Vale silk worms dragging their long bodies over the branches above their heads. 'Run,' Jhona yelled releasing an arrow into the side of one. Causing its white puss like blood to spurt out as others slithered down from the tops of trees. Dropping lines of their silk from their rears as they went. Bethany soon felt something grip her left hand. A strand of silk had caught her and without thinking she reached over with the other to free herself. Only to have both become matted in the silk as it began to retract and pull her up into the waiting mouth of the worm dangling above. Wasiz swung his dagger about but like Jhona and Richard found almost every movement would lead them to find another strand of silk wrapping itself around them. Within a minute each was being pulled into the treetops and Banbury's swearing alone would do little to stay their fate. All but one could and thankfully he knew when his brothers had great need of him. Breaking past bracken Caspian lead the other horses to them. His white coat glimmering as he went, its great shine blinded whatever foul senses the creatures used to see. Letting him soon pull Bethany from the silk's grasp dragging down the Vale worm that had been attempting to consume her to the ground for him to trample. With her hands free ice soon coated Bethany's palms and shards of ice cut the others free letting them scramble to the nearest steed. 'Hurry on, before more of the horrors of this place show themselves,' Banbury declared once Richard had yanked him to Comet's back. Once they were back in the saddle the silk worms were quickly left behind and thankfully Caspian hadn't forgotten the path back to Vurcun, but news the Envoy had lost his precious cargo would quickly reach him.

Deep within the Vale lies the Paratis. Calenir and Kenthor returned to find only members of the Night's Scar patrolling the fortress. Making Calenir even more eager to reach her father and take control of the fortress, before any others could. Dismounting the pair hurried to the main hall, but upon entering both their paces slowed. The air was thick with ash, going on they saw it piled in heaps all around. The only remains left of a slain vampire, but not killed by silver had these been for in the air with the ash shadows flew and crawled over the walls. At the head of the hall her father sat upon his throne, but far from the man she knew was he. He once looked as a king would upon his throne. The master of the dreaded night was he and

225

from his seat of torn skin and plucked teeth he once ruled all about him. Far from those days was the man Calenir saw when she ran to him. 'Father what has happened?' Calenir asked going to him as Kenthor stood back, sword drawn. 'Happened, well I don't, I don't think I know,' the Grey Count replied. Looking up to his daughter she saw shadows darting around within his eyes and as he spoke black liquid dripped from his mouth. 'What have they done to you?' Calenir said holding her father's cold face. 'I have done nothing to him,' the chilling voice of the Envoy echoed from behind the great throne as he emerged. Raising her sword she went to strike the vile figure down but shadows covered her arms and legs and held her back. 'Release him, let him go and forget this madness,' Calenir demanded. 'It is not I that leave your poor father in such a sorry state. Sadly the news of his traitorous daughter seems to have broken his feeble mind. Such woe did he feel upon hearing the news of your clandestine meetings with the Balmoths. His dead heart broke even more so when he learnt you were turning his own generals against him.' The Envoy approached her and forced her head around to see Kenthor lifted up by shadows. Flowing over his mouth they silenced him as others began to burrow under his skin. 'Don't, don't do this. Take the Paratis. Keep the Vale,' Calenir begged as Kenthor's muffled wails filled the room. The Envoy though didn't say a word as the minutes passed, he didn't cackle or gloat. He just watched like he was observing them for some sick experiment. Until after what felt like hours for his victim, Kenthor's body began to fade and all that remained of him was ash. All strength to weep or wail for her love was gone when he passed leaving her ready to meet a fate she was sure was now certain. The Envoy though soon found his head turned as a member of the Night's Scar, their leader in fact, Calsum Votter marched into the hall. Calenir remained bound by shadows as they spoke but even from her restraints she could tell the Envoy had quickly become extremely displeased. A foul vengeful scream came from him making Calenir force her head around to see him gripping Votter's throat and knew there was only one thing that could have riled him up so. 'Seems your plans are not so perfect,' Calenir mocked past cheek's stained with tears for her love. Shoving Votter away he stormed back to her and the Envoy hissed. 'You think some rangers can help you. You truly believe your Balmoths can do anything but die slowly just as he did.' His hand then raised but for whatever reason he thought better of it. Lowering his arm he chuckled and turned to Votter. 'Summon the legion, this has given us a fine excuse to visit Vurcun has it not.'

Chapter Fourteen
Vurcun's Fall

With the others away Stephanie found she was pacing back and forth in the Tapped Toad. Until hooves drew her back outside to see them rushing to dismount. 'Are you all okay?' She asked running over.

'More importantly did you succeed?' Wendolin added hurrying over from the tavern's porch. 'I believe so,' Wasiz said and all quickly retreated back into the tavern as those who returned continued struggling to remove the Vale worm's silk from themselves. Once inside Wasiz placed the chest onto a table and opened it. 'What is it?' Bethany said reaching for it.

'Don't touch it,' Wasiz snapped as he slapped her hand back. 'It's dark magic, a power none should wield.'

'We should destroy it and be done with this whole ordeal,' Banbury said.

'No weapon this world has can break this stone. No jeweller however skilled could change its shape,' Wasiz said lighting his pipe and leaning back in a chair to rest his aching eyes. 'How do you know?' Bethany asked. 'Because I did hold it and it showed me. What it showed me I'm still unsure of but it was enough to discover its true name,' Wasiz said. 'Alike myself it has been given many names over the years. The red life, Norcea's heart. At one point my kind even

228

called it the hope stone. The wise have always sought it but never before has it been found. The name you may know it by is the stone of seeds. Rumoured to be the vessel that first granted the high elves power over the elements.'

'It cannot truly be, this stone exists in the lore of my kind also. Said to grant any who holds it the power to rule over all they see. To remake the world however they see fit,' Banbury said.

'We must contact Elidom, have him send Charlemagne to take this to the high elf's vault,' Richard said. 'Why wait?' Jhona announced. Closing the box he went to the door rubbing his hair clip as he did. Opening the door he found it didn't lead him back to the golden tower within Duniesa. Instead just a black void greeted him. Slamming the door closed Jhona tried again but the same void lay beyond. 'My hourglass had no effect on it. Seems this stone can alter our items. A smarter man might be able to surmise why, but no time do we have for such things,' Wasiz said.

'Enough we must act quickly before this Envoy realises he's lost it,' Richard insisted. But as you know dear reader and what our band would soon discover for themselves is that the Envoy had already been informed. A contingent of the third legion along with the remainder of the Bloodied Spikes horde now approached the town. The gates were barred but soon fell and ravenous hogs charged through killing as they went, followed by warriors of the Vale clad in black steel. No real guard did Vurcun have leaving all within at their mercy. 'They're coming for us,' Krosh yelled running into the tavern followed by Collector Brevoll. 'You pig swilling blagards. You have brought death to us all. They're killing whoever's in their way. The blood suckers have never come in such force before, what have you done?' Brevoll wailed.

'Enough of your crying find what soldiers you have and we will hold them while others get to safety. What's the most defendable place in this town?' Wendolin said. 'Well the Mayor's manor would be the place to go, but he won't like it,' Brevoll answered her.

'Sod what he likes, do as you're ordered. Richard I'll divide the men. I shall take half to slow them, you take the rest and ready this manor,' Thrimore said. 'I'll go with you. Together we can hopefully divide their force and buy the others more time,' Richard said. 'Jhona lead the rest to the manor.'

'I should stay with you,' Jhona argued.

'No lead the others they will need you. We will only slow them Jhona, you must get word to Elidom and hold them off until Charlemagne can retrieve the stone. They must not get it,' Richard demanded.

'I understand,' Jhona said and after the brothers shared a hug Richard left with Thrimore and Wendolin before Stephanie could stop them. 'Where are they going?' She said running over.

'Don't worry they'll be back. Krosh do as your Captain ordered and let us see to this Mayor,' Wasiz said. 'Right you are rotter and whatever tricks you have left best you prepare them,' Krosh replied.

The Bloodied Spikes horde cleared the streets for the warriors of the Vale leaving them free to storm through doors and methodically search each house they found for the item they sought. This slowed the vampires but did nothing to hinder the Bloodied Spike's hogs. 'Slash them all, let the hogs eat their fill,' Duca roared on top of the hog that used to belong to Tartiss. An arrow to this hog's eye would soon end this foul thing and leave Duca trapped beneath it as the few defenders Vurcun had made themselves known. With a great cry Richard's sword cast out a blinding light letting a volley of arrows from the Thorn's bows kill the first wave of charging riders. Swords soon clashed and the battle for Vurcun began with the slaying of the Bloodied Spike's new chief. 'You said they'd scatter,' Thrimore yelled, slicing the neck of an attacking orc as he found his place beside Richard. 'They should have. These must not serve Valcea Ash anymore,' Richard said. 'Then who is their master, because killing their leader isn't making them run this time,' Thrimore exclaimed as the second wave approached. Grabbing an orc's spear from the floor Richard jammed the blunt end into the hog's body and used it to prop up the spear. 'Use their spears and be ready to fight their riders,' Richard ordered making others copy until a wall of dead pigs scored with spears met the charging riders. Hogs were impaled on the spears, but many still bounded on trampling Thorns and leaving them for the foot soldiers to finish off. 'We could use your help here,' Richard yelled to Wendolin who upon arriving had knelt with her hands to the ground. 'There's no greenery around here. Everything in the Vale's as dead as your pale woman. I can't even find a blade of grass and Bethany has the ring,' Wendolin said. Slicing the belly of an orc and then driving his sword through him Richard took the bent blade from his slain enemies belt and threw it to Wendolin. 'Then use a sword,' Richard ordered. 'Blood suckers,' a Thorn yelled as a black blade pierced him. Thrimore fired an arrow to the warrior of the Vale catching him in the throat, but only iron was this arrow and to Thrimore's shock the warrior simply removed it and then bellowed. 'Kill the wood scum but that one, their leader. I'll bleed him myself.' Pulling a spear from a dead hog he ran for Thrimore, but a blinding flash found him before he was able to strike the Thorn down. A deep burning pain started to throb down his side. As his vision returned he saw a silver blade had pierced him and his body was quickly turning to ash. Slicing through the warrior Richard turned to Thrimore. 'Pull them back, get to the others. I will draw as many as I can,' Richard said and before Thrimore could argue both were set upon once more. Slicing the back off an orc Wendolin took the mace from its hand and cracked it around the orc's head. Looking to Thrimore she saw he and Richard had been cut off and the rest of the Thorns were failing. Doing as she hoped Thrimore would want she called out. 'Fall back, fall back to this Mayor's manor. We will slow them as we go.' Leading the Thorns she pulled them back together but as they fell back Wendolin had lost sight of both Thrimore and Richard. 'My lady did you see where the Captain got to?' A Thorn asked.

'No but they are smarter than these. He will find us, worry for yourselves,' Wendolin said as more raging orcs ran to them. 'Don't think of him, just think of surviving this day. Don't let your arrows falter and keep together,' she ordered them as if she was their captain and they followed her command as she was. Together they divided the Bloodied Spike's raiders as they fell back to find the manor's gates.

The Mayor of Vurcun, a Mr Borisea Pompson had hidden away behind the walls of his sprawling mansion. The iron gates of which many of the people of the town now tried to get by for safety. 'Get away, get away,' Borisea yelled from the other side. 'They will only find us faster with all this noise. Get away or the tax men will take the lot of you.'

'You there. Open this gate, your people need your protection,' Banbury yelled to him.

'Begone. It is not on me to protect them. I am not their father,' Borisea spat back.

'You're the mayor are you not? Open up these gates before more are lost,' Banbury ordered but was ignored. Only when Wasiz used his skeleton key to open the lock and swing the gate open did the Mayor speak again. 'Get out, get out. Trespassers, robbers. I'll have you on the gallows for this,' he raged before rushing inside and locking himself away in his office. 'Forget him, get any who can take up arms. Banbury find out if this place has an armoury I need more arrows,' Jhona ordered.

'Look the bell tower. Go send your message. I shall handle this,' Wasiz said. Jhona agreed and soon headed to it. 'How's he meant to contact Elidom?' Bethany asked. 'He will send a message with the wind and we must hope the wind is blowing fast today,' Wasiz said.

Stephanie had taken it upon herself to find the largest room in the mansion and begin moving families there. She soon had the kitchen cleared for an infirmary also. Discovering as she did the town had more sick than well occupants. Most seemed to be in an odd daze and as more passed by her she soon noticed why. She saw an elf man huddled in a corner sniffing on a powdery white stone. Going to him as his eyes glazed over and he slumped down to the floor she took the stone from his hand. 'What's that you have there?' Wasiz asked quickly noticing what she held. 'Give that here, you don't want to get that muck up your nose,' he went on taking it from Stephanie. 'What is it?' She asked as Wasiz gave the stone a little sniff. 'It's troll soot that's for sure, where'd you get it?' Wasiz asked making Stephanie point to the man. 'And where did you get it?' Wasiz said kicking the man's side to jog him from his daydream. One more followed to stir the man making him wave his arms in a vain attempt to bat the pair away. 'Get on, let me sleep.' The man begged as Wasiz took hold of his collar and yanked him to his feet. 'Sleep all you like once you tell me where this came from,' Wasiz asked again and this time got the answer

234

he wanted. 'It was down there somewhere. Now leave me be,' the man said shrugging him off.

'It looks like chalk,' Stephanie said.

'Far from it,' Wasiz said as the pair wandered down the hall the man had pointed to. 'Troll soot is a very potent depressant if it's boiled right. That poor fellows clearly been taking quite a bit for some time.' To the end of the hall they came to a spiral staircase they followed down. 'Why do you suppose he's sniffing that stuff?' Stephanie asked.

'Could have been forced on him? Or maybe he just wanted to escape his miserable life and hide in his daydream,' Wasiz said as they reached the bottom. There a metal door rested in a brick frame and past it both could hear somebody clanging about. 'Best you go back up.' Reaching under Wasiz's cape Stephanie took one of his dagger's and said. 'I'm fine here, just open it.' Adrenaline pumped around her body readying her for what may lay behind as Wasiz took out his skeleton key and unlocked the door. To her relief though they found no dreaded creature beyond only the Mayor. The large room appeared to have once been a wine cellar given the few bottles that still lined the shelves around the walls. It wasn't wine that filled the bottles however, a fact Stephanie soon learnt as the pair entered to find multiple white bags that hung from the ceiling. Each was stained with patches of red, while tubes ran from them to containers slowly milking the ones kept within of every drop of blood their bodies could produce. 'What is this?' Wasiz said. A multitude of sights he had witnessed but very few compared to the one before him

235

now. 'That guard Guniss, he warned us of this place,' Stephanie said as the Mayor noticed the couple. He had been filling a variety of suitcases, some contained bottles filled with the liquid he'd been farming. The others overflowed with silver jewellery and golden coins. 'Who let you in? I locked that door,' Mayor Pompson barked. 'There's no door I can't get by,' Wasiz mocked. Storming before him Stephanie pulled the bag he was filling from his grasp. 'Whatever's wrong with you, how could you do this?' Stephanie said. 'Don't judge me, I did what I had to. They'd have bled us all if not,' the Mayor said snatching it back. 'Seems you've been paid fairly well for it,' Wasiz said as he began sifting through the many necklaces and jewels the bags were filled with. 'Pure silver as well, handy thing for a man such as you to have.'

'Are they alive?' Stephanie asked going to the closest hanging bag. 'I suppose troll soot keeps them good and docile, easier to bleed them that way. Am I right Mr Mayor?' Wasiz said.

'How do we get them out?' Stephanie asked.

'You don't,' the Mayor snapped. 'The tube goes deep into them, remove it and they'll die in seconds. This is the Count's doing not mine. I'm just one of many forced to serve him.'

'And now rather than stay you're taking the wealth and protection he's given you in return for their lives and you're fleeing with it instead of using it against him,' Stephanie argued.

'These aren't just some marauding bandits after the odd bit of coin. They're the Count's own and there's little me or some skirt with a knife could do to stop them,' the Mayor's blustering went on until Stephanie said. 'Wait you're running. So you have a way out?' This made the Mayor fall silent until Wasiz clipped him around the back of the head and said. 'She's right isn't she. Where is it you're rushing to?' Reluctantly the Mayor took hold of all the suitcases he could carry and lead them to a painting that sat at the far end of the room. It showed the Mayor's father and he appeared just as much the pompous twerp as his son. Wasiz moved the portrait aside to reveal a passage beyond. 'It leads out to a quarry a few miles from the red water. From there you can be in Orashon in a two day ride with a fresh mount. So there, I've shown you now let me be off,' the Mayor said to Wasiz pushing his way past. 'Wait we can't just let him go,' Stephanie said.

'Don't worry he's given us a way to clear this town and men like him will soon get what's coming to them without a master watching over them,' Wasiz said.

'I would like to hope so and I suppose you're right. I shall get those already inside and have them start passing through. You go tell the others what we have found,' Stephanie ordered.

'This commanding tone suits you my lady. Let it be as you say and together hope the end of that tunnel leads them to safer places than our path will lead us,' Wasiz said.

High in the bell tower Jhona could see his enemies advancing through the streets below. Sitting to the edge of the ledge he cupped his hands until a small gust of wind flew within his palms. 'Hurry Seers, great power we have found and need your aid. Send the master of the skies, send any you can or more will you lose than just Balmoths and cunning thieves.' As he spoke he lifted his hands sending his message into the air for the wind to carry to its destination. *Let us hope Charlemagne is still spying on us* Jhona thought. Crying then drew his eyes, civilians were rushing to the manor with orcs in hot pursuit. Taking a handful of arrows from his quiver he dropped them around for the wind to take. The bell in the tower chimed as wind rushed past taking up the arrows and guiding them to their targets. Giant bats soaring above that had followed the legions advance soon took notice and with chilling cries swooped from the sky forcing Jhona to take back up his bow. One fell to his arrows, followed by another but the third collided with the bell tower after an arrow struck its eye. Ripping the roof from it and sending the bell crashing through the tower to crater the ground. Flinging his bow over his back Jhona was forced to jump from the crumbling tower grabbing hold of a bat's wing as it flapped past. Taking an arrow in his free hand he stabbed it through the bat's jaw and quickly grabbed its other wing, tearing it from the beast's body. Using its patchwork wing as a parachute to slow his descent he landed upon a town house to see Richard and Thrimore in the streets below. Warriors of the Vale surrounded them, but the ash coating the floor showed what little success they had at killing the pair. Both were almost spent, sweat dripped from each with every thrust or swing of their swords. From every angle another warrior moved for them and both believed they were alone until arrows began to pierce armour and pluck eyes from their adversary's sockets. 'Hurry and get up here,' Jhona yelled down shooting at a washing line that hung over the street, cutting the end to give the others a way to scale the wall to him. Running to the rope both were soon hurrying up as Jhona kept warriors back with volleys of arrows. 'You Balmoths have incredible timing, here,' Thrimore said taking the arrows he had left and refilling Jhona's quiver. 'Balmoth,' a crass voice yelled up to them. More giant bats flew down and circled above while warriors broke into the building to reach the roof as the commander of this force called to them. 'Surrender Balmoths and your deaths will be quick,' General Crathore Blaffer declared. 'And what of myself, for we are not all Balmoths?' Thrimore yelled back.

'Don't mock, lay down your arms and give back what you stole,' Crathore demanded.

'I'd say the chances of that happening are about as slim as you living past this day General,' Richard replied as he saw wiry grey fur approach from their backs. 'Don't vex me Balmoth give it up,' Crathore bellowed, but the cries of his warriors soon made him turn. 'The Beast of the Vale,' one cried as huge jaws wrapped around his waist. Lifting her prey high and with one tremendous bite she tore him in two. 'Kill it, kill the beast,' Crathore ordered as he scrambled to get away. He and his people feared nothing in the Forgotten Vale, apart from her that is. The only creature this land has that can strike fear into

239

any blood sucker. For she feasts on them and thanks to their curse they feel every gnaw, every nibble as she slowly devours their living corpses. Not slow was she now though for before her a banquet lay. Springing up the beast tore warriors of the Vale apart as bats swarmed the roof top.

'Get that gate b-b-b… Sealed,' Banbury ordered as he did his best to assemble the people of Vurcun into a force that stood a hope of repelling the enemy at the gates. 'It's the red lady, open the gates,' a Thorn yelled from the wall. 'Blasted woman, I've only just closed them,' Banbury complained. Opening the gates Wendolin rushed in with Thrimore's group of Thorns close behind. 'They're right behind us make ready on the wall Thorns. Even if our arrows can't kill them we will make every inch they move agony,' Wendolin ordered. 'Where is Richard?' Banbury yelled.

'With Thrimore. We were split up,' Wendolin said as Bethany ran to join them. 'We have the weak as far from this as they can be. Wasiz and Steph found a passage out, she's getting them through now,' Bethany said. The sound of the bell tower tumbling soon distracted them all as dust and rubble coated the courtyard. Before any could respond a yell of, 'Bats,' came from a Thorn as a group flew into the courtyard and with blood red flashes the Night's Scar appeared. Banbury's militias blood was soon coating black blades. One bat flew to the centre of a group and when he changed he threw defenders aside in a mass of bleeding shadows. When they faded Calsum Votter,

Master of the Night's Scar, the first to know the Count's curses revealed himself. Thorn's arrows flew to no effect for shadows spun to them guarding Votter from any attack. 'Fall now sons of Seers, fall to the shadows sons of the forest and daughters of water.' Votter's voice sent a shiver down the spines of all present as water shot from Bethany's hands, but the shadows interrupted it and soon reached to her. 'The ring,' Wendolin yelled. Making Bethany throw it to her just as shadows drew close. Wendolin rose a wall of thorns from the palms of her hands between them, that stretched out in every direction, attempting to encage Votter. 'You can't touch me with your feeble spells and shiny trinkets,' Votter boasted. 'I am the Night's Scar, the eternal night will follow as I go. None can stand before…' He stopped as he felt a pain in his back. Spinning he found a dagger embedded there and a goblin who the vines had let past stood behind him. His shadows tried to strike him but the glowing hourglass he held stopped them from touching him. 'Seems your shadows can't harm me,' Wasiz mocked.

'It matters not, one dagger will not end me,' Votter roared and drew his sword. 'Yes but one with a pure silver neckless wrapped around it should weaken you I imagine,' Wasiz replied. He was right the pain in Votter's back hadn't gone away and his pale skin was slowly turning to ash. Before Votter could react Wasiz took another blade that had some of the Mayor's finery wrapped around it and jammed it between his adversary's eyes. Shadows rushed to aid him, but there was little they could do but swarm around as he wailed

241

until his vocal cords like the rest of him was ash. Unfortunately the rest of the Night's Scar had not been preoccupied with a rotting thief and had fought their way to the gate. The defenders there were forced to flee when the barricade was removed and the Bloodied Spikes joined the attack. 'This courtyard is lost. Krosh, get your Thorns to the passage Wasiz found, I'll hold these gits,' Banbury ordered.

'They're falling back now, but you'll need a back to yours dwarf,' Krosh said.

'Nonsense,' Banbury yelled, swinging his axe he cut the head from an orc. Kicking the headless body back it tipped another letting Banbury drop his axe to the fallen orc's gut. 'They're in the manor we can't hold it,' a Thorn yelled from a balcony above the pair. Running to Banbury and Krosh, Wasiz went, suddenly he felt something tug on him. Seeing a pale hand with peeling skin and black nails pulling on his bag he panicked. Before he could knock it away his neck was gripped and his bag was torn from its strap. Throwing him down a beam of shadows covered him but when the wielder noticed they had no effect they faded and from broken black lips the hooded figure said. 'What are you to wield that strength?'

'Discover my name for yourself. For there are enough to choose from,' Wasiz replied as the Envoy retrieved the case containing the stone from his bag. 'So you're the thief,' the Envoy said as a sickening laugh came from him, but his glee filled cackles would soon be drowned out by the thud of hooves. For not only the Envoy hunted the Balmoths and their friends.

The spreading night had not gone unnoticed and word had soon gotten around that none other than the Balmoths may have a hand in it. Spurring Malcolm to call on what rangers were to hand and ride to their Captain's aid. Barely forty they were and on the barren land that surrounded Vurcun they witnessed the force piling into the town. *We would be no help, even if we tried* Malcolm thought, but more steeds soon crowded around his meagre force of rangers. Clad in golden armour their riders were, while their steeds wore sparkling golden harnesses. 'Who commands this band here?' Captain Slade barked to Malcolm as he approached. 'The Balmoths,' Malcolm replied.

'And where are they? I have business with your Captain' Slade asked.

'There I believe,' Malcolm said pointing to the town. 'Of course they are,' Slade scoffed. 'I suppose we shall see, will we not.'

'See what?' Malcolm asked.

'Who of our parties is the greater?' Slade announced. 'You will ride with us elf,' Malcolm said.

'Certainly not,' Lindow Landon interjected. 'We joined this little expedition of yours to retrieve my sword, not fight the Grey Count's own.'

'If the Balmoths are within Vurcun this thief of yours will surely be with them,' Slade said.

'Then he can keep it, we are leaving this place the Elites have no fight here,' Lindow insisted.

'This is your fight, just as it is ours, are you not meant to guard the elves? You're Elites are you not?'

Malcolm said. 'Not these elves boy,' Lindow replied as he and his men turned their steeds. 'What are we if not a guard to our own?' Slade yelled to him.

'We are the Seer's guard Captain not theirs,' Lindow stated as he rode away. 'You maybe, but not I. Nor am I ready to so quickly give up on my prize,' Slade declared. 'Ready yourselves whoever dares stay. For it is not Seers who need our swords this day. Today war finds us and the Elites will ride below black clouds to face it,' Slade cried out. Drawing his sword and rising it high. 'Coat your blades in the dust I handed out before our ride, here,' he went on. Tossing a draw bag to Malcolm he opened it to find it was filled with silver dust. 'You rangers may travel under prepared but my Elites do not. Coat your blades and it will give us a fighting chance to win this battle.' Rangers and Elites were quickly inline and with silver flowing from their swords and coating their arrows they charged down the slopes and over the plain. What was left of the Bloodied Spikes mounted a counter strike but their worn out hogs were no match for Elite steel and fresh mounts. 'Let us see ranger, for I missed you in the war, so let us battle today and see whose force will go on past here to guard the lands of our fathers.' Rising his sword high Slade declared. 'To their ruin, to their death. We are the slayers of demons, slayers of the mighty and with us the Seer's light shines.' Mounted orcs were cut down and hogs trampled over as they cut a path to the town's gate. Hoping to flee from the beast of the Vale, General Crathore had ridden to the gate but here only death found him as rangers and Elite's bound through. Cut down from his steed, his skin soon sizzled away as silver dust left his body riddled with wounds. 'Richard look, it's Malcolm,' Jhona said as horses charged through the streets. 'I don't know about you Balmoths but I'd say it's time we took the fight to them. May I?' Thrimore said taking the sword from Jhona's belt. Placing both Jhona's blade and his own in one hand he ran to the roof's edge and leapt from it. Grabbing a washing line he slid to the ground landing upon a warrior below. Thrimore booted another into the stampede as he took a sword in each hand. Slicing the neck of a vampire before him with one blade he used the other to hew the arm from another. Before he could make another move and swing for the other warriors charging to him a blinding flash of lighting fried them and left Richard in their place.

Within the manor's courtyard the Envoy could hear their attack on Vurcun was failing, that though mattered little to him, for he had his prize. Others ran to aid Wasiz as shadows consumed the Envoy and he vanished within them. With the Envoy's departure the Night's Scar began to flee the manor and as hooves echoed from beyond the wall the battle for Vurcun was done. They had won but little of the town was left habitable, their relief had arrived too late to save most who lived there. Bodies covered the street and each open door revealed more horrors. The small number that were able to flee would never return but little rest would any of those who still remained get.

The Forgotten Hero

Few would have known it was midday as all sunlight was now hidden behind thick black clouds that jetted out over the Tancoter Mountains. Inching ever northward as the minutes ticked by and the defenders of Vurcun regrouped. From the manor Wasiz went after Jhona returned to him and with the others rushed to rejoin Richard and Thrimore. Wasiz suddenly stopped, letting the rest past he pulled away with Jhona close behind. 'Where are you going?' Jhona asked as Wasiz followed a trail of blood down an alley. Hidden there amongst the rubbish of the town the Beast of the Vale lay. A spear was embedded in her side and blood matted her fur. 'What a state you have gotten yourself into,' Wasiz said but as the pair drew closer the beast used what strength she had left to snarl at the pair. 'Enough of that,' Wasiz went on. 'We have friends, healers who can fix these wounds of yours.'

'Your healers can't help me,' the beast said with a grimace. 'I'm sure they will be able to,' Wasiz insisted. 'No. I just have to change,' the beast replied.

'Change, change how?' Jhona asked. Looking up to him the beast said. 'Like this.' With that wiry fur began to change to skin, paws became hands and feet and all the wounds over her body shrunk as she changed until Jhona's own face looked back to him. 'You're a changeling, incredible, just incredible,' Wasiz said. 'My wounds are still too great. I shall have to become smaller than this to heal faster and conserve what strength I have left,' the beast said using Jhona's voice. 'What's that meant to mean? I'm in better shape than most,' Jhona huffed.

'Perfectly fit you are dear Jhona. I'm sure that's not what the beast meant,' Wasiz said.

'Quite, but a bug will I need to become. Until I rebuild the strength to change again,' the beast said.

'Then change as small as you need and we shall carry you back to the Vale. We owe you a debt of sorts we have to repay after all,' Wasiz said and as he held out his hand the beast changed once again and a stick insect crawled up Wasiz's arm, to hide inside his breast pocket. 'We better get back to the others,' Jhona said. 'Yes, but not a word about our new friend here. Better her secret is kept with us,' Wasiz said. 'You best get yourself higher up see what's happening past these walls, I'll find the others.'

'I have never been happier to see you Malcolm,' Richard said as he put his arm around him. 'And I never expected to find myself happy seeing you,' he went on as Slade approached. 'You're just lucky there's more pressing matters to hand than your arrest,' Slade replied. Around them the Leaflins ran tending to the injured and sending whoever was able to flee through the mansion's hidden passage. Barely a few hours of rest would any get, hardly enough time for each to drink a glass of water. 'Up here hurry,' Jhona yelled from a rooftop as the sound of horns and drums from within the Forgotten Vale reached them. This made most not only the Captains run to the rooftops and the town's wall. 'What is it?' Thrimore asked.

'It's the third legion, they're marching,' Jhona said. Formations marched from the Forgotten Vale, hundreds of vampires passed by dead trees while giant bats and other winged monsters flew above. Their banners though didn't have the Grey Count's mark of a black bats wing upon them. A horizontal bleeding red eye covered black cloth. They didn't yet know it but this was the Envoy's emblem. One he hoped to soon hang from every town and city north of the Vale. 'That's not just the third, there are thousands,' Richard said. 'We must rebuild the gate, make ready for the next attack,' Slade ordered.

'I shouldn't bother, they're not coming here,' Thrimore said. To the north the army march towards the Tancoter. 'They aim to march over the Blenches Pass,' Richard said as he looked to Thrimore. For the first town they'd come by past the mountains and the Erauss woods was the Humtees. 'They aim to march through the Erauss and then I imagine they'll be on their way to Meceller,' Richard said.

'He has it,' Wasiz announced as he reached the rooftop. After meeting the Beast of the Vale he had snuck away from even Jhona and had been planning ever since. 'I wasn't fast enough and the bugger took it from me.'

'He has the stone?' Richard said.

'Why did you not say?' Jhona asked.

'It was not the time to,' Wasiz replied.

'What do you mean it wasn't time to,' Jhona argued but was quickly cut off by another. 'This is done Richard, we lost. We need to retreat, find your Seers and plan our next move,' Banbury said.

'We can't retreat if we don't stop this here we never will,' Richard said.

'Forget your quest, we need to get home before they reach the Humtees,' Wendolin insisted.

'No,' Richard stated. 'Thrimore was right, we need to take this fight to them. If they're marching that means Amunden's Trench is undefended. We should be able to slip in and destroy this gate before he opens it.'

'How do you know he hasn't opened it already?' Banbury said.

'We don't, but I feel like we would know if he had,' Richard said.

'What about our parents, they'll be at the Humtees by sunrise or whenever sunrise is now,' Wendolin said. 'Their numbers will slow them even if we ride the path we came by we should beat them to the Erauss,' Thrimore said.

'You are barely twenty Thrimore, even with Wendolin you can't stop an army,' Jhona said.

'No, but we can hold them. Hopefully long enough for you all to end this,' Slade interrupted.

'I thought you'd have more sense,' Jhona said. 'So did I. You Balmoths must have infected me in some way,' Slade joked.

'Us also, for we have been left idle for long enough. I didn't join you two just to sit in a tavern whilst that Fandisco empties my pockets,' Malcolm announced. 'You realise what you're saying. There will be no aid coming, no help. You will be the only line of defence with nowhere to retreat to,' Richard said.

'We can use the trees of the Erauss. There is a thin path through them where we can ambush their force,' Thrimore said.

'It may work, but all hinges on the clouds breaking,' Wasiz said.

'Then I'll make sure they do,' Bethany declared. 'Me and Bethany will go aid your pale lady while you see to the Envoy,' Stephanie said.

'I'll handle it by myself Steph, you should head back and help mother and father flee,' Bethany said.

'To where? I won't just be running away while you all fight. Wendolin can take care of the Humtees, I'm going with you,' Stephanie insisted.

'Caspian will join you and let us hope we all meet again when this is done,' Jhona said. Horses were soon called from the stable and as one unit the Elites, Thorns and rangers rode from Vurcun. Wendolin lead them upon Comet and as the forces of the Forgotten Vale marched north they dashed around the mountains to ready whatever defence they were able.

'Stephanie wait,' Richard said as Caspian went to her.

'I'm going Richard, I'm not just running off to hide,' she insisted.

'I know and I won't beg you to flee for I know it would be useless. I'm only begging you to come back. There is a life for us when this is done, I swear to you there is. One past wars and strife,' Richard said.

'I'll be back Richard because I know you'll be waiting. Don't fear for me and I shall do all I can to not worry for you. Let us only concern ourselves with what's ahead and together we will best this villain.' Getting into Caspian's saddle Bethany soon joined her. 'When did you become so valiant?' Richard asked.

'When I met the Balmoth brothers,' Stephanie replied with a smile to her love, Caspian spirited the pair away as Richard's friends came around him. 'I didn't think my adventuring with you would lead me here rotter,' Banbury said.

'To certain doom and unending pain,' Wasiz chuckled. 'Where else would following a fool as I lead you?'

'Certain, hardly so,' Banbury barked. 'This Envoy has bet on a lot and played his hand well, but he didn't count on us did he?'

'Let us hope so Banbury, but neither of you have to follow,' Jhona said. 'Me and Richard will face this Envoy.'

'Not without us you won't be,' Banbury said.

'Too right, we started this together and will end it as so,' Wasiz declared. The four of them were the last to leave Vurcun. On they walked into the Vale hoping, wishing even that each would still have the other when this quest of theirs came to an end.

Chapter Fifteen
Standing Before Shadows

'Get into the trees, set traps wherever you can,' Krosh ordered as they rode into the Erauss Wood. 'Ahead,' a scout yelled riding to them. 'They have passed the mountains in record time. We have barely a handful of minutes before they're on us.'

'We will let them march through and stick at their sides at different points along their column. Then draw them into the woods for you woodys,' Slade said.

'Too late they're here,' Thrimore said as bats descended from the sky. Before they could strike the trees stretched over the road blocking some and sneering others in vines. No word did the red lady speak but forward she went as the ones who named her so followed. But a few were the Thorns, yet besides Wendolin, Thrimore felt as if an army of hundreds followed. Elite steel shone beside ranger's bows as the warriors of the Vale marched on and the two forces met beneath the trees of the Erauss.

'Take the left flank, don't let them by us,' Captain Slade ordered. The warriors of the Vale hadn't expected any resistance within the Erauss, leaving the first column underprepared when arrows sparkling with silver dust fell upon them. Others soon joined their advance and the meagre force of elves and wood folk did little to slow them. To Thrimore's back Wendolin had remained and as his sword sung and vines and trees bent to her whims all around them warriors clad in black steel charged on. Monsters flew above plucking Thorns and rangers from the forest floor. Thrimore ducked to dodge a swinging vine only to have his shoulder pulled back by Captain Slade. 'We are out of time, if we had any to begin with,' he said. 'Even with your lady they are too many. Gather the rangers with your own and retreat to the crossroads. We shall slow them until the last.' Before Thrimore could respond Slade's sword was held high and his Elites rallied to him. Together they raised the golden shields they wielded and upon their small line warriors of the Vale were broken. In awe Thrimore was of his bravery and only turned from the Elites when Wendolin's hand gripped his. It was sweaty, almost dripping and looking down he saw the glow from the ring fading as she was. 'Go now, don't let the shadows take us all,' Slade declared seeing Wendolin slump onto Thrimore. Spears then pierced his Elite's line pulling two of his own from it to be hacked at. Raising a fallen shield to fill the gap Slade yelled 'Form a circle, they're to our sides.' Just as a giant bat forced his way past the canopy Wendolin had created and crushed the Elite stood beside him. Tossed down with his allies he was, blood covered his face and then Slade felt the talon of the monster cut through his armour and pierce his chest. The offending talon was quickly removed as others stabbed at the beast to little avail as it trampled him. With their line in tatters and but a handful left Slade and his Elites were doomed. Neither Malcolm's rangers nor Thrimore's Thorns had fled the field. Both had ignored the Captain's order to retreat, but with warriors about them all none could reach them as one by one golden armour fell until like a wave the warriors of the Vale washed over them. 'Hold,' Malcolm yelled. 'Hold them here, we can't let them b..' An arrow to Malcolm's chest silenced him killing the young ranger instantly and sending his body to fall beside others. His lifeless face found Wendolin's eyes as she forced herself to stand. Thorns and rangers rallied to Thrimore and Wendolin but little more could any do as the warriors surrounded the few that remained and General Hervass Hunfor trotted forth upon a steed gifted to him by the Envoy. Rotting skin did this horse have, that peeled off as it went. Revealing its exposed rib cage even more, with eyes as black as the sky that now covered them. 'A worthy act,' Hunfor said looking down to Thrimore. 'But pointless. Like all who are foolish enough to stand against my master your fate is death. Lay down your arms and I shall make it a quick one.'

Black blades and pale faces surrounded Wendolin and Thrimore but before General Hunfor could raise his arm a howl rang out. It was a sound none had expected to hear and as another rippled past the trees leaves fell around them as a warrior of the Vale bellowed. 'Wolves, wolves are..,' A speeding flash of white cast this warrior aside. It soon darted about tossing vampires down as it went, until it showed enough for Wendolin to see it was Salene the White Light of the Fang. With

General Hunfor distracted Thrimore released an arrow from his bow into the General's neck and a second later he and his steed were pulled beneath the ground and pierced with roots. Howls from all about sent the warriors of the Vale into disarray as the hunters of the Fang charged through bracken. 'The wolves, the wolves fight with us,' Wendolin said.

'With the wolves let us see the sun once more,' Krosh cried and as the hunters charged to their backs the few that were left ran on. 'See together Fang Lord there is a change, with my council and me your wolves should be,' the master of the beasts sang as he and Balvor the mammoth slayer watched the battle beyond. 'Keep your songs master and your council. We are simply here to ensure our pact does not die with the Balmoth,' Balvor barked back.

'It's not as fresh or as tasty as elf, but they'll still fill a hole in my gut,' Fengal roared and charged on. His teeth tore heads from bodies while his claws ripped through coal iron armour like butter. 'See the hunters stay together Fengal don't hunt alone. Jerrest with me. We break through to Salene and clear a way for the injured to flee. They are easy prey down there and won't last,' Balvor said.

'As you say boss, but I fear your White Light has already rallied them,' Jerrest replied. Ahead the White Light of the Fang fought beside the red lady and the Thorns mustered to them. Both Wendolin and Thrimore summoned what little will they had to go on as hunters darted past. Still endless was the flow of warriors into the Erauss giving none any rest, but just as quickly as they'd spread the black clouds above suddenly began inching away. As a beam of sunlight broke past the clouds it found Thrimore's cheek and he raised his head to the sun creeping past. 'The sun,' he whispered and then cried. 'They have done it. The skies are shifting. Paratis has fallen, the Balmoths have done it.'

'Not the Balmoths, my sisters,' Wendolin said. The yelps of the warriors of the Vale replaced the valour filled cries of the Thorns and terror inducing howls of hunters. 'Drive them back. Back to their dead trees, back to tell others of the red lady and her Thorns. Of the Seer's Elite and Slade's golden arm. Let them run scared of rangers arrows and hunter's claws,' Krosh declared and on they went with sunlight and wolves to their backs. 'Up here, hurry,' Thrimore said. As others chased down warriors of the Vale he had ran to a tall tree and began climbing it. Before he got half way vines came about his waist and carried both he and Wendolin to its peak. 'It wasn't your sisters Wendolin, look,' the clouds about the mountains and above the woods had started to clear, but above the Vale they were as dark as they always had been. 'Then how did they break the clouds,' Wendolin said as a great light grew in the distance. 'What's that?' Thrimore wondered. 'We need to get down, call everyone back,' Wendolin said carrying the pair back to the ground. Past the mountains and into the Erauss the light spread. Blinding all it passed and when it faded both Wendolin and Thrimore were gone.

Whilst Wendolin fought the Envoy's advancing army her sisters had been rushed to the Paratis by Caspian. An easy location to find was the Count's hold. Even for one who has never visited the Vale. The great towers that cast out the eternal darkness tower over much of the land and the plumes of black clouds pouring from the spire's tips make it nearly unmissable. The land was flat and clear of the Count's men for most now marched under the Envoy's banner. Making their journey slightly less painless, but upon approaching the towers both sisters felt a dread creep over them neither had felt before. 'It's death, this place reeks of it,' Bethany said. Dismounting they left Caspian to hide himself away and made their way past piles of ash behind the open gates. Going on the pair did all they could to conceal themselves, but as the courtyard held little within it both struggled to remain hidden. After a few more feet of timid steps they realised the courtyard was empty. 'Is this not meant to be this Count's fortress? Where is everyone?' Stephanie said. A wail from past the great doors to the Count's keep sent a familiar shudder down both their spines. 'That voice, it sounds like her,' Bethany said.

'You mean, that pale lady,' Stephanie wondered. 'Really don't understand how she and Richard ever became friends.'

'I don't know, she's quite attractive for one of the undead,' Bethany said, a comment that received a glare from her sister and cast away the fear both felt, even if only slightly. Their hearts soon quickened once more as they opened the door to reveal the ghastly show beyond. A sight that would haunt the pair forever more if they weren't both certain they would soon meet their fate. There a table had been laid, a bright purple cloth covered the top with golden cutlery and plates neatly laid out. Strewn with finery the long table was and in the centre lay Calenir. Her body was bare and from the top of her breast to the bottom of her navel her chest had been cut and opened wide to allow for her organs to be removed one by one. A black liver lay on the plate beside her head while one scarred lung rested to her feet. The sisters stood there stunned as a figure standing over the table pulled cord after cord of intestines from her undead body. No clothing did the figure wear only bandages of black cloth covered him from head to toe, leaving no part of his skin exposed. 'It would appear our honoured guests have arrived.' The figure chuckled in a vile masculine voice past the cloth. 'Yes, arrived to feast and celebrate with the others,' he cackled over Calenir's screams. Uncorking her canteen Bethany soon held a sword of frozen ice and regretted giving the ring to Wendolin, while Stephanie wielded the dagger she'd taken from Wasiz. 'Oh come now, let us not cross swords. Such power colliding may break the Count's feeble home,' the figure said. Gesturing to the Count's throne where he sat lifelessly watching his daughter's torture. 'For this is a feast worthy of the Balmoths and their friends I'd say.' As the figure went on more shadows crept around the hall and soon emerged wearing the same as the first. Black cloth covered men surrounded the table marching to stand behind each of the twenty four chairs as the butcher spoke. 'A feast to celebrate his arrival, a feast beyond compare. A fine slice of liver or perhaps a kidney, why not be pushy and take two.'

'Let her go,' Bethany demanded but little attention did any pay to her. 'The spleen is tender but fairly juicy. See this though I do beg you take a nibble on the heart stew, I did make it special. Just for the Leaflins that is, but is still missing a few ingredients. The heart of one of you two would certainly do.' Distracted by the strange man neither noticed another pair of cloth covered men creep to their backs. But as they were grabbed shards of ice shot from Bethany's sword ending the pair and revealing no bodies rested beneath the cloth. For only shadows of their master these were. The others moved from the table as shadows spun around their palms and Bethany released her sword. Flying before them it span creating a shield that blocked screaming shadows from reaching the pair. 'Get to the pale lady we just have to grab her and run,' Bethany ordered. 'What about you?' Stephanie said.

'Don't worry I can handle these puppets,' Bethany declared. Waving her hands the shield broke into a thousand shards that shot around the table. They scarred a couple, but others used the shadows now flowing around them to block her attack. Lunging forward Bethany leapt to the table as the shards of ice reformed to create two short swords. A hand grabbing her leg forced her to cut it from the offending arm. Another swing followed cleaving a man grasping for her in two and leaving her standing over Calenir and the one butchering her. 'Hurry and put her on a plate,' he bellowed before his head was hewed and Calenir's restraint's cut. Jumping from the table Bethany drew away the rest as Stephanie ran to retrieve Calenir, but soon realised there was no way to move her without the rest of her organs spilling out. *I'm not sure even Bethany can heal this* she thought as she reached for Calenir's hand. 'B-blood. I need it,' Calenir said forcing the words past her lips. Taking the dagger Stephanie cut her wrist and held it to Calenir's mouth. After just a few drops Calenir's strength started to return, but then a new feeling joined the usual sensation drinking blood created within her kind. As more passed her lips she felt her body began to change. Organs that had been removed started to regrow, the cut down her chest began to seal. What then followed neither an ailing Calenir nor Stephanie had expected. The sound of bones breaking came from Calenir's back, she then forced Stephanie away as she was pushed up by two long wing bones that had spawned from her shoulder blades. 'What are you?' Calenir wailed as her ears grew to be that of a bat, and her fangs doubled in length. Fur covered her arms and legs as her nails popped off to allow claws to grow in their place. 'That's not wood elf blood,' Calenir screamed, but her speech had become so high pitched only bats would have been able to understand her. The cloth covered shadows who remained had encircled Bethany and as Calenir flapped her newly formed wings Stephanie hoped she was going to her aid. Instead she took off and climbed the great height of the tower going to the very top. Here she burst through floorboards and chiselled stone to find that Sallow had been commanding the Count's warlocks. Upon the top floor of the keep do the Grey Count's warlocks work. Here a cauldron sits in the centre of the room where with their chants the blood within casts out the darkness that now spreads north. Still elf these men were, for only those with untainted blood can cast such spells. The floorboards shattered making Sallow fall through the hole in the floor Calenir had created, crashing before Stephanie on the table below as the others panicked. Calenir's great jaws tore down the warlocks in turn as the beast of the vale would have, until only one remained. Setting her claws around his throat she strained her neck to speak. 'Part the clouds,' she snarled. 'Bring them back to cover only the Vale.'

'We can't, only fresh blood can draw back the night,' he said in a panicked tone. Storming to the cauldron Calenir knocked it over letting the blood pour through the gap she'd created. 'What are you doing? The sun will burn you all, you have no more blood,' the warlock wailed but Calenir in fact had plenty of the blood that would be needed. The pot was pulled upright and while the warlock continued to panic she crammed him into the pot. Multiple violent punches followed until his body was crammed in and she used her claws to slice his throat and waist. 'What is that woman doing?' Bethany yelled kicking back a cloth shadow to the table and ending it with her blade as Stephanie threw the plate that held Calenir's old liver to the face of another. Blood dripped down the hole Calenir created and the pair heard her chanting the words the warlocks had been, but only an elf can cast the spell. As the blood she'd consumed faded from her Calenir's body began to revert to her original state. So when her head appeared though the hole above her face was almost as it was, save for her shrinking fangs. 'I need you up here Leaflin, quickly before the clouds spread any further,' she ordered but neither were in a position to do so. 'What did she say?' Stephanie said as a shadow jumped onto the table to get at her. He though was crushed by Calenir after she dropped from the hole wrapped in one of the warlock's cloaks to conceal herself. She held a book the warlock's had been reading from. A black cloth cover it had, one that held no name. Before Stephanie could react she was pulled onto the table and the open book was pushed into her hands. 'Read from the book before the cauldron and be quick. It will draw back the clouds so they cover only the Vale once again,' Calenir said.

'What, I don't understand,' Stephanie spluttered, but had no chance to argue as Calenir used her incredible strength to propel Stephanie through the hole she'd made and leave her to crash before the bloody pot. Bethany threw one of her blades to Calenir and the pair stood upon the table as the cloth covered shadows summoned shadow blades of their own. 'This is just getting ridiculous,' Stephanie said as she opened the book to the page Calenir had left it on. 'I can't read this,' Stephanie yelled through the hole.

'Figure it out,' Calenir bellowed back as she and Bethany duelled the screaming shadows. 'Figure it out, right it's just that simple,' Stephanie said.

Below a shadow span forth slicing the table into two, separating the pair and casting them both down. Bethany then noticed a light gust of wind part swelling shadows. To her ears it flowed for not only Jhona could speak through the wind. 'A gift I bring to the Leaflins, beneath black clouds let your might sing.' With a flick of Bethany's wrist her sword shattered casting aside the shadows. 'Clear my way,' she yelled as she ran on unarmed to the doorway. 'You Leaflins are as mad as the Balmoths,' Calenir complained slicing her hand she sent blood shooting to intercept clothed men as Bethany reached the doorway and Calenir's side was pierced by a shadow blade. Kicking back the assailant she waved her hand pulling the shadow blade from her side to her hand. 'Not only you command shadows fiend, for I am Calenir, Princess of the Vale, the pale lady. The horror of the dreaded night.' Summoning all of her strength she pulled shadows from all around and as her blood sparked she heard a roar from past the doors none ever imagined they'd hear within the Vale. 'Leave my home shadow you've lost, the Vale's true master is I.' Past the doors Bethany looked to the sky and there she saw the great griffin Charlemagne soaring above. He released his talon and from it a staff fell. Raising her hand the staff slowed until it came to rest in her palm. Ice then covered it as it changed to suit its new master. 'June's staff. How do you have June's staff?' The cloth men wailed. 'It was lost long ago, you can't have that. It, it's, it's just not fair,' with a snigger Bethany turned to the shadow. 'You're right but life rarely is. I'd certainly say this evens the odds though wouldn't you?' Bethany said.

'Kill her, get the staff and kill her,' the man yelled and more shadows fell to become cloth covered men. One tap of her staff created four ice soldiers, the second sent out a wave of spinning water. Calenir cast out those left within her hall and appeared in the doorway to witness great plumes of water casting shadows aside. In the centre of it all Bethany stood covered in the shine of a star. 'Who are these Leaflins?' Calenir wondered as she rushed to join the battle.

Staring to the page Stephanie tried to decipher the words but the strange squiggles that is the language of the undead are almost impossible to read if not taught to. Suddenly though and with no idea how Stephanie began to understand the words on the page. It was like they moved around, putting themselves in order until they became readable. 'How can I read this?' Stephanie wondered but a yell from the pale lady made her hurry on. 'I'm doing it,' she yelled back not realising it was the battle that caused her screams. She then sat before the cauldron and read from the book. 'Lift the sun, forget the stars. Cast out the night above and let the land below be darkened by shadows and never will light shine, never will grass or trees grow and forever will darkness reign.' With her words the blood in the pot began to bubble and turn to black smoke sending plumes into the sky that drew back the black clouds the previous warlocks had created. The Paratis would remain covered in darkness, but slowly dark clouds started retreating to the Vale. 'I've done it, I really did it,' Stephanie beamed and ran to the hole. 'It's done, it worked. I worked it out.'

'There's no end to them,' Calenir said reaching Bethany. But as they spoke the shadows thinned and in the distance past their enemy a light grew but no sun was this. 'Get in and close the doors quickly,' Bethany ordered as the staff she held began to shake as if it was terrified. 'What is it?' Calenir asked.

'I don't know just get in.' Both fell back to the keep's door as ice soldiers followed them to bat away advancing shadows. Calenir ran to a lever concealed behind her father's throne. Pulling it closed many iron shutters that covered the Paratis, as the light rose and the doors closed her father spoke. 'Norcea. It can't be. Does Norcea's light shine once more?' As the light rose to cover the Vale casting the shadows aside and even penetrated the iron shutters blinding all within. It didn't harm Calenir or her father but when it faded both Bethany and Stephanie were gone. 'What? What has happened, my daughter?' The Grey Count spoke in his own voice for the first time in many a year and his daughter's cold hand found his. 'My father, your eyes. They are your own and as black as they once were,' Calenir said.

'I feel as if I was lost. Abandoned on a path no others could follow,' the Count said and his eyes then went to his hall. 'What has transpired? A sickness. An evil has festered here. One that was spawned in the first age and will find us again. For the Necromancer, for

Jandor Grimis was not the fool we imagined he was and return the undying will.'

'Forget the Envoy father. For the Vale is ours once more and in our image and not his will it be rebuilt in,' Calenir said back to her father.

'No, dear daughter. No. For our creed is bound to the shadows that rule him and forever will I be cursed to their cause.'

Chapter Sixteen
The Only Way Left

None of what was happening in Paratis or beyond the mountains Richard and his group knew. Only to carry on past dead trees could they go, all worrying for their friends as they went. All thoughts of others though were soon forgotten when the trees cleared and they came to the edge of Amunden Trench. Below the land had been quarried and the trench had tripled in size. Two miles wide and almost as deep. The land had all been dug out around two tall black spires that rose from the ground to meet at the very top. 'This, this is incredible, to have mined so much so quickly. I never imagined blood suckers had it in them,' Banbury said.

'I don't think it's been the Grey Count's own working here,' Jhona said pointing to a creature lumbering its way around the bottom of the trench. 'What is it? I can't make it out,' Wasiz said.

'Nor would you want to. It's a monster of flesh and bones fused together by some foul spell,' Richard said. He and his brother could both see clearly from even so high up and what both saw made their stomach's retch. Creatures with patchwork skin and contorted bones they were. All varied in size with the largest of their kind standing twenty foot tall before the black spires. There the Envoy stood and before him an alter of bones and blood drenched skin sat that held the stone of seeds. 'There is no way of getting to him without being seen by his creatures,' Wasiz said as they descended into the trench. 'Can you get to it? If I draw his eyes,' Richard asked.

'It will take far more than just yourself,' Banbury said. 'He's right Richard, you can't play the hero alone today,' Jhona told him.

'It's sadly so,' Wasiz said. 'You alone, even with your blade would hardly draw a handful. In order for me to steal back the stone I will need all his monsters charging for the three of you.' At the base of the trench the four wracked their brains for another way but Wasiz saw only one path for he and his friends to follow and would do all he could to force them along it. 'Stand here and dither and we will lose our only chance to take it from him. Together we can overcome this foe, mere minutes will I need and then reunited once more we can...' Before Wasiz could finish a gruesome hand rose from the ground. Great giant fingers of pilfered flesh took hold of him as the Envoy's creation rose from the gravel it was concealed beneath. Rusted metal clamps held this creatures limbs to its fearsome torso. For no head did it have just a circular mouth filled with swirling blooded teeth upon the torso that its arms and legs had been clamped to. A flick of its wrist sent Wasiz flying along with chunks of flesh from the creatures hand as others both larger and smaller than the first lumbered about the others. 'Enough,' the Envoy's voice echoed all around. 'Bring Elidom's pets before me. Let them bear witness to his defeat.' Every side was blocked by the putrid skin and rusted metal leaving

Richard, Jhona and Banbury to be forced on towards the black spires. 'It's b-b... Happening,' Banbury stuttered as black sparks began to burst between the great spires. 'Golems,' Jhona whispered.

'Who?' Richard asked.

'Golems, they're created with pilgrim's ink, but rather than using it to give life to rocks or trees this Envoy has used it on the deceased. Avlor told me of them and the spell is broken by damaging the glyph,' Jhona went on gesturing to the glyph of three skulls under the arm of one of the golems about them. Before any could lunge for it shadows took hold of their feet, floating over the three of them it removed their weapons and forced them to walk on. The shadows about their feet guided them before the Envoy as the flesh golems stood aside and their weapons flew to their adversary. Turning from the alter the Envoy's face was clear to see as they were forced to walk before him. His cape had been removed making all wince when they caught sight of his face. For no eyes does the Envoy have, removed long ago they were. Fused together his eyelids had been, by a thick black wire that held them tightly closed. With a pale bald head that possessed no ears or nose and black lips that dripped vile from his mouth as he spoke. His appearance alone terrified the ones before him, his voice though would send such chills down their spines that most would catch a cold from. 'Bring them forth and let them see,' the Envoy's voice was as foul as he and as their weapons were brought to him by the flowing shadows he chuckled to himself. 'What blade is this?' He said reaching for Richard's sword, but as his hand and long cracked nails got close it sparked. Sending the shadows around it screaming away. 'The Kalarumba,' he hissed and glared to his three prisoners. 'It took much doing to corrupt and then ambush the dwarf's old King. So much so that the shadows took more of me than they ever had before.' As he spoke his hands ran over the holes where his ears used to sit. 'Long and painful was that particular endeavour, but lost my prize was. Lost to you it would seem.' With a flick of his finger shadows reacted. Banbury's axe turned and flew towards the dwarf as the shadows holding him tight moved his left leg to allow the axe's pole to strike through. 'You b-b... Sodding scum,' Banbury wailed.

'Why you? I wonder,' the Envoy cackled past his cries. 'Why did the sword go to you?' Behind him black sparks had continued to grow between the spires as the gate fed off the energy the stone of seeds provided. 'It matters little now anyhow,' he went on turning back to the gate as Richard and Jhona tried to pull away from shadows and Banbury grabbed his axe, desperately trying to pull it from his leg and the shadow's grip. 'For here my master's work will begin and I, Jandor Grimis his most worthy servant, his undying Necromancer has made it so. Let the Seers and their kind be washed away in the darkness. All will be reborn in the shadows clean of Norcea and her people. The orcs were but a test and a way to draw his eyes to us, to the blood and bodies I can gift him. All my works have lead to this day and here the war of the first is won. Some hope we shall have against annihilation.

With this great act I out match even Inkark himself. Ascend higher than Elidom was ever able and do what neither could.' The builder's gate let off one final spark as the red glow over the stone of seeds faded and a portal began to appear between the spires leading to a world none knew. Spinning around the Envoy's arms rose and he declared. 'It is done and be honoured you're here to witness such a sight. Kasseon's world will be reborn upon Alidor and wash away the last light in the universe that offends him.' With that Wasiz had heard enough of this foul man's speech. Around the spires he had crept and as the gate started to open and the Envoy rattled on he snuck to his back. Revealing himself he darted to Richard's sword, scooping it up with his foot he flicked it over to Richard's waiting hand and with a blinding flash of lightening Richard drew all eyes to him and cast the shadow's aside. 'The rangers have come for you villain, your madness will end by my blade,' Richard declared.

'Have at ye foul bugger,' Banbury yelled reaching up all he was able, grabbing a flesh golem and pulling it onto the head of his axe thats pole still rested in his leg. Another flash of lightening freed Jhona and Wasiz soon had his bow flying to him as shadows crashed into the shield his hourglass created. Leaping up and grabbing his bow Jhona landed on the body of a flesh golem. Balancing on one foot he flicked his other leg, spinning on the many chunks of skin. Firing arrows to the great bats descending upon them as he did and then using an arrow he cut through the glyph upon the golem he stood on. 'Why bother thief? The gate is

271

open, your fate is sealed,' the Envoy spat as he reached for the alter to find the stone was missing and passed the shadows he'd sent for Wasiz four daggers appeared. Two the shadows blocked but the others pierced the Envoy's chest and even with no eyes he was able to see the grinning goblin before him who held the stone. 'Because I have a tale to tell,' Wasiz replied. 'For while this world has chewed you up and spat you out as this foul thing that is broken to only serve evil. I found something else.' With that Wasiz's final dagger ended the Envoy but unfortunately Jandor Grimis was not so easy to kill. When one body dies another will wake to further his fearsome plot, not Richard or his friends knew this as creatures from another world began to step through the Builder's gate. Running from the gate Wasiz went to Jhona and grabbed his hand as he stepped off the flesh golem he'd slain. 'Hurry, come with me. I have a plan but we must hurry,' Wasiz said pulling him to a tunnel he had found whilst sneaking about. 'Richard, hurry they don't look the friendly sort,' Banbury yelled waving Richard to his side as the flicking tongues and many legs of Kasseon's spawn bounded through the gate. 'Where's the rotter going?' Turning Richard saw Wasiz and Jhona running away, but his view of the pair was quickly blocked. 'I don't know, he must have some plan, he must have,' Richard said hoping Wasiz did. With a valiant cry and the rest of his strength Banbury pulled the axe's pole from his leg and tossed the axe into the air. 'Go Richard, take it and see to this f-f-fiends.' Falling as he spoke Banbury had little more strength to go on as Richard took hold of the axe and a red glow covered it until it matched his blade. Ahead monsters bounded to them past the spires. Great demonic beasts with many legs and slapping tongues poured forth. The foreguard of Kasseon's army were they and over the lands of the Forgotten Vale they bounded to the only soul still standing. Lightening broke past black clouds as if the very skies above were ripping themselves to pieces. Scarring the land and striking the Spawn. From the tip of Richard's blades sparking electricity danced its way up his arm and with each swing heads fell and limbs were hewed by the flashing blades as Richard used all the might he could muster to stay standing before this onslaught of chaos.

'Hurry it's down here,' Wasiz said leading Jhona away from the fight. 'Where are we going?' Jhona asked but soon realised Wasiz was leading him away. 'Wait Wasiz, what's going on?'

'Don't question it, just don't look back and keep going,' Wasiz said grabbing Jhona's hand and trying to pull him along with him. 'No Wasiz stop, we can't just run off,' Jhona insisted.

'Please Jhona, please trust me we have to leave. We must, there's no other way,' Wasiz begged as his eyes broke and tears rushed from them. 'What has you like this?' Jhona asked.

'They will die Jhona, there's no winning this. Richard, Banbury, the sisters they will all die here. Please run with me. Let us be free of this, the shadows will spread but together we can outrun them, hide ourselves away and never be found,' Wasiz said.

'How are you so sure?' Jhona asked making Wasiz reveal the stone of seeds. 'I've looked. It's shown me this battle a thousand times. Each time we fail, but there is a slim chance of you and I living if we flee now,' Wasiz said.

'That can't be, there must be a way. Is there really no plan or trick you can think of?' Jhona said.

'No, there is nothing,' Wasiz lied, a lie Jhona quickly saw through. 'What is it, tell me?'

'There is a way, but I could not bear it,' Wasiz said. 'I would forget you Jhona and you I. Together we can weave a tale that bends this very world but we'd become strangers to one another. Just shadows would remain of our love. I saw you take the stone, it reacts with your hair clip in some way and you defeat our foes, but I lose you and that I cannot do. I would let this world burn, let it all fall to these shadows if only to keep you. So let us run, run fast and run far to where our love can't be taken. Please Jhona leave with me,' Wasiz begged. 'My dear Wasiz you know we have to try, we can't just abandon them. My brother, Banbury you may love me more as I do you but neither you or I could say love is worth their lives. Besides how could I ever forget about you. You are the only one who sees me as I am, the only one my heart will ever beat with and never could it forget you,' Jhona said as his forehead fell to Wasiz's and both cried. Raising his eyes to meet his, Wasiz kissed him and as the pair embraced the stone of seeds went from his hand to Jhona's. 'I love you my thief, my loving rotter,' Jhona said smiling through tears to him as the stone began to glow in his palm along with the hair clip he wore. 'Your heart is forever stolen, for I shall keep it even after my death. I shall never give it up,' Wasiz said over weeps and in a blinding flash Jhona was gone and Wasiz was left alone. Falling to the ground his cries continued but in truth the rotting thief always knew what his love would do and this was but the first act in the tale they now weaved.

Opening his eyes Jhona found himself on a bright white plain, it was barren save for one other who was as perplexed upon seeing him as he was her. 'Who are you?' The glowing white figure of a woman asked. Jhona didn't reply as she wafted before him, carried by the light that was all about them. 'You've come here seeking power, the power of my heart,' the woman went on. Lunging forward the palm of her hand was quickly placed over Jhona's forehead. 'I see the shadows have returned and my other selves are plotting. Wait. The Leaflins, my Starborn. Finally a way back is clear to me. Let the wizard make his plans and my brother wage his wars, for I shall soon out shine their wicked schemes.'

'I don't wish to plot or scheme. I just want to save my brother, my friends. I just need the strength to save Wasiz, nothing more,' Jhona said.

'And you shall have it son of steeds for granting it will twist the heart to my own end. Drain it to feed on life rather than grant it. With it you may save

275

them, but no longer Jhona Balmoth will you be and all who knew of him will forget the name and face that once was. Your true self shall take your place and what you long to be will be revealed and your mind cleared of the past, a being of pure energy will you become. No longer a Balmoth nor the gift of the zatifas. Only a light made from forgotten power,' she said.

'Just do it, do what you must,' Jhona said. The light grew to blinding levels as the woman's hands cupped Jhona's face. 'Let the stone go to you, let my heart take you and once done hide itself away and feed off the broken world I once so foolishly loved.'

'Where's your blasted brother and the thief got to?' Banbury yelled. 'They'll be back, just get to the..,' Richard said as he was thrown down. Great beams of lightening sprung from Richard's blades but only seconds of time would it buy the pair as creatures poured forth. They swarmed them but before one of their flaying legs cut flesh a light rose from the ground before them. Growing as it went until it exploded throwing the monsters aside to reveal a woman, covering her was a dress of many cascading colours that matched her long flowing hair. 'W-w-w-who the bloody hell is that?' Banbury stuttered.

'It can't be,' Richard said for even changed so he knew this woman's eyes. 'We must run this is the only hope we have, Jhona will handle it from here,' Wasiz said running to the pair. 'What have you done? What the bloody hell have you done? You and your stupid schemes,' Richard yelled.

'It was her choice and the only way,' Wasiz said as Jhona rose before the builder's gate and her emotions settled on one. Her dress turned dark red followed by her hair making her anger clear as the monsters of Kasseon's world bounded to her. Caught in the bright light most were as she drifted to the great gate past the slain body of the Envoy she floated, raising her hands to the gate when she reached it. 'We have to leave,' Wasiz yelled again but Richard shrugged him off and yelled. 'It's Jhona, how is that Jhona?' He said. 'I'll explain, but we have to leave,' Wasiz insisted as the Trench started to collapse into itself. 'I won't leave him,' Richard said running from Wasiz who then had to stop Banbury from trying to follow. 'What trick are you playing here rotter?' Banbury yelled.

'Trust me Banbury, please just this once trust me,' Wasiz begged. Ahead Richard rushed past burnt bodies to Jhona's back. As the light about her grew the gate started to shatter. The light rose to cover the trench as Richard's hand reached her. Spreading further until the clouds above were cast away and even the Paratis was bathed in it before the gate collapsed and the light exploded. Casting its shine to all the lands about it. When rubble settled and the great light faded both the Leaflins, Balmoths and their friends were gone.

Waking Richard found he was sat in tall green grass and beside him a woman sat who stared to him looking quite confused. 'Jhona are you ok? What happened?' Richard asked. 'Who's Jhona?' The woman replied as she stood up and brushed off her dress. 'And who are you? I-I feel like, we are friends, maybe.'

'Yes, we are friends. Great ones,' Richard said even more confused than she was. Then he noticed where they'd been taken. Over the field the Afeun lay and without speaking she stood tall and began to walk to it. 'Where are you going?' Richard asked as she went. 'I'm not sure yet Richard, yes that's it Richard Balmoth the ranger, right?' She asked.

'Yes, that's me,' Richard said. 'Who, who are you?'

'I'm not sure about that. I suppose I'll have to find out,' she replied with a laugh as she continued on to the Afeun. 'Who was that?' Wasiz asked making Richard jump as he appeared behind him. 'You must know,' Richard said back, but then saw tears running down the goblin's face. 'Not a clue,' Wasiz replied as he brushed them off. 'Wasiz do, what do you remember?' Richard asked.

'We were in the Vale, and, you know I'm not sure. Quite strange to think I don't remember our tale,' Wasiz said whilst tears continued to drip from his cheeks. Looking through his tear filled eyes Wasiz saw his map poking out the top of his bag. Taking it out he noticed the zatifas whistle sat in its fold and the name on both had changed. The name of his love had been removed and the name Richard Balmoth had replaced Jhona. 'Seems this is yours, here take it.'

'There you are. Had me worrying more than a pigeon who's lost his nest you have.' A cry from Banbury found them and both saw he hurried his way through the grass to them. His injuries healed he ran to them as fast as he was able. 'It is good to find you two. Although I never imagined you'd have gotten too far,' Richard said as the pair shared a hug. 'Whatever happened Balmoth all I remember is the three of us fighting in the Vale. Then that woman, over there. That's her isn't it, and where's the rotter off to?' Banbury said seeing the woman reach the Afeun's gates and the Elites guarding it started to flee the fortress, and then to Wasiz walking off in the other direction. 'Her we will give some time to find herself, but him,' Richard said and then yelled to Wasiz. 'Wrong way rotter, we still have Leaflins to find yet.' Wasiz though didn't stop walking. In silence he went on and at his first opportunity vanished from the sight of his friends.

Neither Bethany nor Stephanie had any clue how they'd been returned to Meceller. Both woke after the light that grew over the Paratis covered them to find themselves beneath the city's trees. Quickly the pair made their way to the Toppled Dwarf and there had attempted to stay hidden. Unfortunately Bethany's skills didn't go unnoticed. So what was supposed to be a couple of nights in hiding resting up for the ride home turned into two weeks of curing all the many ailments that the people of Meceller came to her with. This lead Stephanie to realise that even her sister's skills had their limits forcing her to forage for herbs and whatever else she could find to cure the ailments her sister was unable to. Along with a young lady called Rebecca Weaver who was an elf from Tailor's Hope. She had originally travelled to Meceller on one of her rare holidays, but after striking up a friendship with the sisters had not been home since. The Caring Hand is what the people called them but in hushed tones to keep the council's eyes from them and the sheriffs unaware of their work. After almost a month past both worried their sister or the others would never find them but little did Stephanie know. For their friends had been searching for the pair and had finally infiltrated Meceller.

Walking back to the Toppled Dwarf carrying what she'd been able to forage Stephanie was until she felt eyes watching her. Looking back she saw a man in a black cape following her. Picking up her pace Stephanie worried the Countess had sent others to retrieve them, this caused her to trip on a protruding root and fall throwing her basket as she did. A hand quickly stopped her from hitting the ground and before she was able to see who caught her she heard Banbury say. 'What sort of a greeting is that then? To think we spent all this time looking for you only to be assaulted with herbs.' Looking up the arm of the one who caught her Stephanie saw Richard smiling and before she could hold herself back her lips were on his. 'I thought you'd gone, returned to your Seers and forgotten me,' Stephanie said. 'Return to them, my lady you are the only master I will ever serve,' Richard replied. His hood fell back and a passing sheriff soon recognised the embracing pair. 'The Balmoth, look there he is,' one yelled as whistles were blown and more hurried to aid him. 'We should go quickly, wait do you know how we fled this place before? Neither me nor Bethany can remember,' Stephanie asked.

'You don't remember Jhona either,' Richard said. 'Who?' Stephanie asked.

'Don't worry I'll tell you later, but we won't be fleeing this time,' Richard said as sheriffs surrounded them. 'Hands up Balmoth the council wants a word,' a sheriff carrying shackles yelled. No reply came from Richard, all it caused him and Banbury to do was remove the black capes they wore and turn them around to show the ranger's green capes they truly were. Whilst Richard retied the cape the sheriff got even more frustrated. 'Stop this show Balmoth come along to your fate.'

'You and your kind are finished here, it is time the wood folk take back their woods and the rangers and King's guard have returned to see it so.' With that others in the crowd revealed green capes. More than just Richard and Banbury had snuck into Meceller and now around the sheriffs a sea of green slowly revealed itself. Flowers spawned on bark as Wendolin and Thrimore followed along with the Thorns wearing the uniform of the King's guard all were. Making the sheriffs quickly realise their time ruling over the streets of Meceller was coming to an end. Caspian charged to Richard's side, he and Stephanie were soon taken up. 'Let the council keep their Evertree and allow the Queen to carry on corrupting your minds if you wish, but I have seen a new Meceller. One with its rangers returned,' Richard declared. 'In the north the fortress of the Afeun has been remade by hands far fairer than any the Evertree could spawn. The Ranger's Academy is open to all who seek a better world, all who wish for the next day to be grander than the last. The Headmistress there will welcome any with open arms. So what say you people of Meceller will you hide behind wooden walls forever more or follow the rangers and together ride onto the next age.'

Bethany watched as Richard began his declaration but before she could join them she was stopped. While Richard had returned for Stephanie another had come for her. 'We must speak,' Elidom Godborn said taking her arm and pulling her away before any saw. 'What are you playing at?' Bethany complained as she was pulled to the backstreets where none could hear them speak. 'I've worked it out what you and your sisters are Miss Leaflin,' Elidom said.

'What? We know what we are Seer,' Bethany said. 'I'm afraid you don't. When we met I felt things for you, things I wouldn't normally feel for a, well a woman,' Elidom said.

'I don't understand,' Bethany replied.

'Nor did I, but have since discovered why. You are no wood elf Bethany Leaflin, nor are your sisters. Why you look as you do I'm still unsure of, but I am sure like my people before you fell from the heavens and were gifted with Norcea's light when you did so. The fact you could wield June's staff proves it. That's why I felt as I did, that's why you can do the things you do. Norcea's light has a way of charming people. I

282

believe it's why Richard fell so instantly for Stephanie and that Thrimore for Wendolin also. I have looked over the stars for many nights and I'm sure of it.'

'So why tell me, why pull me away and speak to me alone. Don't tell me you have instantly fallen yourself,' Bethany asked.

'I'm afraid my feelings towards you are far from that, in truth it is your healing hands I sought. Even for that short moment we spoke in the Fang I felt your heart. It beat in my ears like a drum. It is a good heart, one filled with love and care not tainted by ill deeds as mine is,' Elidom said.

'What deeds could be so dark as to taint the heart of a Seer?' Bethany asked.

'Ones that saw my love lost and my actions scar the world. Ones that make me a man I no longer recognise. So no unlike Balmoth I don't return to plead or confess my eternal love. I just come to find a friend, one who may help my heart beat away whatever it is that corrupts me.'

Meceller rose with its rangers, while in Duniesa within the golden tower caring hands now attempted to keep the Seers in check. Slowly each sister found a place in this rather strange world. Wasiz however had no joy filled reunion, to just walk is all he had done earning him another name in doing so. The weary wanderer they called him, a figure in black who spoke no words and only walked by in silence. On he went as days, weeks and then months passed. Until his wandering brought him back to the Forgotten Vale where the Beast of the Vale watched under dead bark as he drew close. His eyes were bright red, his skin was scarred, his feet torn and close to death the rotting thief was as he fell to his knees before her. 'Help me beast, I beg you, for you are my only hope. My mind is broken and I know not how to fix it. Torn into pieces by a thought I can't find, a tale that's been hidden from me. Something, someone, I don't know.' Wasiz fell upon the ground as the beast looked on and then with a deep sigh spoke. 'There is a face, a body I remember being for just a moment.' As she spoke her body morphed matching the image she had in her head slowly changing shape until a face looked back to Wasiz, one he cursed himself for ever forgetting. 'I remember,' he mumbled. Then with a hop he jumped back up from the ground with a wild glint darting around his eyes as all his memories of Jhona Balmoth came flooding back. Powerful was the spell cast but its caster had not counted on he. One stolen tale after another fell into place in Wasiz's mind until he cried out. 'I remember. Oh yes dear Jhona I remember. How could I be such a fool to have forgotten?'

'Forgotten what?' The beast asked.

'Our tale my beast. A tale weaved by me and my love. One that will spur the very gods and pilfer the tools needed to save our measly world. A tale that only I the world's greatest stealer of stories could tell. For even though we are parted, we still act as one. Yes, onward to the next page. Find a fresh pot of ink and a fine new quill, fill my pipe and together let us see. The stone showed me so much and we must get on, but where to start,' Wasiz rambled as his mind raced. 'Come along then there is much to be done and little time to do it.'

'Why would I follow you, where are you even going?' The fearsome beast grumbled.

'Sit here under dead trees and grim clouds if you wish beast, but I have a better tale to tell. One I feel would suit you really rather well. So come along with me and let us see what kind of tale we can conceive.'

Chapter Seventeen
The Tales We Weave

Months past and none had heard a word from Wasiz, all suspected he had found wealth in distant lands. Aside from Richard who knew the pain his friend had been left with. In Meceller he and Stephanie had remained building what would become the ranger's headquarters within the city, until a pheasant found them carrying a letter neither had expected. It read as such;

Your attendance is demanded at the Flipped Swan on the fourth night in the month of the Steed for a meeting of great significance. Tell no one of your whereabouts and come as discreetly as you are able.

This lead Richard and Stephanie to rush from Meceller. Only three days did they have to reach the Flipped swan and neither wished to miss the event. The same letter was pushed through the letter box of Banbury's cottage leading his wives to charge about packing and demanding all be taken along. While Bethany's was delivered to her in the great heights of the golden tower in Duniesa, by a green phoenix who cast Seer Dune aside to see her letter delivered. Together with Rebecca she'd been growing the caring hand from there, supported by the elf's new King. The last letter proved the hardest to deliver for Wendolin and her Thorns had hidden themselves well. After the show they put on returning to Meceller both she and Thrimore quickly realised the wooden city would never be their home. To the Crimson Grove they went and there with the Thorns that followed the pair would stay hidden from the rest of the world as much as they were able. Some of their following though had found new paths for themselves. A few of the younger ones found ranger's uniforms a better fit and the older which included Phieus Krosh had found their way to the Ranger's Academy's gates, where the Headmistress soon made use of their skills. Most though followed the pair and concealed from the world they became. Crows however have a way of finding even the most well kept secrets and caused the loving couple quite the shock when one burst into the hide away she'd created for them. Like the others they also rushed to the meeting just as unsure of what they'd find as the rest.

Richard was the first to arrive with Stephanie close behind and when the pair saw Wasiz alone in the tavern, hunched over and slowly puffing his pipe Richard worried he was still the broken man that he had left him as. 'It is good to see you my friend, you have had us all worried,' Richard said as he held his hand out to Wasiz. 'Your hand Balmoth,' Wasiz mumbled back. 'After all our trials, all we endured, is a shake of the hand all you have for me.'

'I don't follow you,' Richard said as his hand was batted away and Wasiz jumped to his feet opening his arms wide and embracing the ranger. 'For so long I have wandered and looked forward to this day so very much. Stephanie also a delight it is to see you once more and glowing so,' Wasiz went on as smiles covered their faces. 'You really did have us worried, where have you been all this time?' Stephanie asked.

'Later, later for that when the others have arrived I will speak of it. What of you though? How far along are you, a couple of months I'd say?' Wasiz said as Stephanie blushed and the door swung open and in stormed Banbury followed by his many wives. 'You blasted devil of a rotter,' he said storming to Wasiz and grabbing him. 'Not a letter, not a word, not a single thing to show you weren't sleeping in the Deep,' he went on scolding his old friend. 'Leaving me to the wrath of the wives all this time, some friend you are rotter,' Banbury continued shaking Wasiz.

'I have missed you too my old friend,' Wasiz said. Wendolin and Thrimore both followed and then Bethany arrived and to all their surprise Elidom Godborn had joined her. 'I don't remember inviting you, but I did imagine you'd show up,' Wasiz said to him. 'This is it then, will you tell us what this is all in aid of now?' Banbury asked.

'Not quite we are still missing one,' Wasiz said as the door to the Flipped Swan flung open and all saw it now lead to the newly established Ranger's Academy and through the door the Headmistress of the Academy walked. 'Now we are all present,' Wasiz said and hopped up onto the table. 'My greatest tale is far from done, but for it to be sung there is so very much that must be done.'

'What's he jabbering about?' Wendolin interrupted. 'There will be others red lady, others who will seek the same power as the Envoy and his Marked Men did. The Seer's grow old and the ones who replace them make me fearful,' Wasiz said making all turn to Elidom. 'It pains me to say it, but the thief speaks true. The young in the tower see a different world than myself and Avlor envisioned,' Elidom said.

'They will not act and we can't count on a forgotten hero to save us once more. For this is not their tale, but mine and on us will it fall to play the parts we must. Use the hand we're cast to sway the odds in our favour and stop the world descending into the chaos of darkness once again,' Wasiz said.

'How do you propose doing so?' Richard asked. 'We watch and we wait. We hide in the shadows as they did, we work as one to shift the scales and together, as watchers we will win Richard,' Wasiz said. 'He's mad, just us won't be enough to watch over the whole of Alidor,' Thrimore argued.

'More will come,' Wasiz said.

'Wasiz, nor his plans have ever sent me astray in the past. I can't say I understand what you're trying to accomplish here, but whatever it is you will have my aid,' Richard said.

'Mine also,' Stephanie added.

'I am seldom done adventuring with the rotting thief just yet,' Banbury declared.

'Myself and Elidom will help also, eyes in the golden tower will surely be of use in whatever it is you're planning,' Bethany said nudging Elidom to agree. Soon Wendolin and Thrimore also concurred but both were keen to return to the Crimson Grove. Before Thrimore could go Richard gifted him Wasiz's map saying as he did. 'Let this be a map for your Thorns, so the ones who wish to stay hidden are able. I feel not only rangers will this scheme of his need, but be sure Wasiz never takes it back. For all the treasures in this world would soon be lost if he was ever to turn his eye to finding them and now, without Jhona. That would not take much.'

'Who?' Thrimore asked to which Richard replied. 'A tale for later hurry now or your red lady will leave without you.'

Long discussions followed until one by one the others left after Richard walked out only Wasiz and the Headmistress remained. Walking to Wasiz she stared to him like a ghost had just appeared before her. 'Who are you to me?' She asked as her hair and dress changed to many colours as her emotions tried to settle on one. 'I-I am just a thief my dear Headmistress. Just your thief, nothing more, but I would ask more of you than the others if you're willing,' Wasiz said and pulled out a bundle of letters from his bag. Each had a date and location written on the envelopes. 'I wonder if you would hold some messages in the air for me. Most won't make sense to you, but they will to those who find them,' Wasiz said.

'Who are they for?' She asked.

'I'm not too sure myself, if I'm honest. The tale we write still has a few holes here and there that I will have to fill,' Wasiz said.

'I'm not plotting any fable with you thief,' she replied. 'Are you not my dear Headmistress?' Wasiz said as a glint flashed between his eyes. 'If that's so I suppose you won't send a gust of wind to the Crown City for me either.' He went on writing a date and time on a piece of parchment and placed it on top of the letters. 'The Crown City why? It's sealed away,' the Headmistress asked. 'What sort of storyteller would I be if I told you the intriguing twist. Just spoil all my fun that would,' Wasiz said as the Headmistress looked to him with the same stare Jhona had when they first met many years ago. 'We shall see about this story of yours thief, but I have no love for tall tales and an Academy to run,' she said. Taking the bundle and turning to leave the Headmistress used her hair clip to open a door back to the Ranger's Academy as a fly buzzed down to the table Wasiz sat at. As the Headmistress left it morphed from a fly to take the form of a female elf the Beast of the Vale had become rather fond of. 'You said you'd tell her,' she snapped.

'Calm yourself beast, I will one day,' Wasiz said with a sigh. 'Then why not today and I'm getting tired of you calling me beast,' she said.

'Then what should I call you,' Wasiz asked.

'Mary,' she said in a hushed tone.

'Rather common is it not, I'm sure we can think of a better one,' Wasiz said.

'No, I like Mary,' Mary insisted.

'Kalon yes that's the name of a family of pixies I used to borrow the odd thing from. Mary Kalon,' Wasiz announced. 'You still haven't said why you didn't tell her. Why don't you want her to remember you?' Mary asked.

'Nothing pains me more, but you saw her did you not. The clouds that followed her have parted, she no longer needs her rotting thief to bat them aside. So for the time let us leave her to grow the Academy she loves. Leave her to be all she wishes and in the shadows I'll remain. Just a forgotten memory I will be, but I shall always be ready. Standing up from his chair Wasiz declared. 'Ready to cast dark skies from her if they ever dare return. For her rotting thief, her cunning fool, her eternal love will always be close.' Taking a chest from under the table he retrieved a copy of the stone of seeds he'd made from his bag and placed it within, along with a note and his skeleton key. 'What's that for?' Mary asked.

'Just a game, can't leave Fandisco and Efrain with nothing to do now can I. It's time for someone else to carry the key for a while,' Wasiz said. One lock after another covered the box to dare the pair to look in. Then on to the door Wasiz went after placing the chest onto the bar making Mary rush to follow. 'Wait where are we going now?' She asked.

'You didn't think we were done did you? Oh no we have but one more stop to make. A small change in the story I was shown. Yes, one last twerp,' Wasiz laughed.

The Crown City had fallen into disarray after it had been cast to the sea. Rioting broke out and before long people were starving. Unbeknownst to those upon the island several years after the cage that had been placed around them it had been broken. Letting slaver's sail to the island unaware that with them stowed away the Rotting Thief had followed. The Crows of the Wilds had been chosen to take as many as they were able from the City and after they arrived soon got to work chaining the weak and killing any who put up a fight. Fires burnt homes and flames tore through the once grand city as one after another the humans within were rounded up, leaving only the few able to hide themselves away to remain. Slipping away from the docks Wasiz was soon before a burning home where beyond the flames he could hear a child wail. 'Let us hope I have found the right one,' Wasiz said as a stick insect crawled onto his shoulder. Transforming into a fly and taking flight as he placed his pipe in his mouth and walked on past the burning doorway to find two scorched bodies behind. Almost concealed by the smoke and ash they were but beneath the skirts of the woman something moved. Looking beneath Wasiz found a baby who had barely been born. 'There you are,' Wasiz said to himself. As the child's umbilical cord burnt Wasiz cut it from him and carried the lifeless babe from the burning building. 'Come along it's just a bit of smoke,' Wasiz said rubbing the child's chest once they were clear of the flames. Reaching into his bag he

293

pulled out a vial of dirt. 'That master of the beasts is a funny fellow but his blessing is easily pinched and for one as crafty as I even improved,' Wasiz went on as he poured the dirt over the child's forehead and spoke in a hushed tone, using a voice that didn't sound like his own. 'Let the beasts hear your words, let their world be open to you and all who share your blood. To the ones who roam, fly and burrow this blessing bonds you.' Then with a crooked grin Wasiz went on. 'But I do not just bless you for the beasts, just another master of their kind will change our tale little. So let us use this blessing to bring about something more, let us say, eventful. On you my blessing falls. Not one that will grant great strength or speed unheard of, no mighty arrows will it see you sing. Only a challenge is my blessing, a mystery that no other could find. A tale that will unravel not just a world but the very stars we live under.' Removing his hand from the child's head he saw wide eyes looking back and within the left Wasiz saw a slight glint dart around. 'There we are that was not so bad was it. Come along now we best get you going.' Taking a wicker basket from the floor Wasiz used some rags to make it comfortable and placed the child inside as a young girl's scream echoed to them. 'Damn it,' Wasiz said taking a pocket watch from his bag. 'I'm late, of course I'm late.' With haste he ran to the screams to find a young girl was being dragged from the shore by Crows of the Wilds. Hidden under a broken boat she had been, but was easily found and as she was dragged kicking and screaming from the shore she thought for certain she would soon be dead. One of the men dragging her then released her followed by another until she was freed and she opened her eyes. Around her the bodies of her attackers lay each with a dagger in their backs. Before she could flee a basket was dropped before her and she saw a goblin perched on a stone wall. 'Who, what are you?' The girl stuttered but the goblin just pointed to the basket and said. 'I have saved your life so to pay your debt to me I wish you to take this to the sea. As far out as you can get it,' Wasiz ordered. 'What, why?' The girl argued as more Crows of the Wilds drew close. 'Do as you are told or shall I leave you to their mercy?' Wasiz replied.

'Seeing no other choice she grabbed the basket and then realised what was inside. 'A baby,' she shouted as a Crow approached and more daggers were flung. 'He will be fine, salt water won't hurt him,' Wasiz said forcing the girl on. To the shore she ran and as Wasiz drew away the Crows of the Wilds she waded into the water. Deeper and deeper she went until a gust of wind caught the basket and pulled it from her hands and her head dipped below the water. Woken by a buzzing in her ears she was and found herself back on the shore with no sign of the goblin. Buzzing back to Wasiz the fly had gone after retrieving the girl and now muttered to the thief who was preparing to leave the island after seeing the wind guide the basket over the sea. 'It's done. There's nothing more to do but wait,' he said as the fly landed on him. 'You shan't be able to interfere now, just a guide must you be, for a time anyhow. Save your strength and get that rest you need.

The Forgotten Hero

What do you mean they're staying?' He said as the fly spoke with him. The ships the Crows of the Wilds had arrived on had began to sail away but one remained. 'I see, so they mean to colonise the island with their wretched lot.' The fly hopped on Wasiz's shoulder as he spoke. 'It's not our concern if this is where their kind meets their end so be it, aiding them further will serve no purpose.' This though only made the fly buzz about his face until Wasiz gave in. 'Clear them all out, more boats will arrive soon and the master wants as many as we can nab,' the Crow's commander cried out orders. Until a figure with his face concealed under a black hood found him. He sat on the side of a well smoking a long pipe drawing the attention of him and his men. 'Get that one in cuffs,' he ordered, but all stopped when the figure spoke and a great beast rose behind him. Smoke pooled around the figure's face as he stood tall and removed the pipe from his lips.

Sit yourselves down. Find a comfortable seat and hold your loved ones well. Ready yourself dear reader for I have a tale to tell.

Continued in Alidor The Unlikely Allies

Thank you for reading
The Forgotten Hero
Continue your adventures in Alidor
Follow us on Instagram @alidorbooks
Make sure to sign up to our newsletter, find the details
on our instagram.

The Unlikely Allies Trilogy

Stolen Tales for Cunning Thieves takes you deeper into the world of Alidor with a series of short stories.

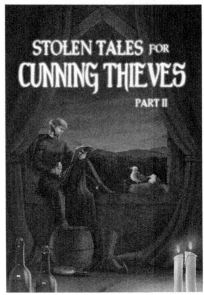

Printed in Great Britain
by Amazon